IRRADIATED

An Alien Perspective

By
Richard N. Boyd, Ph.D.

Irradiated

Richard N. Boyd

Copyright 2021

An Accolade

"It is a great book. Very well written,
Lots of very accurate information.
Best of all, it is solution oriented."

Eric Windheim, BA, EMRS, BBEC, RFSO
Certified Electromagnetic Radiation Specialist
Certified Building Biology Environmental Consultant
Radio Frequency Safety Officer
Lab Leader for the Building Biology Institute

Irradiated

This book is dedicated to Sidnee.

"Fiction is the lie through which we tell the truth"
Albert Camus

Table of Contents

Preface

This book is about the dangers of the radiofrequency, RF, radiation that currently fogs our world. RF is part of the much larger electromagnetic spectrum, ranging from gamma rays of the highest energy, through X-rays, down through the visible part of the spectrum, then infrared, through the RF spectrum, of which millimeter waves are a part, and finally, very low frequency radiation. The RF part is particularly significant to humans, especially in the US, where the telecommunications industry is working hand in glove with the Federal Communications Commission (FCC) to increase greatly the levels of RF radiation. This is to accommodate the ever-increasing desire for greater bandwidth, driven by the relentless marketing of wireless devices. RFR exists not only throughout the US, but in the rest of the planet as well. While some countries have resisted this trend, among them Italy, Switzerland, and even Russia and China, the efforts of the US to bring the world into RF connectivity are driven by economic forces that will be difficult to defeat.

This effort of the telecommunication giants is proceeding even in the face of more than two thousand scientific papers that have shown RFR to be dangerous to biological systems, even at levels far below those approved by the US FCC. Perhaps the source that is most inclusive of medical research is BioInitiative 2012, updated to 2020. It indicates "Extreme Concern" from RFR at levels in excess of 0.001 Watts per square meter. The limit from the FCC, which takes into account virtually none of the medical research, is ten Watts per square meter, ten thousand times greater than the "Extreme Concern" level.

The warning from the BioInitiative 2020 report not only applies to human beings, but also to all animals, birds, insects, and plants. There's a reason that the instructions for a smartphone recommend that the user hold it at least an inch from the head when using it. Since few people actually do that, the telecom giants assume that they can't lose a lawsuit, since they can claim their instructions weren't followed.

The much touted 5G rollout, may well prove to be the biggest threat yet to human beings. These emitters include all the lower frequency radiation that has been around for years but increases the frequency range to include millimeter waves. The popularity of elegant devices such as smartphones, tablets, and computers is what makes these devices so dangerous. And there is already discussion about the next step up in frequency, denoted 6G, sixth generation. But there are mitigation strategies that can greatly reduce the lethality of all these devices.

But one has to wonder about the objectivity of the FCC. One of its four goals, as stated in its 2018-2022 strategic Plan, is "Protecting Consumers & Public Safety." Ignoring all medical evidence that challenges its directives is certainly a poor way to achieve that. A further example has grown to critical size in 2021, that being the FCC's lack of challenge to the 5G rollout, even in the face of the potential disaster it will cause for the airline industry. There is massive concern that weak radar signals from the altimeters in commercial airliners will be affected by the powerful RFR at the 5G frequency. Will it take a crash or two to get the FCC's attention?

Is the intent of this book to persuade humans to give up their smartphones and other fancy electronic toys? No matter how well advised that might be, it's not a realistic possibility. But making people aware of the dangers of the devices they spend much of their time using or carrying close to their bodies might alert them to be more cautious. And that might allow them to adopt mitigation strategies to reduce the most extreme effects of RFR, and possibly extend their lives.

This is a work of fiction. Since it takes place a year or two into the future, and the pressure from the telecommunication companies to increase the RFR they are imposing on humans is enormous, I have assumed that RFR's effects will be even worse in the future than they are now. The names of the characters are not intended to allude to any person living or dead. Furthermore, the real members of the FCC and the telecom industry leaders are probably not as evil as my fictional ones. But the descriptions of the medical effects of RF radiation and the limits on exposure to RF radiation are not fiction; they are buttressed by scientific studies now numbering in the thousands.

Because I often find it difficult to identify human role models with sufficiently high levels of virtue to illustrate the points I wish to make, I have invented an alien to be the principal character for this book. None the less, there did also turn out to be a couple of worthy humans.

Chapter 1. Awakening

Sylvie Sensei woke up Tuesday afternoon in her New York City apartment with a skull splitting headache. This was no ordinary cranial throbbing; it was a serious contender for the headache hall of fame. She had never experienced such intense pain. Was the blare of the police siren that awakened her partly to blame? She knew she had been asleep for more than twelve hours, but that had followed more than two sleepless days and nights. Could the headache be related to the long absence of sleep?

She had moved into her apartment but hadn't organized it yet, or even unpacked. As she began to search her belongings for some headache medication, she spotted the roll of aluminum foil on the kitchen counter. It had been left there by Dustin, who had helped move her things into the apartment a day and a half before. When he laid it on the kitchen counter he commented, "You're going to have an incredible headache before long. Drugs will do virtually nothing for it. But just make a crude helmet out of the aluminum foil; that should reduce the pain to a tolerable level. Longer term solutions are given in your instructions."

She quickly peeled off two sheets of the foil, cut holes for her eyes and nose in one of them, and two more for her ears in the other, formed them around her head, and tucked the sheets around her neck.

"Ahhhh."

Immediately the headache was reduced to garden variety status, and within minutes it had nearly vanished.

Now I remember what Dustin said. It had to do with the pervasive electromagnetic radiation floating around everywhere. I don't know how Earthlings live with this. Actually, some of the

Camitorians who preceded us on Earth indicated that a lot of them don't; a lot of them die from it.

She curled up on one of the overstuffed chairs that decorated her living room to collect her thoughts. They quickly reverted back to the events of the preceding three days.

Chapter 2. Landing

Speaking in native Camitorian, Captain James didn't try to hide his excitement as he addressed his passengers, "My dear friends, this is Captain James. After three decades in transit from our planet Camitor, we have finally reached our destination: Earth. I know you are all anxious to land and begin your new lives here, and we are not anticipating any difficulties, either from the conditions on Earth or from the Earthlings. As you know, there have been hundreds of precursor Camitorians who have preceded you over the past century and, after some adjustment period, have adopted the lifestyles of the places where they landed. They have found that the virus contracted by hundreds of millions of Earthlings several years ago will not affect us, and the climatic conditions on the planet, which were a serious problem in the recent past, have improved as a result of some of the things the Earthlings have done to mitigate the effects of the virus. But the climate problem has not gone away, it continues to intensify."

James was speaking from the command post of his spaceship, surrounded by the many gauges and meters that allowed him to know what was happening everywhere on his craft. The entire room from which he spoke was immaculate, with every object appearing to be brand new, and every surface apparently polished frequently. Captain James was meticulous in maintaining his ship.

The spacecraft had to be large enough to accommodate the needs of its five hundred citizens. Perhaps the most critical things that required continuous monitoring were the oxygen levels at every place in the spacecraft; they must never drop below the level required to sustain life; the air quality; and the bacterial content of the soil in the farms. On as long a voyage as was required for interplanetary travel, the food to sustain the passengers had to be grown on the ship. And any hostile bacterial growth in the soil of even one of the farms could be disastrous. Of course, the rotation of the cylindrical spacecraft about its axis in order to maintain an effective gravity was essential, but conservation of angular momentum guaranteed that would be maintained. The farms, of course, were located at the largest radii of the cylinder so the soil would remain in the field.

Of course, there were grocery stores, repair shops for just about anything imaginable, clothing stores, and so forth. In all the shops, the goods that were available were generally made of the most durable components, but a few frills, for example, simple jewelry and adornments for clothing, were available to maintain high levels of morale.

But the aspects of the spacecraft that were essential for its smooth functioning were either monitored with dedicated meters or additional monitors that were easily accessible by using one of the many onboard computers to access each function. Additional information could be obtained from video monitors from the hundreds of cameras positioned throughout the spacecraft.

James continued, "We are broadcasting what we are seeing as we approach Earth over all the onboard monitors so you can also observe what's ahead. Of course, it's night in New York, but there are enough lights to observe what we're encountering as we approach our destination. When we actually get to our point of disembarkation, we will illuminate our landing spot. So please enjoy the scenery along with us!"

There were already oohs and aahs from the five hundred members of Captain James' ship, and undoubtedly more from the other nineteen ships. As they approached Earth from the night side, the lights from the towns and cities began to be obvious, increasing the excitement of the Camitorians.

"You all have your instructions as to how to disembark, where to get your money, your apartment keys, and a map of the essential features and shopping places near your apartments. Since we do resemble Earthlings in essentially all features except our skin color, which is a bit greener than theirs, applying the makeup with which we've supplied you should make it possible to avoid even second glances from your new neighbors.

"And, finally, we have lived for the past three decades as a family. And I must say," and his voice broke, "I will miss you all as I leave to return to Camitor."

He turned to Sylvie Sensei, the woman sitting next to him, "Sylvie, are you ready for this? You'll all be embarking on an extraordinary adventure! But I can't imagine anyone who would be more capable of leading it."

She swiveled in her chair to face him, "Thank you, Captain. I believe we're ready. We've rehearsed everything to the hilt, although the unexpected can always occur. And it surely will sometime during our stay on Earth.

"But I also must compliment you on leading our fleet of spacecraft to Earth. You did a masterful job, and I am immensely grateful." Their eyes locked for a moment, and Sylvie reveled in his warm confidence and unshakable sense of purpose. She also saw a deep sadness in his return gaze. After thirty years of comradery, who knew if they would ever meet again.

James smiled in acknowledgement, "Thank you, Sylvie. Soon you'll be on your own with your one thousand Camitorians in New York, and of course, the other nine thousand in other cities of Earth. In the meantime, I'll be on my way back to Camitor to collect my next installment of Earthbound Camitorians."

"Good luck, Captain. We'll both need it!"

Camitorians communicated via their brain waves, so the Captain and Sensei weren't actually verbalizing their comments. They could speak aloud to each other if that was necessary, but that was much less efficient than the brain wave exchange mode. If they were within a few feet of each other, they could sense each other's brain waves directly. For greater distances they relied on a communication device, invented tens of thousands of years earlier and upgraded many times since, that they inserted into one ear. It added their low frequency brain waves to three much higher frequency, and intensity, radio waves, which were then transmitted. Since they didn't necessarily want to send out their message to everyone within range, their brains contained a data base that allowed them to select a specific recipient. It did so by instructing the communication device to choose the relative intensities of the three radio waves to be specific to that individual. Camitorians could also broadcast their message when they wanted everyone within range to hear them. In that case their amplifier set the strengths of the three carrier waves to be equal.

For transmission over greater distances, the waves were sent to Camitorian transmission stations to be relayed to the recipient, either directly or via communications satellite. Once the Camitorians got to Earth, they found the Earthling transmission towers and communications satellites to be more than adequate for their needs. But there was a profound difference between all Camitorian communications devices and Earthling smartphones, transmission towers, and satellites. In either sending or receiving mode, the RF radiation levels from the Camitorian devices were at least a thousand times lower, primarily because of their ability to obtain signals from three RF waves. That virtually eliminated background noise. For receiving, if the communications device decided its Camitorian was the intended recipient of a message, it would unscramble the low frequency waves from the three carrier waves and send them on to the Camitorian's brain.

The signals the Camitorians dealt with were vastly weaker than those on planet Earth, as was the interference producing background. Thus, they required many fewer transmission towers and communications satellites, much as Earth was in the 1990s.

Captain James' spaceship and its five hundred inhabitants arrived in Central Park in New York City at three a.m. on Monday January, 2023. It was one of two spacecraft to land there; the two had traveled together since their departure from

Camitor. It was thought this arrival time would cause the least commotion from the Earthlings and allow the best possibility for the Camitorians to melt into the local scene. Anonymity had been chosen as the preferred mode of existence, at least for the short term.

Other pairs of spaceships would land essentially concomitantly in Rio, then in Tokyo, Seoul, and Sydney, followed by Beijing, then Moscow, and finally Paris, Berlin, and London. The landings had been planned for three o'clock in the morning in all the cities, so they were staggered around the globe according to the time zone. The landing in New York was the first, but as successive landings occurred, worldwide news alerted inhabitants of some of the subsequent landing sites.

The twenty spacecraft had traveled closely together in case of a mishap to one of them. In addition to the stars and planets, interplanetary space is flooded with meteoroids of varying size. The hulls of the spacecraft were designed to be self-sealing for small meteoroid punctures, and they occasionally were hit with hull piercing objects. But there was always the possibility, however improbable, of a hit that couldn't be automatically repaired. Then the other nineteen ships could circle the wounded one, which would then distribute its five hundred passengers plus crew members onto the other nineteen spacecraft. Fortunately, this did not happen on this voyage.

People from Camitor had been visiting Earth for nearly a century. Their spacecraft, often observed by Earthlings, were generally filed under "UFOs" Unidentified Flying Objects, by the military establishment of each country, and at first were not acknowledged to the public. However, as the numbers of these sightings grew, it finally became necessary for officials to recognize that alien visits and even landings were occurring, and that the visitors didn't appear to be hostile. At first the world's militaries had attempted to confront the spacecraft and even to destroy them in a few cases, but they soon found that standard military solutions, bullets and air-to-air missiles, didn't seem to have any effect. However, there never was any retaliation, although it was suspected the visitors could have chosen that route with disastrous results if they chose, given that their weapons technology probably was consistent with their highly advanced spaceflight and aerodynamic technology. It was assumed there were aliens of some sort in the UFOs, since no Earthling country could claim technology anything like what was being observed.

The Earthling year 2023 was an auspicious one for both Camitorians and Earthlings. Beginning in late 2019, Earth had been subjected to an extraordinary virus that prevailed for the next two years, affecting hundreds of millions of Earthlings and killing several million. The precautions that had been taken to try to minimize the infections and deaths did have some deterrence effect, especially in the countries where sufficient discipline was imposed to control the virus's spread, and vaccines of varying capability had been developed. But the precautions also had a staggering impact on the economies of the world, plunging many workers around the world into unemployed status, and many others into jobs requiring skill levels well beneath their capabilities, just to survive.

The virus-related deaths did begin to dwindle in 2021, but the virus mutated, so there was a constant effort by scientists to keep up with what the virus was doing.

But by 2023, many more deaths were recorded from something even more mysterious than the virus. The official causes of these deaths were not so different from those of earlier times: heart attacks, diabetes, cancer, strokes, and suicides, but their sharp increase had the medical professionals struggling to understand why. Aside from the official causes listed on the death certificates, there were a number of symptoms that seemed to be precursors of death. These included intense headaches, brain fog, and a wide variety of others, many of which signaled forthcoming organ failure.

There was concern among the arriving Camitorians that the Earthling medical experts hadn't figured out how to deal with the new threat yet, nor had they been able to identify the origins.

None the less, they were confident the precursor Camitorians had found the cause of the newest malady, and managed to circumvent the problem, at least for themselves. But they needed to teach the newly arrived Camitorians how to solve it. And then, if they were amenable to suggestions, the Earthlings.

The Camitorians had planned to begin landing a large number of their people on Earth for some time, although that couldn't happen rapidly. The present group had, after all, been in transit for three decades. Their long-range plan had them ultimately transferring virtually the entire Camitorian population of one billion to Earth. The precursor Camitorians had been sent to each of the ten targeted cities to absorb and understand the local customs, standards, and bylaws, so as to provide the information necessary for the subsequent much larger groups to assimilate as rapidly as possible into the local populations of Earthlings.

Of course, they also had to determine if there were going to be any medical problems for those who would follow them to Earth. There were all kinds of viruses and bacteria that might present dangerous issues for the Camitorians if they couldn't figure out how to deal with them. But they had found in every city they went to that there was nothing for which they couldn't figure out a remedy. The Earth would be safe!

This had been in the planning stages for more than a century, so the landing in 2023 hadn't actually been scheduled to coincide with Earth's current problems.

But the multitude of Earthly problems in addition to the elevated death rates, certainly included environmental challenges and societal issues such as wealth disparity and political unrest. All this made the Camitorians realize that 2023 was the ideal time to land on Earth and, ultimately, make their presence known. Their help might even be appreciated!

Chapter 3. Acclimating

The site chosen for the New York City landing, Central Park, is an extremely popular place for New Yorkers and tourists during the day, even in January, but is not so safe in the middle of the night. Thus, it was expected that no one would be there, save for an occasional policeman. Each of the two interplanetary spacecraft had two lander modules to bring the spacecraft's passengers to Earth. Central Park, as well as the other chosen landing sites, has sufficiently large open spaces that the four lander modules could hover there while the Camitorians descended in their elevators to the frosty grass, relic boulders from past ice ages, New York flora, and pathways. Once on the ground they could disperse on foot in several directions. Central Park is four kilometers long and one kilometer wide and is lined on both long sides by a myriad of apartment buildings. Thus, the Camitorians could get to their apartments with a minimum of walking.

Sylvie Sensei had been chosen to be the overall leader of the twenty-spacecraft mission. Her age, two hundred seventeen Earthling years at the time of disembarkation, allowed her to have been involved in a variety of life experiences, including several major political leadership roles. Her success as a leader always seemed to result from her ability to listen to people of any opinion, and then to merge at least some of their wishes into the final decisions of the group she commanded. It also helped that she had an easy manner and infectious smile that could win over even the most recalcitrant of political opponents.

Because Camitorians had two hundred thousand more years to evolve their civilization than did the current version of Earthlings, they had developed the capacity to solve the majority of their contentious social issues and had built the rules that would perpetuate those solutions into their political institutions. Indeed, it would not have been possible for their civilization, or any other, to have lasted that long had they not done so.

As part of Sensei's life experiences, she had also taken three space flights of more than one year duration. This was deemed to be an essential component for any of the travelers, but especially for the mission leader.

Her academic training had been in genetics, and she had pursued that endeavor on and off for most of her life, often in her free time. However, her leadership skills also placed her at the head of many of the tasks she undertook, usually reluctantly. At one stage she ran for political office, the Camitorian Senate, to which she was elected. She served two six-year terms there, rising rapidly into leadership roles in several of the most important committees. However, she had known since her youth that she wanted to indulge in flights to other planets in her solar system, and preparation for that, along with her genetics research, was what had absorbed many of her years and most of her interests.

Her natural talents were complemented by her energy level. She never seemed to tire, despite a daunting workload. However, this did not necessarily allow her to be patient. She needed to be efficient, and she never allowed a meeting to extend for more than an hour when she was in charge. None the less, she was not abrasive; her outward demeanor generally appeared to be calm, her lavender eyes always seemed to be sensitive to the needs of others, and that lovely smile graced her face far more frequently than her occasional frown.

But on this day in January 2023, as Sensei led her one thousand, Camitorians into New York City, her concerns extended well beyond that group to the other nine thousand Camitorians who would soon be landing at their destinations around the globe. For the New York arrivals, each dozen member subset was to proceed to a predetermined destination under the hovering landers, where they would meet with a member of the advance party, receive some US dollars, a credit card, directions to their apartment, a key, and a roll of aluminum foil. The Camitorians landing in other cities would receive most of the same items, but of course would receive the local currency. They had all adopted names during their travel that were appropriate to their destination and had been practicing the language of their new home so they could adapt readily to it.

When they entered their apartments, they would find enough food and clothing to sustain them for a few days. They were expected to begin quickly to tour their area on foot to discover where to buy food, how to access transportation, and so forth. Instructions were supplied to direct them to the most important places. The advance parties in each city had also discovered that each had places that should be avoided, usually because of safety, so those were also indicated to the new arrivals' maps. All were also informed of the locations of nearby Camitorians, especially of the nearest Camitorian doctor in case he or she was needed.

Obviously two objects the size of the lander modules that hovered over Central Park or any other location on Earth would surely be seen by a few people, even at three a.m. In most countries, sightings of UFOs had become sufficiently routine that they were reported through standard news channels. But these landings were occurring in the dark of night, so there were no reporters to witness them; eyewitness accounts provided all the information. Added to that was the fact that it was January, so the Camitorians could be sure there would be very few spectators to record the many smartphone pictures that would otherwise have been taken of their landings.

The Camitorians were concerned that observation of the numbers of aliens at any location might lead Earthlings to worry that an invasion was underway. Thus, they had developed an electromagnetic screen projected between the spaceship and the ground, which made it impossible to determine exactly how many Camitorians were exiting the spacecraft. The screens were thin "curtains" of intense ultraviolet light that encircled the region directly below the hovering spacecraft. This light ionized many of the atoms in the curtain, producing an abundance of free electrons. They scattered the light, which would otherwise have gone unobstructed from inside the curtain to the outside. The result was very blurred images of any objects within the curtain. Camitorians exited through "doorways" in the curtains.

Despite the winter night, the New York landings were observed by a few motorists and by two policemen, Sam and Joe, among New York's finest, on patrol in Central Park.

Sam and Joe almost in unison, "Holy shit, look at those!"

Sam, spilling his coffee, speaking at machine gun speed, "Are those, UFOs? What the hell! I thought UFOs were just blips in the sky, but those look like honest to god spaceships. What kind of bullshit has our government been feedin' us? Them blips look like they're burpin' out real live critters. And what's that fog? It's only under that ship. And are those people walkin' out of the fog? Do ya' think they're aliens?"

As he was talking, he pointed at the place from which the people seemed to be emerging. Then, "Oh shit, I'd better not point at them. They might point back and make us disappear."

He paused for a moment to catch his breath, "Maybe this is some kinda' government experiment and those are just people. But they must be aliens. Never seen an airplane like that. And how can it just hover? If it was a helicopter is should be making a lotta' noise. If not, it should fall like a goddamn rock. And if it is an airplane, it sure as hell missed the airport. Either way, where are they from?"

Joe, who was having difficulty getting in any words, "Yeah, looks like a goddamn invasion. But I can't tell how many there are. Maybe ten? Or a-hundred? And they look fuzzy; why is that? Don't see any guns but, like you said, maybe these dudes can just point at you and make you disappear. Did they see us? If they did, they coulda' killed us. But they don't seem to be particularly interested in doin' that. At least, not yet. But maybe they're from Hollywood and are makin' a movie. You see any camera crews? Hey, Sam, maybe we'll get to be in a movie."

As soon as the Camitorians had all disembarked, the pilots took the four lander modules quickly back into their respective spacecraft to undertake the subsequent part of their mission: return to Camitor. After the thirty-year return trip, they'll each gather another five hundred Camitorians to bring to Earth. The disembarkation plan had been so carefully rehearsed that setting all one thousand Camitorians into Central Park took only a few minutes.

But this was the United States, where UFO sightings are always investigated by the authorities and then were, for decades, attributed either to natural phenomena or overzealous observers. Only recently had that attitude begun to evolve towards reality, but that change had not had a chance to filter down through all levels of the bureaucracy. Thus, a few minutes later, when Sam and Joe had regained their composure, they reported the events of the evening. "Hey, Super, we just observed two huge goddamn spacecraft hoverin' over Central Park. And two smaller things came out of the bellies of each of the larger ones. Some individuals—aliens?—got off, but we couldn't tell for sure how many."

"I'll need to report this. Sit tight for a few minutes until I get back to you."

Sam and Joe's report wasn't a total surprise. The supervisor's phone had already been ringing off the hook with calls reporting the landers, and the airports had observed blurry anomalous objects over Central Park, despite the landers' stealth technology. He wasn't sure who would be most appropriate to contact, but he figured the Federal Aeronautics Administration would be a good start. The person he talked to at the FAA had also been awakened and had contacted several more people in appropriate federal security agencies. They had a standard plan for handling these situations that had been in force for decades. George Stevens, from the National Security Agency called Sam and Joe. "You guys are good cops, and you've done an excellent job in reporting the UFOs. Although the United States does now officially recognize the existence of UFOs, we haven't yet been willing to acknowledge that they might have anything to do with aliens. Thus, we are going to make you both offers you can't refuse. But there is one condition: that you never ever mention what you saw this evening. You will each be given cash stipends equal to twenty years of your present salary.

"But don't ever forget that you saw absolutely nothing this evening!"

Sam and Joe, in unison, "Twenty years salary, huh? Got it! Never saw nothin'."

Joe, barely able to contain his excitement, "Wait'll I tell the wife about my bonus! Guess I can't tell her how it came about. She'll probably think I got another drug money payoff. I'll have to come up with a good excuse. Got any ideas?"

"Well, we have a few more hours before our shift ends. We damn well better come up with our excuse by then."

The few New Yorkers who had witnessed the landing from a somewhat greater distance assumed that if they ever said anything about it, long-standing attitudes about UFOs would still probably brand them as excessively imaginative, crazy, drunk, or some combination of those factors. However, some did contact the news media, anonymously of course, some with smartphone pictures, to alert the world about the alien landing. The one in Rio occurred not long after New York's, and when the news about two landings hit the airwaves, the rest of the world was suddenly alerted to alien landings, with possibly more to come!

But from the perspective of the United States, it was still possible to keep its head partially buried in the interplanetary sands, perhaps with one eye looking out, and the Camitorians found it easy to merge into the environs of New York City.

Only when all one thousand nouveau New Yorkers had dispersed did Sylvie Sensei meet with Dustin, the advance-party member who had arranged for her apartment. From him she got her key, cash, and credit card. She had brought with her the components of her onboard genetics laboratory that she thought might be difficult to duplicate on Earth. Dustin accompanied her to her apartment to help transport the equipment, most of which was carefully packed in a large box that had wheels to expedite moving it, even if there was a little snow on the ground. Dustin carried one large piece over his shoulder. Sensei explained, "I have no immediate plans to use the equipment, but I still think it might be important sometime for me to have it." She suspected that her knowledge of genetics and an ability to perform experiments might come in handy in her new home.

Dustin replied, "Sylvie, I wouldn't be surprised if your knowledge and experiments turned out to be critical to our merging with the Earthlings! Especially because it might be beneficial to them."

As Sensei and Dustin walked, she was trying to anticipate both the immediate future and the longer term. "The actual length of time we'll spend in our present circumstances will depend on how quickly we can be integrated into Earthling society. This really depends on the length of time required for Earthlings to realize we can solve the problems that have plagued them the most. Certainly a few will see that to be the case quickly, and then our patience will be tested to find out how long it takes for them to convince the others that they should listen to us."

Dustin added, "Sylvie, we'll just have to bide our time. The transition interval may just depend on which Earthlings are the first to recognize the benefits of what we're telling them, and how good they are in broadcasting that information."

"I'm sure you're right, Dustin. But there's bound to be resistance and anger, and many will try to claim that we cannot really understand Earth's problems simply because we are not of the Earth. If they declared war on us, they'd first have to identify most of us, especially those of us in leadership positions, and this might not be so easy since we do look a lot like them."

He pondered that for a moment, "We have to hope we can evade detection for a while so we can avoid any form or retaliation that threatens our survival. Our brain-to-brain communications will make it difficult for them to intercept the messages passing between us and impossible to understand them. However, I'm concerned that all the background radiation may hinder our ability to talk with each other as efficiently as we are accustomed."

She'd given that considerable thought, "Ah, Dustin, but when they intercept those indecipherable messages, they'll know they have found an alien.

"But we do have a defense plan, about which they won't be told unless it becomes necessary. I hope we don't get challenged, since the plan isn't yet in place. It'll take some time to perform the crucial Earthling DNA modifications, chemicals for which would be dumped into their drinking water. The changes include molecular fragments, inserted into their DNA, which could be destroyed by electromagnetic radiation of a specific frequency. Simple emitters would be created to flood the Earth with radiation of that frequency if it became necessary, thus quickly destroying all Earthling DNA and, therefore, Earthlings. There is some radiation of that frequency all the time, but the rate of cell regeneration outweighs that of cell death unless the emitters are turned on.

"Once the modifications are in place, Earthlings would be forced to accept our presence. But we won't put this plan in place unless we are threatened. It's obviously extremely hostile. But we'd like our acceptance to be based on Earthlings wanting to share the planet with us, rather than blackmail."

When they reached her apartment, Sensei was so absorbed with the events of the evening that she failed to observe the number of rooms, how they were furnished, or the view out of the windows. She was certainly on edge over the possibility that something could go awry with her New York based Camitorians, but, happily, there were no immediate problems.

She kept cycling through the events of the evening, "Dustin, I'm still wondering about those two policemen we saw. They clearly had weapons and could have done great harm to us. However, they appeared to be in awe of our lander modules, and the rapidity with which we disembarked and evaporated into the night. And, because of the electromagnetic screen, they certainly were not able to count how many of us there were."

"Right, Sylvie. I've generally seen the New York City cops to be fairly reasonable, that is, not trigger happy. I think we were lucky to have gotten those two, though. We have found that the cops are not always as civilized as they were."

As she was setting things down and opening a few cases, "Well perhaps their inability to act was associated with the speed at which everything happened. I was amazed myself with how rapidly the entire disembarkation evolved; I think that spared us a lot of problems that simply did not have time to develop."

Dustin stayed a few minutes to make sure she had everything she needed, then left her to her thoughts.

The landing in the United States had been done first because it was thought it would take the news longer to travel from there to other countries than the reverse, primarily because of the government's residual myopia about UFOs and aliens. But Sensei continued to worry: *I cannot feel certain of our success for the time it will take for the other nine landings to take place. The advance parties here did an incredible job, and all the New York–based Camitorians have found their new homes. But will that be the case at every site? We must not have even one Camitorian wandering the streets of their new city all night! Surely if there's a problem the local leader will know about it immediately, and I'll find out soon thereafter.*

Finally, by the morning of the following day, she had gotten confirmation from the other nine leaders, their amplified brain waves being relayed to her via Earthling communication satellites, that all ten landings had gone as planned and all ten thousand Camitorians were safe. She was so exhausted that she lay down on her unmade bed still wearing the clothes she had worn for more than two days. She slept fitfully for a short while, then exhaustion overtook her, and she drifted into a deep sleep. She was finally awakened by the blare of a police siren. As soon as she opened her eyes the headache set in with a withering intensity. She quickly remembered the roll of aluminum foil and Dustin's instructions for making a head covering with it.

Once she solved her headache problem, she began to inspect her apartment. Only then did she realize, *this apartment is undoubtedly much nicer than those of the other Camitorians. We couldn't afford to set everyone up like this. I'm on a high floor, perhaps the top floor of my building, with a view of Central Park out these expansive windows.* She walked over to a large sofa across from the windows and sat down, running her hands over the fabric. *And this furniture is both beautiful and comfortable, and all the pieces have the same pattern, presumably of some traditional Earthling design.*

I see from my map that I'm located a few blocks from an entrance to the Park, and a block from a bus stop. The apartment also has several rooms, something that would have been impossible for the past thirty years on the spaceship. This seems excessive. Perhaps Earthlings will realize sometime that they need to limit overuse of resources in a civilized society.

But this means that I can set up my genetics laboratory right here when I get some time to do so. And that is something for which I will make time.

However, the walls certainly are desperately in need of some pictures!

The landings at the other nine sites also went flawlessly, although some were observed by many local Earthlings. This was especially true for those in the southern hemisphere, where summer gatherings were still in force when the spaceships arrived. However, they were so in awe of the landers and the organization of the Camitorians that no threatening incidents occurred. Indeed, in the case of Rio, some of the aliens were presented with floral bouquets that were spontaneously prepared by especially courageous Cariocas as the Camitorians emerged from their electromagnetic cocoons beneath their landers. As the landings proceeded around the world, and it became clear that the aliens meant no harm, a few lucky witnesses even managed to take a selfie with one of the newcomers.

Although the Camitorians greatly appreciated the warm welcomes, their primary desire following their thirty-year trip and arrival was to get to their new homes as quickly as possible. And to get some sleep!

Chapter 4. Headaches

Sylvie was not the only newly arrived Camitorian to experience the headache. In many cases, they awakened the morning after their arrival with something that threatened to split their head into fragments. They had all been forewarned, so immediately implemented the desperately needed aluminum foil fix to circumvent this problem. Those in Seoul, Beijing, Tokyo, and New York seemed to suffer the most, with those in the other locations enduring less pain, in some cases, much less.

The Camitorians who had been on Earth for the decades since the advent of cell phones and other RF radiation emitting devices had partially solved the problem with various shields and clothing that contained metallic fibers. However, it wasn't practical for them to provide these mitigation materials to all ten thousand newly arrived Camitorians. But some solutions had been developed, so they left catalogs and instructions for ordering in their apartments. The ten thousand had been briefed about the issue in the weeks preceding their arrival. Still, it wasn't completely clear to most exactly how strongly they would be affected, and what mitigations would be needed.

Once on Earth, though, word quickly circulated that they had to, in some way, create a partial Faraday cage for their heads to buffer their electromagnetically sensitive brains from the plethora of radio frequency pollution that permeated the environment of every city, and most of the countryside. When they were in their apartments, the aluminum foil metallic helmets seemed to at least make the situation tolerable. They amused themselves by sending cranially transmitted photos of themselves with their variously decorated aluminum foil helmets. Earthly flora and fauna were popular adornments.

Although a solution sometimes just creates a new problem, this was not the case for the Camitorians. Since most of their communication signals were emitted and received via sensors in their ears, a small hole in whatever they were using for head covering was adequate to permit their communications as usual. This didn't completely solve the problem; there was still so much electromagnetic noise, so-called white noise, that their communications were sometimes garbled from what worked on Camitor without further modification. This was especially true in New York, Tokyo, Beijing, and Seoul, the cites with the most RF emitters.

To circumvent the noise, they learned they could send their communications via carrier waves of highly defined frequencies. Once everyone in a single locale knew those frequencies, they could lock their sensor in on them, thus tuning out most of the extraneous noise. Although there was always some white noise at every frequency, the precise frequency selections alleviated most of the background.

After spending most of the morning communicating with the leaders in the other nine cities, Sylvie decided to brave the headache enough to do two ventures out. The first was to a grocery store Dustin had recommended. He had indicated it had a wonderful produce department, and Sylvie couldn't wait to see how well Earthling vegetables could satisfy her vegetarian diet. Few of the things she found there looked even remotely familiar, but she realized she'd have to learn which items she liked best by just tasting them. She also quickly discovered that it was risky squeezing the produce to see if it seemed fresh; squeezing carrots produced a rather different result than squeezing tomatoes.

The second trip was to a local art shop that was indicated on her map. Her wish for some artwork to decorate her barren walls had become so intense that it simply had to be satisfied. As she entered the store, the proprietor gave her a cordial greeting, "Good afternoon, Madam. Please just look around as you wish. I will be here to answer any questions you might have."

"Oh, thank you. Let me just browse a bit, and then I may wish to purchase something."

She spent a good hour looking around, ignoring the headache, but enjoying especially the most brightly colored paintings. She was surprised that few of them seemed to be paintings of something, but she liked the way the shapes and colors had been matched and mixed. She was a bit surprised at the prices, but she finally selected two paintings that seemed to fit her budget and were small enough for her to carry back to her apartment.

"I'd like these two."

"Okay, I'm sure you will enjoy them. These are acrylics done by a local artist. He's well known for his unique style and bright colors. Here, let me wrap them up so they won't get damaged. And the price is as indicated."

"Here's the money to pay for them." She had to examine each bill carefully to determine its value.

The salesman didn't want to pass on a potentially extraordinary opportunity, "Are you new to the area? I've not seen you here before."

She decided to humor him, "I did arrive just recently, and this is the first time I've been in your store."

"Are you feeling okay? You look a little bit … uh … green."

Hmm, I thought this morning's makeup would last through the day. That's apparently not the case. I'm not quite ready yet to let it be known that I'm an alien.

"I'm quite healthy, thank you."

He didn't give up easily, "Where did you move from?"

That ended the humoring, "Oh I'm sure it's a place you haven't visited. I'm also quite sure you've never heard of it."

With that she hurried out the door with her purchases.

Chapter 5. Camitorian History

The situation that was forcing the Camitorians to abandon their planet and migrate to Earth had been described to them by Professor Koming, a legendary two-hundred-seventy-three-year-old Camitorian astrophysicist. He was both a famous scientist and an extraordinary talent for explaining science to Camitorians. His appearance would best be described as "rumpled." He did get an occasional haircut and beard trim, although his students concluded that he himself trimmed both his hair and his beard, but probably not more frequently than twice a year, and using the Camitorian equivalent of sheep shears. The shirts and pants with which he clothed his lumpy body always seemed to be wrinkled. However, his eyes were not consistent with the rest of his appearance; they were intense, somewhat kind, and always sharply at attention.

He gave regular talks to Camitorians about astrophysics and astrobiology that had become quite popular and accessible. To view the lectures, RF signals from the transmission stations were converted to audio and video by the transducer in their ear to signals that produced three-dimensional holograms they could view with any backdrop, including their hand, or even with their eyes closed as their brain reconstructed the images.

Koming would occasionally interrupt his lectures with a light cough, which wasn't necessary, but he thought it gave special significance to what he had just said and gave his audience a few seconds to digest his comments. Whether it did either was debatable, but the Camitorians had come to expect the occasional coughs, usually with amusement.

Koming thought it might be interesting for listeners to hear some of the questions children might ask. So, he arranged to include the interactions between his great-great granddaughter and her daughter following the lectures.

All Camitorians had been alerted to the importance of the messages of Koming, so every adult reserved one of the time slots when his talks would be broadcast. Although his talks were pitched for adults, most children also planned to watch them. It was useful for the adults and children to watch the lectures together, since the youngsters would often have questions that helped them gain understanding. Besides, he was entertaining.

First Koming Lecture

"Good evening, my fellow citizens of Camitor. I will be presenting news that, while sad for continued life on the planet we and our ancestors have enjoyed for two hundred thousand years, should give all of us hope for a future in a new home.

"I will be comparing two planetary systems: ours, Camitor, and another, Earth, which orbits about a star the Earthlings call Sun. We will need to get used to the Earthling names for their star and planets; we are planning to move the entire population of Camitor to Earth. But let me not get too far ahead of myself.

"As you know, Camitor is one of seven planets that orbit our star Seduline. The Sedulinian system was formed about nine billion years ago out of the gas and dust produced by earlier generations of stars, which had enriched the interstellar gas and dust with all the elements of the periodic table.

"Camitor is the third planet as one moves outward from our star. Seduline's stellar system was initially awash with the detritus that accompanied its formation. In addition to the planets, there were meteoroids, asteroids, and comets, and one of these frequently crashed into a planet with consequences that depended on the size of the incident object. However, these cosmic messengers also brought water, as well as the amino acids and the nucleobases that comprise our DNA and RNA. Despite the hostile conditions of outer space, these basic molecules of life are formed there. The water that was delivered to most of the planets in the Sedulinian system by asteroids either boiled away or froze, with the exception of that on Camitor, where it remained liquid in most places, maintaining its ability to support life forms. In time the hits from the space objects lessened, and life could finally begin to develop and evolve with only occasional interruptions.

"Both Earth and Camitor rotate about their axes; Earth rotates with a speed that makes its days about ninety percent as long as a Camitorian day. Camitor's axis of rotation is nearly perpendicular to its plane of rotation about Seduline, which means each place on our planet has only one season year around. On Earth, however, the axis of rotation is tilted by twenty-three degrees with respect to the perpendicular to its plane of rotation about Sun. This produces warmer and cooler seasons in most places. Earth also rotates about Sun at a speed and distance such that its years are ten percent longer than those of Camitor.

"Our star, Seduline, was born several billion years before Sun was born, which means it is that much farther along in its stellar evolution. Sun and Seduline have about the same mass and they and their planets were formed of the same elements. These include the hydrogen, oxygen, nitrogen, and carbon on which are based Camitor's and Earth's life forms, the oxygen we need to breathe, calcium for our bones, iron for our blood, and so forth.

"As Seduline and Sun condensed, heated, and became stars, they began to consume their hydrogen, converting it into helium via nuclear reactions. Stars of their mass spend ninety percent of their lives consuming their core hydrogen. After roughly nine billion years, most of the core hydrogen will have been used up, and the central part of each star will contract and heat up. This temperature increase will permit the stars to begin to convert what will then be their core helium into carbon and oxygen, now by a new set of nuclear reactions. ... cough, cough ... When this happens to Seduline, it will expand to a size that may envelope Camitor. We will return to this in my third lecture.

"Planet Earth is roughly the same distance from Sun as Camitor is from Seduline, and the two have about the same mass. Earth underwent an early history similar to Camitor's, namely, with many bombardments from meteoroids, comets, and asteroids that brought it water and the basic molecules of life.

"Life was then able to develop, initially as very simple single-celled entities. But these ultimately evolved into an incredible variety of living beings on Camitor and, several billion years later, on Earth. Although the DNAs of Camitorians and Earthlings are made out of the same nucleobases, they have significant differences. Evolution would not be expected to produce identical results in two completely independent biospheres from the plethora of possibilities. Although it might appear unlikely that there would be any resemblance at all between Camitorians and Earthlings, perhaps the requirements for the life-forms at the top of each food chain demand some basic similarities. … cough, cough … They just happened to make creatures on the two planets that look a lot alike. This will turn out to be important for us.

The video switched to the living room of Koming's great great granddaughter.

"Mom, if the core of Seduline is contracting, why is the outer part of the star expanding?"

"Well, the higher temperature of the contracted core sets off a new set of nuclear reactions which will produce more energy. That produces more radiation pressure, and that's what drives the outer portion of the star to greater radius."

"Wow, Mom, you're really smart. Is that because you're a descendent of Prof. Koming?"

"Actually, I learned that in my astrophysics course."

Second Koming Lecture

"What do Earthlings look like? Well, they have most of the basic components of Camitorians, such as two eyes, a nose, a mouth, two arms, and two legs. There are two sexes, and births

37

of Earthling babies are much like those of Camitorian babies, which is to say Earthlings have reproductive systems that are essentially identical to those of Camitorians. The babies even have the same gestational periods. However, Earthling babies grow from the moment of their inception inside the mother, unlike Camitorian babies, which often grow in gestation pods. Earthlings obviously need to reproduce to keep things going, so they have hormones that drive their sexual urges, just as we do.

"Earthlings also have hair, and they are slightly larger on average than we are. They have four fingers and a thumb on each hand, as we do, and five toes on each foot

"Earthlings sustain themselves by consuming foods, which provide the amino acids that their cells combine to make proteins, as is also the case for Camitorians. They also breathe oxygen from the atmosphere of their planet. Earthling DNA has many components in common with Camitorian DNA, although there are a few important differences. One makes it possible for us to live much longer than Earthlings. Although ages of several hundred years are not uncommon for us, Earthlings typically live only eighty Camitorian years, and there are large differences in life expectancy between different regions.

"Another difference is that Camitorians are much more resistant to damage from radiation, certainly from the cosmic rays that rain down unavoidably on both planets. This radiation impacts life span. Furthermore, the cell damage it produces can be quite different in various parts of the body. It is particularly serious in Earthling brains, as their brain cells are not readily repaired or replaced when they die, as are cells in other parts of their bodies, and in all parts of Camitorian bodies.

"There is no way to shield us or them completely from these cosmic rays. The ability of Camitorian DNA to repair cell damage has several consequences, one being the much longer typical lifetimes we enjoy compared to those of Earthlings. Another is the implication that radiation damage repair has for space travelers. … cough, cough … Spacecraft are continuously bombarded with high energy particles, which cause showers of radiation when they impact the shells of the spacecraft. These burrow through any bodies they intersect, inevitably causing cell death. Since space travel can entail transit times of decades, if your body cannot repair the damage from this radiation, you do not have much of a chance of making it to your destination.

"The inability of Earthlings to live for many years impacts how they organize their lives. For example, Earthling women are typically fertile from about thirteen to forty-five Camitorian years, as opposed to the twenty to more than two hundred years for Camitorian women. But Earthling women's bodies compensate for their shorter reproductive lives; they have thirteen estrus cycles per year, as opposed to Camitorian women, who have only two.

"A couple on either planet could easily conceive dozens of children, which could produce a population explosion that would quickly overwhelm the ability of either planet to support its people. Unlike us with our two-child limit, most Earthling countries have not addressed this situation in a meaningful way. While Earthling birthrates are not at the level that will produce an immediate worldwide disaster, some countries already do have serious problems feeding their populations.

"Camitorians and Earthlings reach physical adulthood at about the same age, so they go through their education and then into the work world at about the same time in their lives. Having grown to adulthood, Earthlings tend to marry and raise families sooner than we do. If your expected lifetime is as short as that of Earthlings, you would probably choose to get on with life sooner than you otherwise might. And the possibility of marriages only lasting several decades imposes less caution in choosing a mate than if you might have a marriage lasting hundreds of years!

"I'll return to astrophysics and its implications for the inhabitants of Camitor in my next lecture."

The screen returned to the living room, "Mom, do the people on other planets look like us?"

"I don't think so. There are many ways evolution could lead to the most developed beings, and it is not likely that they would come out looking nearly the same in very many cases. It is really a fluke of nature that we ended up having such a strong resemblance to Earthlings."

"Wow. That's cool."

Third Koming Lecture

"As I noted in my first lecture, when Seduline moves into its helium burning phase, its core helium nuclei will undergo a new set of nuclear reactions. The additional radiation produced creates a pressure that will force the periphery of the star outward, producing a star that is called a red giant. The temperature at the surface of such stars is lower than it is in the preceding phase, making them appear redder. However, since their size, hence surface area, has increased, their total energy output has increased.

"This increased size is ultimately going to be a problem for us. The red giant's outer surface will extend close to, possibly even beyond, the orbit of Camitor. ... cough, cough ... In either case, at the resulting high temperatures all life will be destroyed.

"So, we have developed a plan. With our telescopes and space probes we identified potential candidates for our migration, then visited the most promising ones to be certain that the conditions would support us. One of our early visits to Earth resulted in disaster, as the spacecraft crashed near a place the Earthlings call Roswell, New Mexico, in the country they call the United States. But before it crashed it sent back data, suggesting Earth was a pretty barren place. Fortunately, we didn't give up, and subsequent visits identified greener and wetter places in many other Earth locations. Since water appears to be essential to sustain any form of life, this is clearly crucial.

"Once we identified Earth as the most promising planet for our migration, we sent one thousand Camitorians there to ten different locations to see how well we would adapt, to learn the local customs and rules, and if things went as we hoped, to serve as the welcoming committees for the larger contingents to follow.

"In a few billion more years, Sun will also become a red giant, and will expand to near the orbit of Earth, destroying all Earthly life. But this gives the Camitorians who have been transported to Earth millions of Earthling generations to exist before the helium burning phase of Sun becomes a problem.

"What is the timescale for our migration to Earth? While it is difficult to tell exactly how much longer we have before Seduline becomes a red giant, we do know that when its outward appearance indicates it has begun its transition, we need to have already evacuated Camitor. Our computer models of Seduline predict the conversion to a red giant will begin in about three hundred thousand years. But space travel takes a long time, and we estimate it will take most of that time to transfer everyone to Earth. So, the transfer needs to begin now. We have already begun building the first spaceships that will transport us to Earth, the planet we have chosen for our new home.

"But what do we do about the several billion Earthlings? We are far more technologically advanced than they are, so we could simply annihilate them and take over. But after a short debate, no, actually just a discussion because there was no dissent, we concluded that mass murder would not be acceptable. We have been around for two hundred thousand years and have developed into a citizenry that has never known anything but peace. Our forebearers realized early on that our survival depended on it. Thus, the annihilation scenario would be invoked only if it became necessary for the defense of the Camitorians who were there.

"Instead, we plan to try to coexist with Earthlings. So, we have to decide how difficult it will be to simply persuade the Earthlings that we should all live together. We found, from some Earthling history books, that this might be difficult. ... cough, cough ... They showed Earth to be in a nearly continuous state of war, which in some instances involved many Earth countries.

"Although the Earthlings seem to be working diligently to destroy themselves and their planet, we have had much longer to solve the root problems of greed, aggression, and excessive

41

competition, than the Earthlings have, and to replace them with civility and cooperation. Whether or not they could solve these by themselves is something we will never know. But if we assist them, perhaps we can extend their lives by the same number of generations we have enjoyed, and even allow us to live in peace with them. That is our hope.

"Finally, since our lovely planet will begin to be enveloped by Seduline in roughly three hundred thousand years, we must abandon it. So, the strategy adopted by the Camitorian general council is to move as many of us as possible to planet Earth.

"Why was that planet selected out of half a dozen good candidates? We found that every transition scenario we came up with involved merging with the existing population. Earthlings bore the strongest resemblance to Camitorians, making Earth the easiest place for us to coexist with the local population. Our advance parties have not necessarily found Earth to be accommodating, but they believe ultimately, we Camitorians will be able to blend in with the local populace. Furthermore, transit time to Earth is only a small fraction of a typical Camitorian lifetime. Thus, Earth was the obvious choice for our new home.

"Best wishes for a safe voyage."

Once again in the living room of Koming's relatives, "Mom, why does it take so long to get to Earth?"

"Well, I think you know the answer to that. Stars and planets are very far apart, and our rockets can only go so fast."

"Why can't we make them go faster?"

"I think you know the answer to that also. Remember that we cannot exceed the speed of light. In fact, the faster you go the more difficult it becomes to go still faster. Right?"

"Oh yeah, now I remember. That relativity stuff."

Chapter 6. Finances

The precursor Camitorians needed money to operate immediately when they arrived on Earth and had no obvious way to obtain it. They developed two strategies: counterfeiting and larceny. Both rankled their basic commitment to honesty, a Camitorian requirement for their civilization to have avoided self-destruction for two hundred thousand years. But they had to indulge in these undesirable strategies long enough to exist until they could get jobs and start producing income.

Obtaining jobs was easy for the Camitorians. The qualifications for virtually any job would be trivial for them, especially in the sciences, given that they had so many more generations to acquire knowledge than was possible for Earthlings. But they had to be careful not to exhibit too much of it or their bosses, and certainly their peers, would quickly realize that something was amiss.

Of course, they needed identification in order to be hired. That meant obtaining social security numbers in the United States, and similar forms of ID in other countries. But a little hacking of the social security system's computers took care of that problem. The Camitorians found the security systems used for Earth's computers to be archaic by their standards. Hiring also depended on having a bank account to which deposits could be made, and the fraudulent social security numbers took care of the ID needed for that. Creating bank accounts required a bit more hacking, this time into bank computers, a fairly routine exercise, which also allowed them to establish modest bank balances.

That allowed them to obtain credit cards, which kept them solvent until their salary deposits began. However, when the very first handfuls of Camitorians arrived, close to fifty years before Sylvie's group, credit cards had not become popular.

Quick inspections of shopping malls made them realize they needed to get some cash. They had brought small, sophisticated printers with them, anticipating that they would need to copy whatever the local currency was at each location, but they had to acquire the samples to copy. All this required was a little 'forgot what happened' mist sprayed on an isolated Earthling in a parking lot, extracting their wallet, removing a few denominations of bills, copying them, putting the bills back into the owner's wallet, and finishing the escapade with a bit of 'I'm back now' mist.

Thus, the precursor Camitorians obtained some of the currency in each country. Of course, that concern applied only to them; when Sylvie's group arrived, the precursors could supply them with all the cash needed to get them started.

But the precursors did have to counterfeit many more bills, changing serial numbers as they printed multiple copies, to achieve solvency during their initial weeks on Earth. The small printers they brought with them were sufficiently elegant that they could even simulate the necessary watermarks. The Camitorians realized that larger denominations were much more likely to be scanned for authenticity than smaller ones, so they never printed anything larger than twenty-dollar bills in the US, or their equivalent elsewhere.

The Camitorians quickly became aware of the greed that was usually involved in amassing, or suddenly obtaining, large sums. Following the flow of financial assets and understanding the Earthling financial systems became an endless source of entertainment for a few of them. Every so often they couldn't help but do some discrete transfers to even out wealth disparity, then use the funds to contribute to foundations that helped alleviate the suffering of Earth's neediest.

However, the sporting aspect of their efforts increased when they observed that transfers of huge sums of money in some of the accounts barely registered before the money was transferred to another account in some other bank, usually in the Cayman Islands or similarly remote place.

Gene Commins, one of the New York based precursor Camitorians, had a particular interest in correcting disparity. He couldn't help but notice the many homeless and destitute people on the streets of his neighborhood. He sent out some brain waves.

"Dustin," Gene, had inquired nervously of the person in charge of the New York based precursors, "would it be inappropriate for us to do a bit of an intercept of those huge, and probably illicit, money transfers? I've seen that they occur incredibly quickly, at least by Earthling standards. So, it would really be an interesting challenge to try to spin off some small fraction of those funds before they got transferred. If we did so, we'd be helping to mitigate two Earthling problems: wealth disparity and grand larceny."

Dustin pondered the question for a few seconds, "Gene, you've raised an interesting question, which doesn't have an obvious answer. But for my understanding, you believe the funds are illicit because they move so rapidly?"

"Well, that and the fact that the sources of the funds are not traceable. Legitimate funds have traceable sources."

"Okay, I understand. Let me not answer your question immediately but do go ahead and figure out what you'd have to do to remove some small fraction from those transfers. And to not get caught!"

With Dustin's cautious approval, Gene and his friends proceeded to develop algorithms that identified unusually large sums as they were being received and transferred and would switch a percent of each one to their own account. This all had to happen in the short time the money resided in their bank. Then the funds from their account were transferred anomalously to accounts of non-profits that were helping to feed and house the most destitute.

He reported back to Dustin, this time going to his apartment to give him an account in person, and exuding more confidence, "We've figured out all the tricks we need to divert funds from the rapid transfers of huge amounts of money. Actually, I've a confession; we've already begun to do the transfers. Our algorithms worked like a charm, as the Earthlings say."

Dustin gulped, then replied, "I don't know if I'd have approved of your doing that. But since you've already done it, that takes the decision off my back! However, I'm still uneasy about it, even if it will help needy Earthlings.

"But I must also note that we've been struggling a bit to provide for our basic necessities. We're finding the rents in New York to be extremely high, and I've gotten reports of similar problems in Tokyo and Paris. And the problems will only balloon when the groups of ten thousand begin to arrive. Your efforts become more defensible if you're willing to have your endeavors support Camitorian expenses in all these locales. Could you just create another account that could be a general purpose Camitorian account and transfer half of the money you acquire to it?"

"Of course. This is all to promote the Camitorian enterprise on Earth!"

"But what are the chances that you'll be caught?"

"Oh, I think the risks are nonexistent. Our algorithms are untraceable with the security the Earthlings have in their banks. Furthermore, the transactions we're stealing from must be illicit, so I doubt if the owners would want to invoke the authorities in figuring where the small amounts we pilfer from them are going."

"Ah, good thinking. I'm sure you're right."

Chapter 7. Decisions

It took a week or two of settling in for most of Sylvie's newly arrived ten thousand Camitorians to orient themselves to their environments and local customs. While each had received years of briefing and instruction on their new country's language and protocols, some were still struggling with their transition. The precursor Camitorians developed a peer support system that proved invaluable to those who needed a bit more adjustment assistance.

Sylvie was looking out her window one morning, admiring the beauty of Central Park in the winter, especially of the snow on the conifers, while working on a decision. *I'm wondering if our transition to becoming Earthlings, and especially to gaining Earthling acceptance, would be expedited if we allowed ourselves to be identified. We have encouraged everyone to remain inconspicuous, but is that really the best thing for all of us to do if we're trying to attain our ultimate goal? I need to consult with the Camitorian hierarchy.*

She sent a message to the leaders at the other nine landing sites:

Dear Nouveau Earthlings,

Although we were encouraged prior to our arrival on Earth to blend in with the Earthlings as best we could, I'm wondering if this is the optimal way to bring about our ultimate mission. What we hadn't anticipated before we left Camitor was that Earth would be in the throes of crises. I believe we have the ability to understand the root causes of some of Earth's problems, and if we proceed cautiously in opportune ways, we may be able to help Earthlings escape from their troubles. We might even gain some valuable positive recognition for our efforts, which ultimately could assist in our gaining Earthling acceptance. Our eventual plan to transport all one billion Camitorians to Earth will certainly be expedited if most Earthlings accept us.

However, I fear the Earthlings will panic when they realize how many of us we plan to add to Earth's population. That won't actually be a problem, since we have ways to increase food production and improve living quarters that Earthlings don't know about yet. But perception too often becomes reality, and that is what I'm most concerned about.

Thus, I'm wondering if some of us, specifically the leaders of the Camitorian enclaves in each of the ten cities we inhabit, should make it known that we're from a planet other than Earth, and that we have knowledge we're willing to share that will greatly benefit Earthlings. Might it be useful if we identified ourselves to help to produce positive feelings from the Earthlings?

Please let me know your thoughts on this matter.

Sylvie

The replies were virtually instantaneous. Igor Vivanovich, the leader of the Moscow contingent replied, "I can believe that this might be a good strategy for most of us, but not me. I have learned that in Russia, people who represent any sort of threat to the existing government, or even a slightly different way of thinking, tend to either disappear or get killed. From what I've been able to figure out, those who just get killed are the luckier ones. Russian prisons are not nice places! For the moment, at least, I need to let the rest of you carry our message to Earthlings!"

Bai Xinyang, the Camitorian representative in China, after hearing Vivanovich's concern, concurred. "I believe a similar situation exists for me. It would be dangerous for me if the authorities here knew I was an alien."

Takashi Hamamoto, the leader of the Tokyo group, offered a neutral opinion, "In Japan it would not be unsafe if I made it obvious I was an alien, but I do not believe it would be of any consequence. I might be ignored. I am certainly willing to go public, but I predict it will take a long time before that will have much effect here."

In Paris, Francois Dupre expressed a view that seemed typical of most of the others, "I think it would be a good idea for most of us to make ourselves known. I believe the risks are minimal, and we do have succession plans in place in all ten of our cities in case misfortune befalls the leader. Perhaps the second in command should remain unidentified in case that situation does come about. But I believe the answer to your question is 'yes.' In the interest of the ultimate Camitorian transition our leaders must begin to make our good works known."

So, Sylvie sent a follow up note.

Dear Nouveau Earthlings,

The consensus is that we as leaders should make ourselves known as Camitorians, with the exception of those in Russia and China. The Russians and Chinese authorities must be aware that there are aliens in their midst. After all, there were landings in both places that they could hardly have overlooked. They may make an effort to purge us. But we have to wonder why they have not already tried to do that. Until we have an answer to that question, no Camitorian in Moscow or Beijing should make himself or herself known.

For the rest of us, though, we seem to agree that the Camitorian leaders should make public the fact that we're from an advanced civilization, and that makes it possible for us to present useful ideas to Earthlings.

In particular, I'm making plans to try to address the problem that many Earthlings, especially most city dwellers in the United States, seem to have. As many of you know, we Camitorians have also experienced the problem. This is the proliferation of radiofrequency radiation and its effect on living beings. Our precursor Camitorians figured out a patchwork solution, that is, creating shielding for our bodies and homes, especially for our brains. But the solution for most Earthlings will be to reduce the intensity of this radiation in the environment. If this problem can be solved by reducing it in the United States, I believe that solution can be exported to virtually every other country. I've learned that several countries have already attempted to mitigate the problem to some extent.

As a result of the comments from her fellow Camitorians, Sylvie decided to expedite her conversion from closet alien to emergent Earthling-Camitorian in the most direct possible way. She first created a short video, describing why the Camitorians had to leave their planet, showing some pictures of the outside and inside of the spacecraft, and finally a picture of herself with her light green complexion in a Central Park setting with the New York City skyline in the background. Then she contacted a local TV station, "Hello, Channel Seven. This is Sylvie Sensei, and I'm one of the aliens you undoubtedly heard landed in Central Park a few weeks ago. I've just uploaded a YouTube video you might want to view, after which I'd be happy to come for an interview at your earliest convenience." Her phone rang five minutes later.

"Hello, Ms. Sensei, this is Chad Burton, a newscaster from TV Seven. Thank you for alerting us to your video. But you don't have to come to us, I'll be at your place, complete with camera crew in about half an hour if you just tell me where you are."

She gave her address. *Well, that didn't take long! I was concerned they would think the video was a hoax. Apparently, that was not the case. Let's hope this works out as I'm hoping it will.*

Burton was true to his word. After introducing himself, he began, "Hey, are you really from another planet?"

"I am and am happy to have arrived on Earth."

He was bubbling over with questions, "We heard that spaceships landed in other cities; how many cities now have aliens?"

"Oh, a dozen or so." *I need to be vague to protect those in Moscow and Beijing.*

He persisted, "Exactly how many?"

"I can't say for sure, since they may have dispersed by now." *That isn't likely, but maybe it'll change the subject.*

"How many are there of you in New York?"

I was afraid I'd get that question sooner or later. She paused for a moment, then answered, "I've heard estimates like one hundred or so. They'll not make even a tiny dent on New York City's population."

"Can we identify them? Do they look like you? Are they also a little bit green?"

She had not applied her de-greening makeup, "Yes, we tend to be slightly green." *However, you'll not see them without their makeup!* "But I've also noted that some New Yorkers are sometimes a bit green." *Does he have a sense of humor?*

"Are you going to save our planet?"

Guess I can't count on the sense of humor. "We do have some suggestions that we believe will improve the quality of life for Earthlings. I'll be introducing those in the weeks to come."

"Thanks; you'll be on Channel Seven at six o'clock."

"Thank you for your questions."

Thus, Sylvie suddenly became famous, at least in New York City. She was immediately contacted by two more talk show hosts, each of whom couldn't wait to interview of an honest to god alien and get it on their station's broadcasts as soon as possible. Sylvie quickly realized that she needed to start planning a schedule before it got out of control, so she began writing down her appointments. Her next interview would be the following morning with MSNBC.

When Sylvie awakened the morning after her first interview, she had a few second thoughts. *I hope this was a good idea. I'm certainly trusting in the good nature of Earthlings to accept us, but I'm feeling uneasy.* She reviewed the information she would be sharing, then took a long look at her image in the mirror. Her lavender eyes were full of purpose. *Guess I'm ready!*

She called an Uber to take her to the MSNBC studios, where she was greeted by her interviewer, Loren, who ushered her to the interview site. They were seated on opposite sides of a table. Sylvie was surprised at how the only polished areas of the studio were what the TV audience saw, the rest being littered with what she presumed to be the junk from other shows. Sylvie was surprised that the cameras were so close. She found them to be somewhat intimidating, as they looked to her like huge eyes. Initially Loren asked the same basic questions the ABC TV newscaster had asked, and she gave the same vague answers. When she was pushed to provide more definitive information, she refused, finally saying either that she was not sure or that the information was classified.

Loren leaned forward, elbows on the table, and introduced a new line of questions: "You used the word 'classified.' That has a military ring. Are the Camitorians planning an invasion? Some sort of military action?"

Sylvie had been anticipating that question, so she swished a wayward lock of hair to its proper place, put on her most serious expression, and replied, "No, we've no such intentions. Camitorians are peace loving people. We're here to help, and we believe with our advanced technologies, especially in genetics, we can. Two medical problems Earthlings seem to be facing are the elevated death rates of heart attacks, diabetes, strokes, and cancers. The other is the lingering effects of Covid-19, the epidemic that has abated, but seems not to have been completely vanquished. We believe we can help Earthlings solve both problems. I'll be contacting agencies soon to try to suggest ways to do so, although the second one will require a bit more work on my part. I am a geneticist. Earthlings need to realize that Camitorians have had two hundred thousand more years than Earthlings to learn how to deal with problems in genetics and a lot of other areas, and we believe these problems are solvable."

She paused briefly and continued, "This certainly doesn't address all Earth's problems; global warming comes to mind as another that needs work. But we believe we need to work first on those that are most intense and immediate, and which we think have near term solutions."

He closed the interview, "That sounds promising. We surely can use some help! Thank you for the interview."

The following day she had the Fox News interview. This time she and the interviewer were seated next to one another. The first few questions were repeats, and she was becoming proficient at dodging them. She was pushed a bit on how many Camitorians were on Earth, and she tried to avoid using the word 'classified,' but ultimately had to resort to that again. That lit the fuse the interviewer had been trying to ignite, "When you say 'classified,' that means that you have some sort of secret endeavor going on, some clandestine activity. Is this military? Are you going to attempt a takeover?"

"No, we're a peaceful people. We come in peace. We're here to help, not destroy. ..."

The interviewer leaned toward her, "But suppose you were attacked? Suppose the countries of the Earth got together and rounded up all you aliens with the intention to eliminate you. Surely you would defend yourselves. How would you do that? With your technological capability I can't believe you don't have some incredibly sophisticated defense."

Hmm, defenses are not in place yet and for that matter may never be. I hope that we would not have to resort to that sort of thing anyway. So, I'll just bluff. "Well, our defense mechanisms are not something I want to talk about. They would be extremely lethal, and would surely allow those Camitorians who are here to prevail over your several billion Earthlings. But an attack would not be in the best interests of Earthlings. We have accrued knowledge over the two hundred thousand years we have been a civilized society that could be incredibly helpful to Earthlings."

The Fox News interviewer, apparently thinking he would catch her by surprise, leaned even closer, "Suppose I grabbed you right now. How would you defend yourself?"

She leaned away and fixed him with her gaze, "I don't think you would do that. You'd be fired for sexual assault. From what I've heard, you wouldn't be the first."

That ended the interview. Abruptly!

She had many more invitations for TV interviews, spanning most of the globe. But not in Russia or China. In places where one of the other Camitorians had been identified, she and the local Camitorian's images would be projected simultaneously on the screen, hers via Zoom. She would think her answers to questions and transmit them to the local Camitorian via satellite, who would give her answer in the local language. Of course, they were really just doing that to show how they communicated, but it blew the citizens of that country away to realize that they were communicating through their brain waves. Before each interview, Sylvie would discuss in detail what the local Camitorian thought to be the dominant issues in that country so she could anticipate potential questions. She wanted to be sure to avoid local speed bumps and present as positive a front as possible.

The head of Security in the United States was expressing a concern to the President, "Madam President, I think we need to head off a potential problem. Sylvie Sensei, the alien woman, is beginning to make a huge splash around the world. That means she'll be the center of a lot of attention. From what I've observed, that'll probably be overwhelmingly positive, but certainly there will always be a few nut cases who would do anyone harm if it would get them some attention. I believe she needs a Secret Service detail, and a well-protected limousine service to transport her around. What do you think?"

The President didn't need much time to come to a conclusion, "I agree. She's a complicated resident of the United States, albeit not one with a passport or visa, but it would be a terrible black eye for the United States if something bad happened to her on US soil. Furthermore, it might deprive the world of desperately needed solutions to some of our problems. I'll authorize what you're requesting."

So, Sylvie got Secret Service protection whether she wanted it or not.

As she opened her apartment door to leave her building the next day, she found a group of tall men dressed in uniforms there. After recovering from her shock, "Who are you people? You look very official."

One of the men moved forward, "Ms. Sensei, I'm Buzz, and we're your Secret Service detail." He introduced the others. "We've set up a guard around your apartment building twenty-four/seven, and we'll escort you anywhere you want to go."

This is absolutely crazy. "What if I want to just go for a walk in Central Park? That's what I was planning to do."

Buzz was prepared for her reaction, "Three of us will escort you. The expression on your face suggests that you'd prefer not to have us accompanying you everywhere, maybe anywhere, but this is by order of the President of the United States. While most Earthlings are decent peace-loving people, there are a few who will do terrible things just to get attention or to stake some sort of misguided claim. Apparently the President felt that all the publicity you've been getting lately would make you a possible target for some bad person. Anyway, please let us help you in whatever way we can."

She paused a moment to let all that sink in, "Buzz, this seems really weird and unnecessary to me, but I guess I don't have a choice. Anyway, I'm sorry to put all of you out."

"That's okay, Ms. Sensei, that's our job."

Chapter 8. Light Green Children

It was fine for the adults to apply makeup to obscure the fact that they weren't Earthlings, but that was more complicated for the children. These were the products of marriages or romances that occurred during the final stages of the trip from Camitor to Earth. Anticipating that these kids would have every intention of mingling with their classmates, the Camitorians had developed a makeup that, once applied, could survive a hard day's mingling, even with the most extreme tussling and perspiring that the kids might endure. In the cities where it really was imperative that all the Camitorians remain incognito, Moscow and Beijing, the children would have their industrial strength makeup applied to all exposed surfaces each morning, and then sent off to enjoy their day without producing any concern in their parents.

However, in all the other cities, where there were no obvious threats to the Camitorians, the children forced the issue soon after their arrival on Earth. This was first reported to Sylvie by Francois Dupre. "The Camitorian children in Paris do not seem at all concerned about their light green color. It appears that, when given a modest amount of interaction and exposure to their French peers, they quickly abandon any pretenses of being non-Earthlings, even taking some pride in their slight light greenness. Indeed, when they first saw an old video of Sesame Street's Kermit the Frog singing 'It's not so easy being green,' they found that to be hilarious and completely irrelevant to their situation.

"But that has forced their parents to emerge from their closets. The only ones that could maintain the fiction of being Earthlings, albeit with face makeup, were those who were not involved in a family with children."

Takashi Hamamoto joined in the group discussion, "I have to second Francois' comments, but need to add to his observations. In Japan, novelty can bring very positive attention, and it'd be difficult to find something more novel than being light green. The Camitorian youth have been accorded extremely high status here because of their natural coloration. Many Japanese children have attempted to mimic the tone of the Camitorian children; that seems to be developing into a cult phenomenon. It might also be noted that the Camitorian children's well-developed mental capabilities accord them additional prestige. None of the children would think of obscuring their greenness."

Gunther Zweig, the head of the Camitorian delegation in Berlin, chimed in, "I completely agree with Francois' and Takashi's comments about the youth, and the fact that their parents have been forced to admit to their own Camitorian heritage. In Berlin we have seen an additional, shall I say, problem with staying in the Camitorian closet. This has involved the situations our people encounter when they enter the work world. Of course, their well-advanced mental capabilities make it easy for them to do extremely well at their jobs, in some cases, so well that it quickly becomes obvious they are from somewhere no Earthling has ever been. That quickly leads to their having to confess that they are not from Earth. However, that makes it possible for them to just do what they did best, letting their capabilities have free rein, but being careful to avoid situations where they are pitted against Earthlings in problem solving cases."

He continued, "But an additional feature of the work world has surfaced. In their working environments, the Camitorians were bound to develop friendships with Earthlings, and those sometimes have led to romance. In the liberal atmosphere of Berlin, that was sure to blow their cover sooner or later, either when the Camitorian had to admit to an extraterrestrial origin or when the Earthling had an opportunity to observe the Camitorian with less clothes than would be required to cover all his or her light green skin."

Francois added, "I found Gunther's comments amusing. We have also seen frequent situations in France involving romance between Earthlings and Camitorians where the fact that the latter was an alien became obvious even in the dim lights of a romantic setting. In some cases, I'm told, the Camitorian tried as long as possible to avoid admitting to not being of Earth, but finally succumbed when his or her hormones overcame the continued wearing of the clothing required to retain anonymity."

That brought many appreciative chuckles over the Camitorian leaders' communication lines.

Sylvie paused for a moment, rubbed her hand across her brow while collecting her thoughts, then summarized everyone's comments, "In New York there has also been a general move toward admitting our heritage. We have generally found that the Earthling response was positive, especially when they had reason to appreciate our advanced capabilities. They were also impressed with our ability to communicate by just thinking our thoughts, and sometimes asked us if we could try an experiment to do that with an Earthling. As far as I know, that has failed thus far, but we should keep trying. You never know when we might encounter an Earthling with a sufficiently developed brain to make that happen, assuming that might be one of the outcomes of greater brain development resulting from evolution.

"None the less, it appears that in most of the cities where we placed Camitorians, many, perhaps even most, have quit worrying about remaining anonymous, and have simply taken advantage of the natural assets we have. However, I must say that the situation Takashi noted for our light green children in Tokyo may be the best possible acceptance we will ever receive."

There was general agreement that, except in Moscow and Beijing, that there was little risk, and possibly even benefit, with making one's Camitorian heritage known. But sooner or later Sylvie and her fellow Camitorians would have to face the Russians and the Chinese without their flesh-colored makeup.

Chapter 9. Sylvie's Experiments

Sylvie couldn't wait to test some of her ideas in genetics. First, she had to gather samples so she could establish the DNA factors that were common to most Earthlings, and compare them to those common to most Camitorians. Then she could begin to understand things like the differences in sensitivity to the Covid-19 virus between the two races. And the differences in brain structures that allowed the Camitorians to think their messages to each other while Earthlings had to rely on verbal speech. Camitorian geneticists had analyzed their DNA in much greater detail than had Earthlings, so the genetic components that ruled brain function were well established. This was complex, as several different parts of the genome could contribute to each function, and there could also be subtle differences between the DNA of any two Camitorians. Sylvie needed to find the corresponding features that applied to Earthlings.

It wasn't difficult to collect a number of samples of Earthling DNA. These were largely gotten from samples of hair. One source was beauty parlors, where the Camitorian would offer a small stipend to the operator in exchange for a handful of the hair of her or his patrons. But most of the samples were obtained worldwide from students, who would offer a stipend to the managers of coffee shops, then set up shop with a sign 'One Dollar for One of Your Hairs, Limit Two.' Other students were all too happy to contribute to a worldwide science effort, especially for a reward.

She was concerned that she would not be able to draw conclusions about United States DNA just from those that inhabited New York City. So, she dispatched some of her colleagues to other places around the United States, Chicago, Los Angeles, Atlanta, some smaller cities like Peoria, some more rural places, like a western Nebraska town or two, and even a few places in Texas, to extract hair samples and bring them back to her laboratory. She also asked some of her colleagues who had landed in other cities around the Earth to analyze the hair samples they collected. In most of those places there was at least one Camitorian who could perform the analyses well enough to provide the results she needed.

Of course, occasional trips to barber shops or beauty salons also yielded samples. The Camitorian simply befriended the hairdresser, agreed to pay a bit for fresh hair samples, which were going into the trash anyway, and collected the results.

After getting results of analyses of thousands of samples of Earthling hair, Sylvie created a distribution of the genetic markers that contributed to hearing from sound, and those that were involved with brain wave activity. What she found was remarkable; a small fraction of Earthling brains was probably capable of transmitting and receiving brain wave radiation much as the Camitorians were. She thought, *Presumably the reason this mode of communication never took root here on Earth was that very few Earthlings were able to communicate that way. But I wonder if some of the couples who often claim to be anticipating each other's thoughts are really just having them transmitted to them. None the less, it appears that the structure of Earthling and Camitorian brains is sufficiently different that I'm not sure we could ever hope to communicate with Earthlings through brain wave transmission and reception. Maybe that will happen sometime, though.*

Sylvie then studied correlations between the sensitivity of Earthling brains and the potential for diseases such as heart attacks, diabetes, strokes, and various cancers. She discovered a stunning result. *Good god, the potential for all these diseases in many Earthlings is strongly correlated with the sensitivity of the brain to electromagnetic radiation.* She realized this information would make her a prophet of doom; she could predict those Earthlings that were most likely to suffer those diseases resulting from exposure to excessive electromagnetic radiation.

Given the comments she had received from the precursor Camitorians regarding their headaches in relation to their proximity to smartphones, she bought such a device along with a meter that measured the amount of radiation the phone was producing. She was stunned to realize that they were emitting huge amounts of electromagnetic power. *Obviously if Earthlings have a high sensitivity to RF radiation, and they are frequent smartphone users, they may have a real self-inflicted problem.*

Now what do I do with this information? She got on the internet and discovered that the Federal Communications Commission set the guidelines for smartphones, among other devices, as well as for both the large transmission towers and the small cell devices that sent and received the electromagnetic radiation.

She also spent several days researching data bases with any available information about RF radiation studies and the FCC's involvement setting standards and authorizing the sale of bandwidth. What she found shocked and alarmed her!

So, she drafted a letter to the FCC.

Dear FCC Commissioners,

As you know, aliens from the planet Camitor, of which I am one, recently landed on Earth. We came from many different walks of life. My area of expertise is genetic research. Our civilization has been evolving two hundred thousand years longer than that of Earthlings, so has had many more generations to acquire knowledge than has yours. Thus, our expertise in areas such as genetics has advanced well beyond that of Earthling scientists. This is not to disparage their efforts; we have just had a lot longer to achieve our understanding than your scientists have.

Thinking it might be useful for me to continue my research once I got to Earth, I brought the essentials of my genetics laboratory with me. I've collected thousands of samples of Earthling hair, from which I've deduced many basic features of Earthling DNA. Remarkably, there are many more similarities between Earthling and Camitorian DNA than differences. Perhaps the most significant difference is in the ability of Camitorian brains to send and receive brain wave signals; this allows us to communicate by just thinking our messages. Remarkably, a small fraction of the Earthling DNA samples I analyzed suggests that a tiny number of Earthlings might also be able to communicate the same way. In a few cases such communications may already be taking place, although the Earthlings may not be aware they are using this very efficient mode of information transmission.

In my studies I also looked for correlations between the capabilities of Earthling brains and the susceptibility of their organs to diseases such as heart attacks, various cancers, diabetes, strokes, and several other diseases, as well as the ability to procreate, and found that those with the highest sensitivity to radiofrequency electromagnetic radiation, RFR, were also those with the strongest correlations to most of the aforementioned medical problems. I learned that Earthling death rates from these diseases have been increasing sharply in recent years, especially in the cities, and urban birth rates have been dropping. So, I decided to see if there were concomitant increases in the amount of RFR.

I was stunned to learn that there has been a huge increase in the RFR to which Earthlings are exposed just in the past few years, especially at 5G frequencies. Your group authorized the communications industry to vastly increase the number of wireless transmission facilities and communications satellites, as well as the intensity of the radiation the facilities can emit. This has spread RFR around the Earth and has increased its intensity in most places, certainly by large factors in Earth's cities. The reasons for which these increases were authorized may well have been noble but, with all due respect, I believe your conclusions were based on faulty logic and highly selective data. You continue to insist that there is no evidence of medical issues from RFR, despite thousands of studies that conclude the exact opposite. You base your conclusion on assumed exposure time of thirty minutes per day. I have learned from people with teenage children that this exposure time may be wrong in many cases by at least a factor of ten. And the same error factor may well apply to many busy adults.

You've long claimed that the only relevant medical effect of RFR is temperature rise in the exposed tissue, but most medical research studies have found much more complex things than a simple temperature rise. And these occur at RFR levels in many cases more than a factor of one hundred below the levels you have concluded are safe, and have authorized the telecommunications industries to assume. There are many well-known health effects that can be caused by RFR, such as difficulty concentrating and sleeping, brain fog, headaches, nausea, and exhaustion, but at a more microscopic level, oxidative stress seems to be the outcome of many of the studies. As you may know, this results from RFR's inhibiting the body's ability to balance its reactive oxygen species. While the physiological effects of oxidative stress include the short-term ones mentioned above, longer-term ones are also experienced. The result that has been found is a breakdown of bodily systems, beyond what the body can repair, which can result in the aforementioned major medical issues.

Thus, the effects of RFR at levels far below what you have assumed to be safe have been disastrous for some humans and, since cancer takes years to develop, will ultimately be fatal to many others. This was brought to your attention in a legal challenge issued in 2020 by the Environmental Health Trust and the Children's Health Defense, to which a verdict was reached against you in 2021. You apparently decided to challenge the suit, and that is still being processed. Unfortunately, my studies indicate that the incidences of those illnesses will continue to worsen, especially if you continue to persist with your currently recommended radiation level maxima.

As mentioned above, thousands of research studies, spanning several decades, have been performed to determine the effects of RFR on humans, but also include studies of RFR's effects on other animals, birds, insects, and plants. Profound adverse effects from this RFR have been found in all of these systems. And as you may know, but have apparently chosen to ignore, medical effects of RFR have been well demonstrated, and summarized in the *BioInitiative Report 2020*. This document lists and summarizes research studies showing that RFR causes oxidative stress, sperm/testicular damage, neuropsychiatric effects including EEG changes, apoptosis (cell death), cellular DNA damage, endocrine changes, and calcium overload. In considering the evidence of harm, scientists and medical associations around the world have called on governments to ban or limit the use of RFR, most specifically Wi-Fi, in schools and to replace it whenever possible with hard-wired networks. Unfortunately, you have ignored these scientifically well-founded recommendations in establishing your limits for the United States.

Most studies of living creatures have been done on lab animals, since experiments with Earthlings can only be done in environments in which it is often difficult to impose the usual scientific controls. None the less, those studies do document RFR's effects on living beings. But in a growing number of cases, effects have been observed on Earthlings as a result of their living near cell towers or small cell emitters. Perhaps the most troubling results show the effects RFR has on children, as studies of RFR related behaviors following installation of a cell tower near a school unmistakably document its effects. This is related to the thinking of scientists that exposure to RFR is most dangerous at times of most rapid cell division, as occurs in children.

One symptom of excessive RFR exposure that Camitorians also suffer from is massive headaches, although there may well be other less obvious symptoms that signal future organ failure. This would certainly be consistent with my research results, since any Earthling with the enhanced sensitivity to RFR would surely develop intense headaches. Indeed, we Camitorians found that we suffered extreme headaches immediately upon arriving on Earth, but we have devised ways to deal with that problem. We've discovered that there are commercially available shielding devices, including wearable fabrics that have some metallic fibers, which can greatly mitigate the effects of the radiation. But these are stop gap, temporary solutions, which have reduced the RFR effects in our brains and bodies to a tolerable level. I mentioned earlier that we communicated by brain wave transmission and reception. However, the ubiquity of RFR has badly disrupted that mode of communication. We are often reduced to speaking—verbally— to each other. But that's not the most important effect of the radiation. Had we not reduced the level of RFR to our brains and bodies, we might be suffering the same enhancement of diseases that Earthlings are. My research and that of thousands of Earthling scientists has shown that we are all, Earthlings and Camitorians alike, being negatively impacted by the high RFR levels. In order to mitigate the damage being done and the resulting enhanced death rates, steps must be taken immediately to reduce this serious threat to the health of all living beings.

I propose to meet with you, show you the results of my research, and suggest a solution to the dilemma in which Earthlings and Camitorians find ourselves.

Yours sincerely,

Sylvie Sensei

Upon receipt of the letter, the Chair of the FCC, Clyde Jenkins, sent a copy of it around to the other members of the Commission, and added a few comments. One would expect that he might be a little short on objectivity with respect to challenges such as the ones Sensei presented. He was after all, as were most of the other commissioners, an employee for one of the telecom companies until he accepted the FCC post. Some were still receiving stipends as rewards for their efforts.

They had a Zoom meeting to discuss Sylvie's letter. Jenkins cleared his throat and began, "I can't believe that our actions could have created medical problems. Well, okay, we did gloss over the data coming from the world's laboratories about the effects of RFR, and we did duplicate one experiment that showed dramatic effects, or at least we sort of duplicated it in a way that was guaranteed to produce a negative result. But this alien woman's assertions are terrible if they're true."

Now he was warming to his subject, "But how could they be true? All our friends are in the communications industry, and they're not bad people. They're just trying to maximize profits for their shareholders. That seems appropriate in a capitalist society, so we've always gone along with them. Hell, most of us worked for one or another of the companies before we took this job.

"But I guess we'd better meet with this woman, or whatever she is. We've swept every other challenge to our authority under the rug, and I presume we can do the same with this one."

There were no dissenters; his conclusion was met in most cases with reluctant agreement.

The Chair sent an email to Sylvie inviting her to a private meeting with the commissioners the following week, to which she agreed. Jenkins had allotted twenty minutes for her presentation, and another ten minutes for questions. However, there were so many questions, some in the form of interruptions of her presentation, that her talk took an hour and a half, and additional questions and comments took another hour. Jenkins was becoming increasingly agitated as time wore on; two of the commissioners were obviously impressed with her research and concerned about the effects she described. Finally, she suggested a moratorium on further telecom development, a reduction by at least an order of magnitude in the allowed electromagnetic intensities, especially in cities, and a follow-up study in two years to see if the medical problems had been reduced.

Jenkins leaned forward in his chair, seeming to be preparing to attack, and asked, "Ms. Sensei, what you have described is obviously meticulous research. But in the end, I have to wonder why you think what you know about the genetics of the people from your planet should have any bearing on Earthlings?"

She perceived that this was the final question, so she offered a summation, "Mr. Jenkins, if you just look at the other members of the Commission, and then at me, you'll see that there is virtually nothing that would allow you to say that your fellow commissioners are not Camitorians, or that I am not an Earthling, aside from a slight difference in skin color. But this is only the periphery of the situation. My analysis has shown that Earthling and Camitorian genomes have far more similarities than differences. Of course, this is as might be expected, just from looking at the two species. Camitorians have had more time for our DNA to evolve, and that has produced some differences. However, these are small. And many of these differences occur between the complexities involving the effects of different components of the genome on various markers. Were you a geneticist I believe you would be stunned at the similarities between the DNA of our two races. I'm absolutely certain that my conclusions apply to both Earthlings and Camitorians."

Two of the commissioners, Linda Forrester and Rob Thompson, applauded her presentation. Jenkins did his best to shut that down as quickly as he could, gesturing to them while wearing an expression of great displeasure.

Jenkins had intended for that to be the end of the FCC's considerations of Sensei's presentation, but after she had been dismissed, Ms. Forrester shifted to the front of her chair, with her hands on the chair's arms, and suggested, "I'd like for an Earthling doctor to come and advise us as to the veracity of Ms. Sensei's comments. I believe there is enough truth in what she said that we should not ignore it. Her presentation made me very uncomfortable about our past authorizations of the number of RFR emitters, their intensity limits, and the number of satellites connecting to them. I'm also very uncomfortable about the legal challenge we made to the suit we lost in 2021. I fear that we may be killing off Earthlings with our intransigence. In a few years the only 'people' left on Earth may be the Camitorians, simply because they know how to protect themselves!"

Jenkins leaned back and to one side in his chair as if to maximize the distance between Forrester and himself. He wasn't surprised at her comments; she was often a thorn in his side. He replied, "Since you're so damned concerned about the effects the alien woman described, I'll arrange for a doctor to meet with us. But do realize that we can't back down on our recommendations without a huge fight. Our friends in the telecom industry have already committed billions to push things to the limits we gave them, maybe even a bit beyond, and we wouldn't have a friend left in the world if we backed those down to accommodate Ms. Sensei's concerns."

Forrester countered, "I'm concerned that we may have selected the wrong people to be our friends."

Jenkins proceeded to interview several doctors, focusing his attention on those with the least desirable reputations. He finally located one, a Dr. Ambidoger, who was willing to assert that the sharp increases in deaths from the various diseases were a myth. Jenkins got him to testify to that in another meeting of the FCC. Of course, his testimony allowed Jenkins to conclude, "Well, we see from Dr. Ambidoger's testimony that the medical issues Ms. Sensei is concerned about don't exist. I therefore conclude that we declare the whole exercise with her to be a waste of time and move on to more important business."

With that, Linda Forrester and Rob Thompson stood up and resigned in disgust. Unfortunately, that left Jenkins' electromagnetic hypocrisy intact, and the telecom industry with no real constraints on what they wished to inflict on Earth's inhabitants simply to enhance the bottom lines of their friends. At least until the legal challenge got resolved.

The FCC's response was not a surprise. Their health guidelines relied on the obsolete scientific assumption that the non-ionizing RFR can be harmful only if it causes an arbitrarily chosen thermal change in tissue. That assumption had been shown to be false in many studies, even before cell phones were widely commercialized in the 1990s. Contrary to the FCC's position, in the 1970s, the Russians had already acknowledged that the RFR emitted from radio and microwave frequency based technologies can be harmful at levels that are at least 1,000 times lower than the levels that create thermal effects.

Sylvie had done some internet sleuthing and had found that, despite massive evidence of medical harm, in December 2019 the FCC published a decision that there was no evidence of harm from wireless technology. This led them to conclude that a review of its health guidelines, which were established in 1996, was not warranted. This is what precipitated two lawsuits, by Children's Health Defense and Environmental Health Trust, which were ultimately combined. Although the main brief in the case was submitted in summer, 2020, and a verdict against the FCC issued in 2021*, the FCC has insisted on maintaining its dangerous RFR limits. This has been supported by the telecommunications industry, since admitting to the medical evidence would cause them to revise virtually everything they've done in the past decade. Legal truth and justice can proceed very slowly in the US.

But that was not the end of the matter for Forrester and Thompson. Forrester was a tall woman with a commanding demeanor, a perpetually intense look, and a voice that demanded attention. She had a history of supporting causes in which she believed, and often which she felt were not receiving appropriate recognition. She had been involved in her teen years in protest marches to make politicians aware of the need for climate change legislation. She concluded while in college that she needed to get a law degree to be most effective in the efforts to which she

*Since the case against the FCC is pending as this is written, I have had to speculate on its ultimate conclusion. However, it is expected that the FCC will do everything it can, including appeals and cherry-picking data, to oppose any judgements against them.

planned to dedicate her life. Her efforts caused her to quickly become recognized as a disciplined and dedicated force on any issue she chose. Because she had become an expert on litigation that involved radiofrequency emissions, she had been appointed as a Commissioner for the FCC, much to the chagrin of its members who represented the telecom industry.

Forrester's personal life was limited by her dedication to the causes on which she focused her legal efforts. She did have occasional dates, usually with men who were involved in the same litigation she was. On the same side, of course. But her closest friends tended to be her female law colleagues. What little leisure time she had was consumed by her passion for painting seascapes, of which she had many.

Rob Thompson did not have the sort of appearance that would make him stand out in a crowd. He was of average height, had sandy hair, and generally maintained an 'aw shucks' expression. He could be very engaging and had a natural ability to make people he was interacting with feel at ease. His early years were spent in Berkeley, with both parents attending the University there. They made sure that he was taught to seek the truth and reality in any situation even as he was growing up. He also attended law school and joined a large law firm upon passing his bar exam. One of the cases his firm litigated was in support of a telecom giant. Although he was instrumental in winning a decision for his client, he became increasingly uneasy about the case as it developed. However, because of his involvement on it, he had been appointed to the FCC. His enthusiasm for the efforts of the telecom giants had faded considerably, even as he began his term as a commissioner.

None the less, he was determined to show that a telecom company need not be so focused on its bottom line that it ignored the dangerous aspects of its business. So, he started his own company. By the time he and Forrester resigned from the FCC, his company, headquartered in Silicon Valley, California, had grown to about one thousand employees. He had carefully selected his managers from his competitors, usually hiring those who had also become disenchanted with the predatory attitudes toward humanity adopted by the larger companies. The result was a workplace that fostered collegiality over competitiveness and tended to engender employee loyalty most other companies could only dream about.

Rob's management style involved hiring the best people he could find, then getting out of their way and letting them do their jobs. Of course, he did impose some oversight, but each exercise of that nature usually involved congratulations on a job well done, along with a few tips for future progress. Employees tended to view these exercises as an opportunity to report on their efforts to the boss, rather than anything involving a belt or a woodshed.

Rob might have been suspected of being a favorite of the ladies, and many would have happily accepted marriage with him, but he just hadn't met the right one yet.

Chapter 10. Collaboration

Sylvie answered the corded landline in her apartment, "Hello, this is Sylvie Sensei."

"Ms. Sensei, this is Linda Forrester. I was one of the FCC members who was so positively impressed with your presentation last week that when Chairman Jenkins managed to decide we could ignore your testimony, I resigned from the FCC. I've been in contact with Rob Thompson, the other member who concurred with you. In a follow up meeting, Mr. Jenkins invited a completely inept doctor to discredit your work, after which Jenkins concluded we could completely forget about what you had to say and move on to new things. That comment is what led the two of us to resign." The tone of Forrester's voice was serious, and it sounded as if she had been rehearsing her words for some time. She frequently rubbed one hand across her brow as she was speaking. *I've never talked one on one with an alien; I'm not sure what to expect!* She took a deep breath, "Mr. Thompson and I were wondering if we could get together with you and discuss where we are in our thinking and how we might proceed."

Sylvie was pleased to receive some positive feedback from her presentation, "Yes, Ms. Forrester, I remember your excellent questions and comments directed at my presentation. I also recall Mr. Thompson making several incisive comments.

"Although I'm sorry to hear that Mr. Jenkins has dismissed the whole effort, I was pretty sure that would be the outcome. And I'd very much appreciate your bringing me up to date. I'd also be delighted to meet with you. I'm in New York City. Can you come to my apartment?" Sylvie's voice was calm; she hadn't expected a call from Forrester, but she wasn't entirely surprised by it.

Forrester was relieved at Sylvie's positive response. They agreed to meet the next day. But that wasn't going to happen. Sylvie had been told by her security folks that she needed to alert them to anyone who she was meeting or who was visiting her. When she told Buzz about the meeting to be, he responded, "Ms. Sensei, we'll have to do some checks on the two people you mention. This won't be as detailed as such checks often are, but we can just do a three-day check if you allow us to be in the room with the three of you."

Sylvie tried to hide her annoyance, "Oh, this is much more involved than it should be. These are excellent honorable people and are certainly no risk to my security. But we would like to get together as soon as possible. So, I guess we must have you sit in with us. I'm afraid it will be pretty boring for you; the discussion will be quite arcane."

The meeting was postponed for three days. Thompson and Forrester arrived at the appointed time, endured a pat down, and then were allowed into Sylvie's room. As they seated themselves, they noted that the apartment was nicely furnished, the living room in soft blue French Provincial decor, and that it had a stunning view of Central Park. Forrester commented, "These furnishings are beautiful. I am particularly fond of the French Provincial design, and the gentle curvature of the legs accents wonderfully the soft blue upholstery. And where did you get those unusual paintings? I especially love their bright colors."

Sylvie replied, "Thank you for your comments. I must confess that the apartment was fully furnished when I arrived, so I presume one of the Camitorians who preceded me chose the furniture. But thank you for telling me that its design is called 'French Provincial.' I was pretty sure it had some design name, but of course did not know what it was. As for the paintings, I got them at an art store just down the street. It was my second trip out for shopping, following only the trip to the grocery store."

Forrester and Thompson smiled.

The security detail looked bored.

Sylvie had a pot of tea and another of coffee, which she offered to all her visitors, along with some cookies that were apparently homemade. Forrester and Thompson murmured appreciatively over the treats, Forrester in particular commenting that she especially liked oolong tea. Thompson thought to himself, *this woman is incredibly composed. She seemed almost like an automaton when she made her presentation to the FCC. But now she just seems very relaxed and, ironically, human, like an extremely thoughtful Earthling, but totally in control. And, blond hair, with a swatch that frequently needs to be swished back into place; almost lavender eyes; and a megawatt smile; how do aliens end up with characteristics like those? How is anyone on any planet so lucky as to end up with such beautiful features?*

Forrester, hands gripping the arm rests of her chair, began, "Rob and I would like to discuss some ways to move forward with your efforts. Since we have both resigned from the FCC, we are now free to speak our minds. So, we'd like to propose a way for us to circumvent the FCC, bring your efforts and plans to the public, and then force the FCC to go along with your proposals.

"By the way, I realize that English couldn't possibly be your native language, but when you met with the FCC, you appeared to be at least as fluent as the rest of us. So, I must ask, do you understand everything I'm saying?"

Until Sensei spoke, Thompson realized he had not been listening at all to Forrester's remarks. *Must not let this alien woman be such a distraction.*

Sensei replied, "Oh yes, but thanks for asking. When our fleet of spacecraft was about two years out from Earth, we began to detect signals from the most powerful Earthling radio and television stations, using our onboard radio telescopes. We had been alerted by precursor Camitorians that there was not one common language for Earthlings. We had to wonder how people from different countries were able to communicate efficiently with each other. Anyway, the Camitorians heading to each country had to learn its specific language by listening to its radio and TV stations. Of course, I must note that sometimes required a lot of filtering."

Thompson and Forrester laughed.

She continued, "Since Camitorians communicate by thinking their messages, they are not restricted to only using words. Thus, we can think images or even pictographs to transmit, if those make our messaging more efficient. But when we need to learn a new Earthling language, that can proceed very swiftly, since our brains can store large vocabularies. So, the only thing we need to practice is pronunciation."

She shifted her focus, "Anyway, I'm delighted to learn that you have been planning a way to circumvent, or perhaps confront, the FCC. I believe that would be very much in the interest of Earthlings. What do you have in mind?"

Thompson offered, "Ms. Sensei, I thank you for meeting with us. I wish to add my appreciation to that of Linda for your FCC presentation. We both believe your intentions are completely altruistic, and I hope together we can find a way for us to make your case to the public, as well as to the industrial people who are responsible for immersing the planet in electromagnetic pollution.

"By the way, we are going to be working pretty closely together on this project, assuming you agree to go forward with our suggestions. So please address me as 'Rob' and Ms. Forrester as 'Linda.' I'm not sure what the protocols are for Camitorians, but may we address you as 'Sylvie'?" Thompson may well have had more than conversational convenience on his mind as he tried to make their interactions less formal.

Forrester surmised his intention. She smiled.

Sylvie warmed immediately to that suggestion, "Thank you, Rob. Sylvie is fine with me. And I'm pretty sure I'll want to go along with your proposals. Please tell me what you have in mind."

Linda, now leaning back in her chair in a more relaxed pose, replied, "Our plan has several facets. First, we'd like for you to cast your presentation as an op-ed piece. We would try to get that published in as many newspapers in the United States as possible. Second, Rob and I would write a companion op-ed piece that would detail our thinking, and note that we felt so strongly that the FCC was making a disastrous error in not taking your presentation and your suggestions seriously that we had to resign as Commissioners.

"Third, we would send our two op-ed pieces to as many doctors as possible to try to enlist their support. It would be important to contradict the testimony of the doctor that Mr. Jenkins brought in to evaluate your presentation. He is hardly a stellar member of the medical profession; a little checking showed that he has lost his license to practice in two states. But getting doctors to undercut members of their profession is difficult, so we would need to get a large fraction of the American Medical Association to support our efforts. Finally, we believe the medical associations of other countries may not be quite as hide-bound as that in the United States, so we would appeal also to many of them to elicit their support."

Sylvie laughed, "I'd not heard the expression 'hide-bound' used previously, but it is pretty obvious what it means."

Now Rob chimed in, "Linda and I understand the work you've already put into this, so what we're requiring is just a summation of your efforts, although we realize this is not a trivial task. We would take care of submitting our op-ed pieces, and also contacting all the people we would need to support our efforts.

"I should also note that anything Linda and I write will be passed by you for modification or approval. You're the expert, but we would assume the roles of politicians here. So, I hope our plan sounds like something on which you can join with us. Is that a possibility?"

Sylvie needed no time to reply, "I'll be delighted to do what I can to support your effort. And thank you for thinking of a way to move ahead on this. I was not at all sure how to proceed following what I sensed to be the negative reaction of Mr. Jenkins, but I think you have designed an excellent plan, providing American doctors are not too hide-bound." She couldn't resist using the word, and that evoked smiles from Linda and Rob. "And I'd like for you to provide editorial comments on what I write. It'll be much easier for you to determine what Earthlings, especially Americans, will understand than for me."

Their meeting ended with many expressions of admiration for each other. Thompson was especially effusive about Sylvie's efforts. But he had to be somewhat circumspect so as not to say what he was most enthusiastic about.

And the service detail folks still looked bored. Attentive, but bored. But they did enjoy the cookies.

Sylvie rewrote her presentation to cast it in the form of an op-ed piece. She worked hard to make it not too technical but sent it to Rob and Linda to proofread and possibly scale down even a bit more. They were honored that she asked them to edit what she wrote and did have numerous suggestions. In the end all three were happy with what they planned to submit.

Linda and Rob had contacts at the Washington Post and New York Times, so were pretty sure the op-eds would be published together in those papers. But they could only hope they would be accepted at most of the other newspapers.

The readers of the New York Times, as well as many other newspapers, were greeted by Rob and Linda's op-ed piece on July 17, 2023.

"There can be no doubt that this is a time of crisis. We have been struck the past few years by two correlated disasters, the first being the Covid-19 epidemic, and the second being the collapse of the world's economies as a result of the responses to the epidemic. Fortunately, the effects of the virus have receded over the past year, and the world's politicians seem to be coming together, albeit slowly, to develop economic recovery plans.

"But what we want to address in this op-ed piece and the companion one by Sylvie Sensei is a third worldwide disaster: the sharp increases in death rates due to heart attacks, diabetes, strokes, and cancers, and an apparently associated plunge in birth rates. These problems have been especially prevalent in cities. The medical profession has struggled to determine the cause or causes of these problems, but there can be no doubt that these effects are real. Suddenly, just as the world was looking forward to a sharp drop in deaths from the Covid-19 epidemic, the death rates have surged as a result of this mysterious malady.

"We were members of the United States Federal Communications Commission until recently, when we resigned in protest to the FCC chair's response to an identification of and suggested response to this malady. Sylvie Sensei is a geneticist from planet Camitor and is part of a group of aliens from that planet who landed on Earth half a year ago. Because Camitor has had a developed civilization much longer than Earth, its scientists are greatly advanced compared to ours. Thus, Ms. Sensei was able to perform experiments with equipment she brought with her from her home planet that allowed her to observe similarities and differences between Earthling and Camitorian DNA and correlated bodily functions. Her advanced knowledge of the effects of different genetic components also allowed her to determine the many genomic pieces that drive the functions of the organs in both Earthling and Camitorian bodies.

"Her article describes some of the details of her work. But the bottom line is unmistakable: the brains of Earthlings have a direct bearing on the health of the organs in our bodies. And we Earthlings have, in recent years, produced an incredibly destructive effect on our bodies, especially on our brains, resulting in the enhanced death rates from many different diseases, and in loss of reproductive capabilities as well.

"We are referring to the huge increase in the amount of radiofrequency radiation, RFR, that blankets the Earth. Several years ago, the US FCC authorized a sharp uptick in radiation output from large towers, small cell devices, transmission satellites, and Over the Air Transmission Devices (OTARDs), which can be created by individual RFR users/creators, producing this huge increase. While many countries outside the US have tried to resist, the enhancements inflicted by the United States telecommunications companies have produced similar increases throughout much of the world. These increases did produce the FCC's desired effect, that is, to greatly enhance radiofrequency communicability to all the world's citizens, but they also produced an extremely powerful and harmful effect on Earthling brains and bodies. We note that the huge increase in deaths due to previously well-known causes are often accompanied by headaches and other debilitating brain associated effects.

"The Camitorians who have arrived on Earth recognized the cause of the problem, and they devised ways to mitigate the effects of the RFR on themselves by using shielding, and by eliminating wireless devices in their living spaces. In fact, this was the approach some Earthlings who were affected by the RFR have taken even before the Camitorians were known to be among us. But this has become more difficult in recent years because of the increased amount of this RFR. Ms. Sensei's work was not able to determine if simply shielding Earthling brains would eliminate the problem, or if it would continue due to direct effects on other bodily organs from the RFR. Some Earthlings have had to relocate to remote areas to escape its effects.

"There are some things that can be done immediately to alleviate the problem. First, the FCC should get its head out of the electromagnetic sand and develop more stringent limitations on the intensity levels from the telecom industry. These changes will have virtually no effect on either social or economic Earthly endeavors. Second, Earthlings should use their smartphones, which are very intense RFR emitting devices, as infrequently as possible, certainly turning them off at night, but also during the day when they are not in use. When they are on, they should be set on airplane mode. Third, they should not carry their smartphones next to their bodies, and they should never hold their smartphone closer than an inch from their head. Fourth, they should replace all cordless telephones with corded land lines and hardwire the internet connections to their computers. Indeed, any device that is normally thought to require connection to Wi-Fi should be hardwired if at all possible. Fifth, OTARDs should be outlawed.

"Finally, this increased RFR is having a devastating effect on other species on our planet. Research conducted by thousands of scientists in many different scientific disciplines has documented its effects on bird migrations; insect populations, on which much of the food chain relies; bees, and their importance to our food supply; and plants.

"The unwillingness of the FCC to recognize the importance of Ms. Sensei's research work and her suggested mitigations is what led us to resign our commissions. We hope that you will take these recommendations more seriously than the rest of the members of the FCC, and that you will see fit to write to us regarding your thoughts on this issue.

"Linda Forrester and Rob Thompson"

And they gave a postbox address and e-mail address where they could be reached.

Sylvie's op-ed piece, as well as that of Rob and Linda, ran in about half the newspapers to which they were sent. Reactions to them ran the gamut from recognizing that the Camitorians probably would know more about genetics (and lots of other things) than Earthlings, to essentially the Jenkins assessment of how aliens could be expected to understand Earthling bodies. Fox News didn't say anything about the op-ed pieces, but just offered that they didn't appreciate an alien, for god's sake, telling Earthlings what to do. They were probably sulking from the way she ended her Fox News interview.

However, that was only Forrester's and Thompson's shot across the bow of anti-science. The American Medical Association has more than two hundred thirty thousand members, and Forrester and Thompson sent letters that included both op-ed pieces and the following note to every one of them:

"We have recently been made aware of the damaging and potentially fatal effects of RF radiation via a presentation to the Federal Communications Commission by Ms. Sylvie Sensei. We feel compelled to alert you to this situation by making available two op-ed pieces, one by Ms. Sensei and the other by ourselves.

We believe these demonstrate how the FCC made its decision to invalidate the research and recommendations of Ms. Sensei. A doctor was invited to a subsequent FCC meeting by Chairman Jenkins to provide expert evaluation of her recommendations. That was Dr. Ambidoger. He basically dismissed the medical crisis evidenced by the enhanced death rates that are facing the world, and recommended that the FCC ignore Ms. Sensei's work and arguments. As many of you know, Dr. Ambidoger has had his license revoked in two states in the US. In trying to establish his medical credentials, we were unable to determine where he went to medical school or if he was ever enrolled in any medical institution. We do not believe his credentials give him the qualifications to comment on any aspect of medical science."

When the Chair of the AMA received the letter, he immediately responded that the AMA did not wish to become involved in political issues, and therefore would not choose sides in political debates. However, within two weeks, two thirds of the members of the AMA had responded in strong support of Forrester and Thompson, and especially of Sensei. When apprised of this, the AMA Chair immediately wrote a letter in strong support of their effort, noting especially that the FCC should reconsider its recommendations to the telecom industry as an urgent matter of national health.

Forrester and Thompson had also contacted the Chairs of many foreign medical associations. Virtually all of them wrote very enthusiastic letters supporting their efforts, as well as Sensei's scientific findings.

The Chairs' letters, along with copies of the thousands of letters from doctors, were sent to the President of the US. Her response was to demand that the entire FCC resign, and that Forrester and Thompson be reappointed with Forrester as Chair. She then requested suggestions from Forrester and Thompson for additional new FCC Commissioners. They suggested no one who had any present or former affiliation with telecommunication companies. In addition to the suggested FCC Commissioners, several doctors were suggested as potential consultants. The new FCC was approved by the Senate with minimal discussion.

Of course, the new FCC followed Sylvie's recommendations, scaling back the authorizations for allowed RFR emissions by a factor of one hundred, and encouraging the telecom industry to replace Wi-Fi transmissions with fiber to the premises whenever possible. The telecom industry howled in self-perceived financial pain and threatened more lawsuits. However, they weren't sure they could muster the necessary legal arguments to counter the new reduced limits.

Sylvie had recommended that the medical statistics be revisited in two years. She did not expect sharply defined effects to appear immediately, but reduction of the allowed RFR limits was only her first step. She intended to educate people on how they might reduce their personal contributions to the Wi-Fi soup, and also reduce its effects on their own health.

Chapter 11. Telecom Industry Retribution

"How the hell are we going to counter the testimony of that damned alien woman, and the newly constituted FCC? This is a disaster. We can't let a few people with what they are calling heightened sensitivity to electromagnetic radiation screw up our profits. Who knows what the real causes of their problems are, but didn't the old FCC give us the guidelines that they deemed to be safe, and which we've used to develop our network and products?'' The speaker was Tom Mack, CEO of the world's largest telecommunications company, and he was speaking on a conference call with three other telecom CEOs. Mack considered himself the leader of this group. He had risen to his position partly because of his heritage, and he assumed that made him a kind of king. His education had involved prestigious schools, finally culminating in his MBA from Harvard. Then he joined the telecom company his father had founded, eventually succeeding him as CEO.

He continued, "And where the hell is that goddamn Rob Thompson, our version of Benedict Arnold, when we could really use his support in the issues we face?"

Jack Rathbone, one of the others, commented, "He's probably out hiring away your best employees. He's done that to all of us.

"But back to the issue you raise, we've got a hundred of the best lawyers in the land, or at least the most highly paid ones, working to claim the new FCC has no authority to regulate what we do. Of course, Congress passed a bill a few years back that gave the FCC that authority. Thus, our current legal efforts are a little tricky, because our lawyers had asserted that the decrees of the previous FCC were quite legal and binding even before Congress gave them any authority. And we were abiding with the rulings from that FCC. But most elected officials believed the FCC had legal authority. And our customers were just so enamored with their smartphones that they never challenged us."

Jack Rathbone was also from a wealthy family, which allowed him to attend prestigious private schools. His education reflected west coast values, as his MBA was from Stanford. His business acumen was quickly recognized in the first company he joined after graduation, and he quickly rose to the top. When he was chosen to be CEO, it surprised a few of his competitors for the job, all of whom had thought themselves to be in line for it, but his success in subsequent years leading his company proved his selection to have been the correct choice.

Matt Barkem, another CEO, offered, "We need to use our tried-and-true technique of disinformation. I'm sure we could drop in some appropriate lies to our standard fake news sources. We could promote a conspiracy theory where Sensei's front and center for an alien takeover or Earth. Or that she's just taking advantage of the alien landings to claim that she's one of them, but that she's really just a light green Earthling nutcase who's trying to make a name for herself."

Matt Barkem's family had pinched pennies to make it possible for him to attend Oberlin as an undergraduate, where the very humanistic attitudes appealed strongly to him. He then was awarded a fellowship to work on his MBA at Berkeley. The company that initially hired him gave lip service, but not much else, to nurturing its employees, so after a few years he joined another telecom company. He had never bought in to the dog-eat-dog attitudes of corporate America, but his Board of Directors were impressed with his attitudes toward his underlings. They decided he would provide the leadership that would get the best from the company's employees. And he seemed to place appropriate importance on expanding the company's bottom line. So, they made him CEO.

Jim Curson, the fourth CEO, took a different tack, "I don't think we're going to get away with discrediting this FCC while claiming the previous one was perfectly legal and authoritative. Furthermore, if this discussion ever hits the news, they'll tear us apart for our hypocrisy. I'm not especially bothered by that sort of accusation, but the public reaction to it might cost us money."

Jim Curson had a rather different background from the other CEOs and was sometimes regarded by the others as a pariah. His upbringing was at the lower end of middle class, and he learned early in life that being an accomplished street fighter was the way to succeed. His education, including his MBA, took place at state universities. He was never popular with his peers, continuing the combative ways of his early life into his mode of operation within the company that hired him. When its Board of Directors chose him to be CEO, there was considerable argument and dissent, but it was thought that he might be an effective leader as CEO until a better candidate came along. However, his successes as CEO seemed to justify the votes of his supporters, even though based to some extent on the general success of the telecom industry.

Curson continued, "I think we need to come up with a way to get the new FCC to bend to our wishes. Fear is really a good motivator. I don't make this suggestion lightly, but there might have to be some dying here. If the alien woman were to have an accident, that would take her out of the picture, but I don't think that would change the FCC's rulings. However, if Linda Forrester also had an accident, I believe the other commissioners might have a change of heart. I'd lump Rob Thompson with the other two, except that he's one of us in a sense. So, whether he agrees with us or not, I'd give him a pass for now.

"As for Matt's suggestion about a disinformation campaign for Sensei, I think that would be essential. Otherwise, when we knocked her off, it would turn her into a martyr. That would most likely backfire."

After a short pause he went on, "I thought I heard a couple of gasps when I mentioned dying. I surely wish this weren't necessary but, gentlemen, we do, after all, have to worry about our bottom lines and our shareholders. As well as our children's inheritances. And, let's face it, we have already caused a lot more than two deaths as a result of our RF radiation enhancements!"

Now there was an even longer pause in the conversation. But after some seconds, Tom Mack said, "My colleagues, I believe we need to think about the issue that was just raised. And I believe our next meeting should be in person in an electronically isolated room."

They met three days later, this time in the plush, reserved-for-CEOs-only, conference room in Tom Mack's building. As Curson entered the room with a worried look on his face, he said to Mack in a low conspiratorial voice, "Jeezus, I hope our last call wasn't being recorded or overheard. Sorry I didn't think of that before I made my comments."

Mack, remaining expressionless, replied, "Yeah, we wouldn't want to be discussing assassination on a recorded line! At least that discussion didn't go very far. We'll have to see if the gasps that resulted from your comments were of shock at your suggestion or concern over the possibility of being overheard."

They all seated themselves, and Mack called the group to order, "Okay, gentlemen, we can now discuss Jim's suggestion over our conference call to eliminate the alien woman, and possibly the current head of the FCC as well. Is this something that you are fundamentally opposed to, or were you just nervous that our call might not have been private?"

The other three members affirmed their willingness to consider assassination, although Matt Barkem noted, "If I were opposed to the very idea, I sense that just because I'm attending this meeting, I might be signing my own death warrant. You guys are a tough bunch of hombres."

That was met with chuckles by the other three. But it wasn't obvious whether his primary motivation for going along with them was concern for the telecom industry or for his own life.

"Okay," Mack concluded, "I guess we are in agreement that we need to hire someone to take out Sylvie Sensei. Yes?"

They all murmured their affirmations, although with varying levels of enthusiasm.

Mack was warming to the task, "Okay, the next question then, is how the hell do we go about hiring a hit man? I don't have any experience in this. Do the rest of you have any ideas?"

After several seconds of silence Curson offered, "Well, I my next-door neighbor in the Hamptons, who has a much grander house than I do, is a reputed Mafia boss. I don't really know the guy. But he probably knows me in about the same context, that is, from our respective levels of infamy. If nobody has a better idea, I can try to contact him and see if he can help us."

All agreed to authorize Curson to contact his Mafia neighbor.

Curson deliberated, working up a sweat, before making his call. Finally, "Mr. Cambrioni, this is Jim Curson, your next-door neighbor."

"Yeah, Curson, I know who you are. We been neighbors for more than ten years, ever since you bought that pile of crap next door to me, and you've never contacted me before. By the way, I wish you'd upgrade your shack. It's a disgrace to the neighborhood. But I have to wonder why you're calling. What the fuck do you need from me?"

"Understood, Mr. Cambrioni. As you might have guessed, I have a question I hope you can help me with. Some of my associates and I need to look into the possibility of making someone go away. Far away. Permanently. I don't know if you would have any information about that sort of thing, but given your alleged past, I thought …"

"Goddammit, I don't know why the hell you'd assume I'd know anything about hit men. Sure as hell never had anything to do with that sort of shit."

"Oh, I'm sure that's the case. I apologize for having it sound as if I was insinuating that you might."

"But you might try calling Vladimir Levchenko. His nickname is 'The Russian,' which I guess is obvious. And for Christ's sake don't tell him who advised you to call him. You don't know me, and I've sure as hell never heard of you. Except from the scandal pages of the newspaper."

"Got it, Mr. Cambrioni."

And he gave Levchenko's phone number to Curson.

Curson had been apprehensive about calling Cambrioni, but that paled in comparison to how he felt about calling The Russian. After an hour of hesitation, he dialed his number.

"Russian here."

"Mr. Levchenko, this is Jim Curson. Some of my colleagues and I need to look into making some people disappear. Permanently. I got your name from the grapevine as someone who might be able to help with this."

"Oh, don't know about doin' stuff like that. But might be able to find someone who would. Who gave you my name anyway?"

Curson wasn't prepared for such a direct question. "Oh, he asked me not to divulge his name."

"Well, then, it's been nice talkin' with you."

"Wait, wait, we need to do some business here."

"Okay, my business is based on trust. So, either you tell me who gave you my name or we don't do business."

"Jeez, okay. My neighbor, Cambrioni."

"Yeah, thought that might be the case. I'm sure he'll be demandin' his cut. But let's get back to the business at hand. You and I need to meet so you can tell me who's to get rubbed out. Then we need to settle on a price, half paid in advance, and the other half at the successful conclusion. Meet me at Sam's Bar and Grill in downtown Jersey City tomorrow evenin', nine o'clock. You can't miss me. I'll be the only one in the bar wearin' a Cossack's hat. I don't like crowds, so come by yourself."

"Got it. See you tomorrow evening."

Curson thought about his forthcoming "date" all day with great apprehension. Evening came, and he drove to Sam's. The bar was in a very seedy part of town and, although he'd worn casual clothes, he had a feeling he'd stick out in Sam's like an extremely distressed thumb. It didn't help that he drove his Bentley. He would have liked to have brought someone else along, or told the cops where he was going, but one of those things wasn't allowed and the other wouldn't do for the project at hand.

The bar stank of cigarette smoke and spilled beer. Curson spotted The Russian immediately upon entering, sitting by himself at a table. He didn't seem to be that tall, but was built like a fire hydrant, with a barrel chest and biceps like stovepipes, all well exposed in his sleeveless T-shirt. He had a long scar on one side of his face, and he looked like he hadn't smiled since he'd reached puberty decades ago. *Good god, I'd better not make this guy unhappy!* Curson walked over to the table and pulled up a chair.

"You're Curson?" The Russian's voice sounded like a rasp working on metal.

Curson tried to sound tough, "Yeah."

"You got anyone with you? Anyone waitin' outside?"

"No. Just me." And then he wasn't sure he should have confessed that he had no backup. He was suddenly drenched with sweat, and frequently had to wipe his hand across his brow.

That seemed to amuse The Russian. "Goddamn, but you do look nervous. Anyway, I done some checkin' on you, and you are some rich son of a bitch. But that only matters when we start talkin' money. So, tell me who you want bumped off, and I'll decide if I know anyone who might be willin' to do the honors."

I wonder if this guy reads the newspapers. I wonder if he can read! "Well, let's start with our number one target. Ever heard of Sylvie Sensei?"

"Jesus Christ, you want to knock off the goddamn President of the United States? That'd be easier than dustin' her."

"Yeah, I was afraid you'd say something like that. So, is that impossible?"

"Didn't say it was impossible. Anything is possible for a price. But don't think I could find anyone to do that for less than a hundred million."

Curson gulped, "One hundred fucking million? That's one hell of a lot of money."

The Russian backed up his chair and stood as if to leave.

"I'll have to check with my colleagues to see if we can raise that much. When can we meet again?"

The Russian sat back down. "I'll give you a week from now to raise the cash. Meet me here a week from tonight, same time. I'll give you instructions where to wire the half that precedes the action. In the meantime, I'll check with the guy I have in mind for the job to be sure that price is good with him."

"See you then." Curson got up to leave, still unsure if he would be able to exit the bar alive. *Wish I could find someone else to carry out this interaction. This guy scares the shit out of me. And a hundred million ... ?*

Curson reported back to his three colleagues, again seated in Mack's insulated room, He tried to appear in charge of things, but recurring thoughts of The Russian made that very difficult. He was developing a tic over his left eye. "Okay, I'm risking my life to save our bottom lines. I suppose that's a fair bargain, although not necessarily from my perspective.

"What I learned in talking to some thug named The Russian is that he, or someone else, would want one hundred million to knock off Sensei. That's only half of the people we want to eliminate, but she's certainly the more important, and undoubtedly the more costly. And that assumes the price doesn't go up. He sort of suggested that he'd need at least that much. That's only twenty-five million for each of us, which isn't exactly chump change, but is still only a fraction of our annual salaries. And The Russian only wants half of that now, or twelve and a half million. So, I guess that's not too much."

There were a couple of gasps and some murmurs, but not much else in the way of pushback. Mack asked, "How's he going to knock her off? I suppose these guys use guns, but maybe they have other ways."

"He didn't say, and I didn't ask. I assume they'll take care of the details. Jeezus, you must understand how creepy it was talking to this guy. Would one of you like to take on that job?"

Matt Barkem, becoming more accepting of the situation, replied "No, he's your neighbor's referral." Then he wondered aloud, "Twenty-five million is only a small fraction of the net worth of each of us, but our money doesn't sit around as a liquid asset. I'll have to sell some stocks, and I hate to just do that at whatever price the market has for them. I guess we don't have any choice on timing. We need to do this for our shareholders."

Curson replied, "Yeah, we need to be able to wire half of the hundred million to some account The Russian will give me the number for when I meet him again in just six days.

"God, but that guy is creepy."

A week later, he had purchased a used Ford, which he thought would be less conspicuous than the Bentley and drove back to the bar. The Russian was waiting for him, so Curson sat down and began, "Okay, we have lined up half of the one hundred million, so give me the account number and I'll do the transfer."

"Well, the guy I thought might do your job wanted more. The price is now one-hundred-twenty million. But you had no trouble gettin' the first part so I'll assume you'll also be okay with the new price. Here's the account number for the transfer. It needs to be done by noon, day after tomorrow."

"I thought we had a deal at one-hundred million."

The Russian backed his chair up and gave Curson a look that would probably cause many hearty souls to faint.

"Okay, okay. One-hundred-twenty million. I think I can do that. But if there's a problem, I won't be able to make the transfer by noon on the day after tomorrow."

The Russian leaned forward and growled, "I don't like people who ain't agreein' with me. You get what I'm sayin'?"

Curson definitely understood what he was saying. "All right, all right, I'm pretty sure I can raise the additional money." Curson was wondering if his heart would last long enough to get out the door. But if he succeeded with that, his life still depended on the willingness of his colleagues to come up with the remaining cash. *I must not displease The Russian!*

Back in Mack's conference room the following morning, Curson reported to his colleagues, "Okay, guys, I need an additional two and a half million from each of you now. The Russian just announced that the price had gone up to sixty million for the first installment and, as far as I could tell, if I didn't agree to the new price the deal would be off and I could be in danger. With a permanent result. At least it would undoubtedly be quick."

Mack asked, "Didn't you negotiate the price? After all, he was the one who was raising the ante."

Curson inhaled deeply and his tic was getting more persistent, "I think if you'd seen this guy you'd understand why I didn't have any option but to go along with what he said. Either we wire sixty million to the account he gave me or I have to enter the witness protection program."

They agreed. After all, it was only another two and a half million from each of them for now.

As Curson made the wire transfer, he thought, *I wonder how we're going to find out when they've executed Sensei. I guess we'll read about it in the newspapers. Then I'm sure The Russian will contact me for the remaining sixty million. I certainly won't have to contact him!*

Chapter 12. Socializing

Forrester had to overcome her apprehension about Sylvie's possible reaction to what she was about to request, "Sylvie, this is Linda Forrester. I hope this isn't too much of an intrusion on your life; I know you must be extremely busy. But I was hoping that we might get to know each other better. Some of my best friends are people who come from very different walks of life from mine. And I can't think of anyone whose origins are even close to being as different from mine as yours."

She took a deep breath, "So I hoped we might get together for a lunch. Could you do that sometime this week?"

Sylvie had enjoyed her interactions with Linda and Rob, so she had no hesitation in accepting, "Linda, that's a wonderful suggestion. I'd certainly be interested in getting to know you better, too. You seem to have very strong principles, and that's something I admire in both Earthlings and Camitorians. Although I'm guessing I'll quickly become busier than I am right now, I could meet you for lunch tomorrow. Would that work?"

Sylvie had eased Linda's apprehension, "Terrific. I'll pick you up at 11:30."

"You know about my security detail. They not only guard me at home, but also follow me around all the time. I hope that won't be too much of an inconvenience?"

"We'll figure it out. I don't think we should let that get in our way."

"Great—see you at 11:30."

Once again, the timing turned out to be far too optimistic. This time the security folks wanted two weeks to do their security check. It might have been shorter, except that some of the issues they discovered Forrester supported had tainted reputations. At least in the eyes of those who thought socialists were a threat to the US's way of life. So, they waited until she got their reluctant approval, and rescheduled their date.

After finally gaining approval, Linda was able to accompany Sylvie to their luncheon restaurant. It was more a teahouse than a restaurant, but the little sandwiches they featured were thought by both women to be adequate. Lacy curtains decorated the windows, and the décor could best be described as 'quaint.' Although Forrester had thought the security detail wouldn't be a problem, she'd never before been surrounded by large men wearing dark suits and carrying weapons. And they insisted on being in close proximity to the two of them.

"Linda, I'm sorry these men have to take tables on either side of ours. We'll just have to ignore them if we can. For what it's worth, I've never found them to be especially interested in my conversations. At least as far as I could tell."

"I'll do my best, but this isn't going to be so easy."

She leaned forward in her chair, "But let me ask you a question, and maybe that will help. Do Camitorian women get together for social lunches?"

"Sometimes we do, but it'd more likely be a business lunch. I've learned that Earthling men get together for business lunches, but that's less frequent for women. Or perhaps the Earthling men and women do not have business lunches together. That seems odd to me. On Camitor business lunches usually include both men and women. I suppose that's because our men and women have job equality, so business cannot usually be conducted with just one sex.

"But, Linda, wouldn't that work for Earthling business lunches?"

"Well, on Earth, there are wide variations in the equality of the sexes as far as status in businesses. Women are making progress on this, but men still pretty much dominate the business scene. In some cases, there is more equality, but men often seem to want to do business just among themselves anyway. They've selected a different venue for that. Business lunches have been replaced by golf outings."

"Oh, how strange. Yes, I know what golf is. I find it difficult to see how men could reach agreements when they are doing their best to compete with each other in a game. They must come to some ridiculous agreements."

And the two of them shared and explained many equally different and odd concepts. After a pleasant hour and a half, they agreed to meet again in the near future.

Another call on Sylvie's landline came two days later, "Sylvie, this is Rob Thompson." He wasn't sure if he needed further identification to remind Sylvie who he was, but she took care of the issue.

She straightened up in her chair, a smile on her face, "Of course, Rob, I recognized your voice. How nice to hear from you."

"Sylvie, I was wondering if we could do a dinner together. I'll be in New York in two weeks, and I'd love to treat you. I don't know what protocols are for Camitorians to get to know Earthlings, or if they even exist but, well, I was hoping we could get to know each other better."

The smile was becoming larger, "Rob, that is a lovely invitation. I'd be delighted for us to evolve from working associates to friends, and if the protocols don't exist, we'll just have to make them up. Please give me a couple of possible dates, and I'll arrange my schedule to include a dinner with you."

"I'll be there from the sixteenth through the twenty-first of this month for some meetings but could extend that a bit if necessary. Would some time in that window work for you?"

"Wonderful, Rob. The evening of the eighteenth would be perfect. But I should warn you that I have a security detail that never lets me out of their sight. They have to have dinner at the same restaurant just so they'll be always present. Is that too much of an inhibition for us to become better friends?"

Rob took a deep breath, recognizing the implications of that, "I'd heard you had heavy security, so I was assuming I'd have to ignore it. We'll make it work."

"Thank you so much for calling, Rob. I'll look forward to our get together. Is that what Earthlings call a date?"

"Yes. Exactly."

When Sylvie informed her security folks of a new date, to take place in two weeks, they groaned. But Rob's approval turned out to be much easier than Linda's. His track record was strewn with considerably fewer political land mines.

In any event, Rob and Sylvie had two weeks to think about their forthcoming date.

I wonder what Earthling men expect when they have a date. If we go to a fancy restaurant: dinner, cocktails, and wine, I will have to know if Rob expects me to share the cost. He did say he wanted to treat me, so maybe he's planning on paying. But should I offer to split the bill?

I wonder if he's expecting any intimacy. Camitorian men are respectful, but aren't usually bashful, so I guess I'll not be too surprised at anything he wants or does. But I wonder if Earthling male anatomy is similar to that for Camitorian men. I guess I'll find out soon enough if our relationship evolves to that level. But what limits should I set on the evening? We'll just have to see how things evolve to find out. But if we come back to my apartment afterward, perhaps we can be together without the security detail, and then those decisions will be ours to make. Whatever happens, I know I admire Rob a great deal, and will continue to do so no matter what happens.

I wonder what she'll be expecting of me. I surely have infinite respect for her, but I'm not sure how that translates for Camitorians. Anyway, I can't imagine pushing the limits of physicality with a woman whom I admire so much, or with any woman, for that matter. I hope she won't be offended if I don't try to push our relationship too far too quickly.

And could the anatomy of Camitorian women be just like that for Earthling women? From what I've observed, it surely looks like there are many similarities. I wonder how Camitorian men would handle a situation like this. Anyway, I'm just pleased she accepted my invitation. I just hope her security detail isn't too inhibiting!

Rob had planned to pick her up in his car, but when he arrived at her apartment, he discovered that her security detail would be driving them to the restaurant in two limousines. That was his first taste of his new reality.

When they arrived at their restaurant, Rob indicated their reservation, and they were seated in a plush booth decorated in maroon velvet. The booth would have allowed them to sit as closely as they wished, but they maintained a respectful separation. Several security men were seated at the usual adjacent tables. They had much to talk about, she with many questions about Earth and Earthlings, and he with questions about Camitor. Male-female protocols never came up, either in their discussions or in their minds. Rob wasn't sure how the restaurant knew to hold those adjacent tables for the security people, but somehow Sylvie's guardians figured out how to be as close as necessary to her. Anyway, the security folks were delighted to accompany her to such an elegant restaurant. Rob wondered; *I hope I don't have to pick up the check for these security guys. They look like they could eat a lot!* But in the end, they paid for themselves. And, somehow, despite their presence, Sylvie and Rob were able to focus just on themselves.

Rob was usually a fairly gregarious sort, but he found himself having difficulty finding anything to say. He was so distracted by Sylvie's blond hair, lavender eyes, and an expression that always seemed to be on the verge of shifting into her dazzling smile, that his tongue seemed to be anesthetized. But finally, he managed a question, "Sylvie, is Earthling food anything like the food Camitorians are used to? Are you having any difficulty with the food you've encountered? Or, specifically, with the menu here?"

Sylvie appeared to be relaxed, leaning back in her booth seat, "Most Camitorians are vegetarians, but I've been able to find enough vegetables and other things in the grocery stores to make what I like. Sometimes they're strange looking compared to what I'm used to, but when I taste them, I find they are mostly acceptable. And the menu here seems quite able to accommodate my tastes. We do indulge in alcoholic beverages, certainly including wines. But from the menu I'd guess that most Earthlings eat a lot of animal protein. Is that the case?"

Rob was beginning to relax, but he wasn't sure how to handle that question, "That's probably correct. I certainly enjoy a good steak once in a while. I hope that doesn't offend you."

"I understand that a steak comes from a male cow. Is that correct?"

Rob decided to just go with the flow, "The steaks we get in restaurants usually come from a steer, which is a male that has had its testicles removed so it cannot reproduce. Females are used to produce milk or for subsequent breeding. But some steaks might originate from some other kind of animal. Sometimes it may refer to a mushroom. Or even to a tomato!"

She seemed unfazed by his answer. "Oh, that's confusing. Anyway, the steak from an animal might have offended me a few months ago, but I've gotten more accustomed to Earthling habits, so that's no longer the case. You certainly need to continue doing what you've always done, at least food-wise, and I don't think I've any right to try to convince you otherwise.

"In any event, I should note that I'm enjoying the wine you ordered. I believe Pouilly Fuisse is my new favorite!"

"I'm delighted that you like the wine. And I understand your concern about Earthlings being such carnivores. Perhaps I'll forego the juicy steak tonight and have something that isn't quite so obviously a recent part of an animal."

Sylvie decided to address something that had puzzled her, "Rob, I've observed that Earthling men often hold doors for women, at least my security detail certainly does for me. I find this a bit odd; it suggests that men think women are intrinsically weaker, and need help with many things. Camitorian men would never suggest that Camitorian women were weaker than they are."

"Oh, Sylvie, when an Earthling man holds a door for a woman it's not a sign that he thinks she's incapable of doing that for herself. Rather, it's a show of respect. In many cases Earthling men don't hold doors for women, but you shouldn't be offended if they do. They're trying to please you, not to suggest that you can't open the door yourself."

"Thank you for the explanation, Rob. I guess there are many Earthling habits to which I need to become accustomed."

They each took a couple of bites of their dinner, then Rob asked, "Sylvie, I've heard it rumored that Camitorians live much longer than Earthlings. Is that true?"

"Well, for example, I am considered early middle aged among Camitorians at my two-hundred-seventeen Earth years."

Rob was, unfortunately, taking a sip of wine just as she said that. He choked, and it was a minute or two before his voice and aplomb returned to normal. And one of the security men cracked a smile, suggesting he might be tuning in more than Sylvie realized.

She smiled as he regained his composure, "Oh, Rob, I'm sorry. That must have been a shock to you. I hope you don't now think me to be an old lady."

"I couldn't possibly think of you as an old lady. You seem more like a thirty-year old Earthling in every respect: beauty, vivaciousness, and any other factor I could come up with. And your intelligence and savoir faire are at a level that even the most sophisticated seniors can only dream of. Let's forget I asked you about your age."

"Rob, what's savoir faire? That sounds like a French word."

"Sorry, I shouldn't spring too many words on you. That's French for 'know now'."

"Okay, that's very kind of you. But getting back to our discussion, I must ask how old you are."

"I'm forty-seven, but somehow that seems older to me than your two-hundred-seventeen."

And so it went until they finished their dinner and it was time to leave. The men of the security detail had done a background check on Rob to ensure he wasn't a threat. But they also apparently discussed how to handle the two of them in one of the limousines. In any event, they were allowed to sit in the back seat of their limo, with the driver and one other guard in the front, and the second car following behind. Rob had held the car door open for Sylvie, and she smiled her understanding. Then he climbed in after her. Once seated, Sylvie and Rob surreptitiously held hands. The guards kept their eyes looking forward, figuring the second car could watch out for threats from the rear.

When they got to her apartment, one of the two guards who had accompanied them asked if she was okay. She assured them she was and invited Rob in for a nightcap. The guards took the hint and assumed their post outside her apartment.

They were both so uncertain about what to expect physically that they decided not to proceed beyond more talk over a glass of port that Sylvie had somehow discovered in a local liquor store. But as Rob was about to wish her goodnight, he decided that there was no question about a kiss. Sylvie didn't need to wonder about that either. It was the culmination of a wonderful evening for both of them.

"Rob, I hope I will see you again soon."

"I live on the west coast, in San Francisco, but I do get to New York often. I'll give you a call next time I'm planning a trip here. But sometime I'd like to show you the sights of California. It's very different from New York."

"I'd love to see California. I've heard so much about it. Would you be willing to be my tour guide? Would you be willing to usher an old lady through California?"

"Absolutely, young lady! But for now, goodnight, Sylvie."

Two days later she picked up her landline, "Hello, this is Sylvie Sensei."

"Sylvie, it's Rob. I just wanted to say how much I enjoyed our evening together. And I'm looking forward to many more."

"Oh Rob, I loved our time together also. Thanks for setting that up."

"But Sylvie, I have a question for you. Ever since I got back to my condo, I've had a nasty headache and I've been experiencing brain fog. I suspect it's related to a new small cell emitter near my bedroom. San Francisco is loaded with RF transmitters, both the towers that transmitted all the signals up to a few years ago, and the more recent powerful small cells which, as you know, also transmit the previous generations of frequencies along with the higher 5G ones. The headache has been bad ever since they installed the small cell closest to me. It's only thirty feet from my bedroom which, unfortunately, is consistent with what San Francisco allows. I know the intensities aren't locally regulated; they just have to be consistent with FCC limits. Our recent FCC order lowered the limits for telecom; I wonder if this small cell is consistent with those levels."

"Well, I suggest you get out your RFR meter and measure the RFR levels. Have you ever measured it before?"

"Actually, no. I never worried about it until I got the headache."

"Well, once you've measured it, multiply your reading by two and a quarter to correct for the square of the thirty-foot distance from your bedroom to a distance of twenty feet from the transmitter, since that's the distance from the emitter where your

FCC imposed its limits. As you know, the outputs are more complicated than just an r-squared falloff."

"Oh, right. I've seen the radiation patterns; they have a number of lobes that is determined by the antenna configuration. But this should at least give me an approximate answer as to whether or not the company is abiding by the FCC limit.

"Holy shit! That's ten times the FCC allowed level. And I may not even be at the maximum in the radiation distribution. No wonder I have such a bad headache.

"I'll call the company that installed the small cell and demand they either remove it or reduce the levels. My company installs fiber to the premises, but I guess I'm stuck with that emitter thirty feet away whether my building gets fiber or not.

"But I wonder how many Earthlings continue to suffer headaches because they aren't personal friends of Sylvie Sensei?"

She laughed, then replied, "It'll probably take the company a while to make the change. In the meantime, you need to get some shielding cloth to drape around your sleep and work areas as soon as you can. I assume you've already eliminated Wi-Fi and hard-wired all your electronic devices; is that right? And what about your smartphone; do you keep it on airplane mode? In the meantime, you can wear an aluminum foil helmet around your condo. It will really help."

Then she giggled, "But you would look pretty silly if you wore it outside."

Rob's visits to New York gained in frequency like a metronome set to gradually increase its rate. The next time they were together, Rob reported that he had observed a workman at the small cell device near him, and that the radiation levels in his condo had indeed been reduced. So, he had been able to remove the temporary shielding without causing a return of the headaches. Also, of course, the aluminum helmet.

Chapter 13. RF Radiation Mitigation Strategy

Having persuaded the FCC to issue reasonable guidelines for the large towers and small cell devices, and sharing those rulings with the medical and political leadership of other countries, Sylvie decided to next try to educate Earthlings about the uses and misuses of their electronic devices. She convened a meeting with Rob and Linda to discuss potential strategies.

They arrived, endured their security pat downs, and were admitted to Sylvie's apartment. The three of them were now very comfortable with each other; Rob and Linda sat back comfortably in their chairs. Sylvie served them oolong tea and coffee, along with some brownies. Linda inquired, "Sylvie, these brownies are incredible. Where did you get the ingredients for them?"

Sylvie smiled, "I used some spices that originated from Camitor, but were actually grown on our spacecraft. I packed an assortment of them before I left the ship. So, you really are enjoying Camitorian cuisine now. Or perhaps I should say you are getting the benefits of outer space!"

Rob just smiled appreciatively, which was fortunate, as it obscured the silly grin that might otherwise have resulted from his gazing at Sensei. He hadn't yet gotten beyond the unfettered admiration he had for her. He doubted he ever would.

After a few sips of tea, Sylvie began, "I believe the purpose of our effort should be to help people realize they do not have to give up wireless devices, to which many have become totally dependent. With reasonable precautions they can continue to use them safely. Our efforts thus far have certainly been public, but I suspect they have affected only a tiny number of people."

Rob managed to redirect his attention to the task at hand, so offered, "We can flood the news, TV and newspapers, with more interviews and op-ed pieces, but I believe that Earthlings have become so addicted, especially to their smartphones, that we're going to have to attack the addiction before we're going to make much progress. Case in point: me. Even though I turn my smartphone off most of the time in my condo, I still have it with me at all times, and I always look immediately on receipt of a beep to find out who's calling and decide if I should respond. I'm a terrible example of unwise use of smartphones. Hence my conclusion that perhaps we have to point our fingers inward before we become too critical of the general public!"

Sylvie raised her eyebrows at Rob, and Linda laughed. "I'm afraid I'm also a fairly prototypical Earthling. I'm only slightly more careful than you are, Rob. I at least turn the damned smartphone off or have it on airplane mode some of the time, and then check occasionally for accumulated messages. But I also have it with me all the time. Sylvie, help!"

Sylvie laughed at their confessions, then asked, "How much of an effect do you think we have had on the public with our op-ed pieces and letters to the doctors? Surely all that effort must have done something."

"Well, our efforts did do something," Linda noted, "it got our FCC to issue vastly more reasonable guidelines. But that doesn't prevent the wireless devices from being dangerous. As far as the general population, though, we need to figure out what fraction of the population read the op-eds that were published, and also how many doctors actually read our messages. I'm guessing that we're up to no more than a few percent of the population. Then we need to figure out what fraction of that few percent did anything about what they learned from our efforts. If we take Rob and me as examples, the fraction of those who have actually changed their habits may be indistinguishable from zero!"

Rob added, "Although I did shield my condo at Sylvie's recommendation, which mitigated the electronic junk that pervades my portion of the San Francisco atmosphere, my smartphone still emits a lot of radiation all by itself. I hadn't realized how bad those devices are until I measured its output.

Even worse, I found that when I use it inside my now somewhat shielded condo it works harder than when I'm outdoors, and that makes its output even greater. But how many people are going to buy a meter to show how dangerous their favorite toy actually is? Especially when they may not want to know the result."

Sylvie rearranged the rogue swatch of her hair, which Rob observed appreciatively, then said, "We really have our work cut out for us."

Rob stood and paced a bit, "I'm reconsidering my previous statement. I think choosing the smartphones as our initial point of attack might be a mistake. We first need to convince people that exposure to RFR can be a general problem, and that their health depends on their keeping that to a tolerable value."

"I agree, Rob," Linda offered. "Then we need to suggest mitigation strategies to help them see how they can lower the potentially dangerous levels to something acceptable."

Sylvie's expression brightened, "Somewhere in the mitigation strategy discussions we can begin to talk about smartphones. And once we get there, we can start on the other wireless devices people are using. I like what you two are suggesting. So how do we get started?"

Rob, still pacing, noted, "A lot more people get their information from TV and the internet than from newspapers, so I suggest we concentrate on those venues. We could create a bunch of infomercials. These could feature the head Camitorian in each location, or perhaps just you, Sylvie, since you're probably better known than any other Camitorian even outside the United States. Either way, it might also include famous scientists to create the backdrop for what the Camitorian is discussing. I've had some interactions with an ad agency in New York that I think could produce some really provocative spots."

He reseated himself and continued, "We'll need some money, of course. We probably don't have any friends among big telecom anymore, so I don't think we can hit them up for donations. I'm guessing our best source would be the President.

She apparently approved the funds for your security, Sylvie, so maybe we could get her to go for this program. Unfortunately, it's going to cost a bundle.

"And, Sylvie, I think you are the person who should meet with her. You would surely have the greatest impact."

Linda seconded the nomination.

Sylvie replied, "That'd be good. I've been looking forward to meeting her. From what I've heard of her principles, she and I will have a lot to agree about."

Ever the opportunist, Rob suggested, "We've been talking the entire afternoon, and it's approaching dinner time. I have a favorite restaurant near here, and I propose we all head there for dinner. My treat." He would have liked to just take Sylvie, of course, but didn't see a way to not invite Linda also.

However, he hadn't given Linda enough credit for seeing the reality of the situation. She had also noticed several very friendly glances between Sylvie and Rob. "Thanks, Rob, but I'm pretty tired. I think I'll head back to my room."

So, Sylvie and Rob dined together again. While their dinners together were becoming frequent, their conversations never deteriorated to the commonplace. They always had many important issues of the day to discuss. The security people were becoming accustomed to being present but looking the other way. Or at least appearing to.

Linda had arranged for Sylvie to have a secretary, courtesy of the FCC, so she got an appointment for Sylvie to meet the President, who was surely as curious about meeting Sylvie as the reverse. So, Madam President had to do some homework. After studying the two op-ed pieces in the Washington Post, she decided she needed to learn more about effects of electromagnetic radiation.

She called her scientific advisor, Nate Morgan, in for a discussion, "I've gotten the message from things I've read that RF radiation can be harmful. Is this for real? Do I need to be concerned about this for Americans?"

Morgan was comfortable speaking with her, as she took science seriously, and consulted frequently with him. "Madam President, I believe that you do need to be concerned. The science referred to in the op-ed pieces is real, and some European countries have taken it seriously enough to put limits in place, at least for children. And they've enforced them. But even those don't completely solve the problem.

"As you know, our telecom companies were required by the recent FCC directives to reduce RF radiation in the US, but the industry's installation of tens of thousands of cell towers and small cell devices in the past few years has blanketed the US with RF radiation. And there are now thousands of 5G-related and even 6G-enabled satellites circling the planet. The small cells, installed to emit the millimeter radiation, also emit all the lower frequency stuff as well. Mitigation of the RF radiation will therefore be very difficult. And the industry has done nothing to address people's addiction to their smartphones and other electronic toys, all of which can be very dangerous. In fact, they've been encouraging it. I guess the reason for that is obvious."

"Ah, yes. Profits. What do you recommend we do?"

"I'd have a conversation with Sylvie Sensei to find out her thoughts on these matters. She certainly has the ear of everyone involved, possibly except for those in intelligence."

"Our meeting is already scheduled. But you mentioned intelligence. Have you gotten any vibes from the NSA or CIA since the limits on RF emitters were lowered? "

"Naturally they squawked when the new limits were first announced, but I've not heard anything from them since. I suspect they're working to see if they can circumvent any damage the lower RF levels will have on their monitoring abilities. Anyway, if they do have a problem, we could raise the limits part way back to what they were. Even raising them a factor of ten would leave the limits a factor of ten below what they were."

"I'm uneasy raising the limits at all, unless we are absolutely forced to by the NSA and CIA. But I like your recommendation; Sensei it is. Can you anticipate what she will suggest? Or request? Would it be expensive?"

"I'm guessing it might involve some sort of educational program, and that means a media onslaught. And that will be very expensive, if it is to be effective."

"Okay, thanks, Nate. I'll do a bit more homework, especially about costs, before my meeting with Ms. Sensei."

So, Sylvie and her security detail headed for Washington, first by limo, then by commercial airplane to Reagan National Airport, then by previously arranged limo to the White House. She had heard about the mass transit trains in Washington and asked her security people if they could use that to get from the airport to the White House, but they decided security would be too risky on the crowded trains.

She was amazed by the huge government buildings she passed in the drive as her limo headed toward the White House. As she entered the Oval Office, the President motioned for her to take a seat in an area, away from the Resolute Desk, that had two overstuffed chairs and a small table, thinking that would be more comfortable for both of them.

Sylvie couldn't help but be impressed with the trappings of the Oval Office, and she did stare a bit.

The President smiled, "What you are seeing are the relics of our nation's history, and of past presidents. Some of these oils of past presidents are so institutionalized I couldn't remove them if I wanted to." Then she asked, "Would you prefer coffee or tea? Or something else?"

Sylvie opted for coffee over her usual tea. "In my time on Earth I have acquired a fondness for coffee, light roast. So, if you have that, it would be wonderful. If you do not have that, any coffee would be fine."

"Oh, I think that's exactly what we have." She had her secretary pour both of them a cup of coffee, then opened the discussion, "Ms. Sensei, it is truly a privilege to meet you. You have had a tremendous impact in your short time on planet Earth, and I want to thank you for your efforts. And, of course, for the genetics research you have been able to perform that led you to identify the cause of the medical problems that so many Earthlings are having. We've named that The Earthling Headache, although my political opponents would rather saddle me with that name."

Sylvie laughed, took a sip of her coffee, then responded, "Madam President, I believe the privilege is mine. And before we get started on the issue we need to discuss, I want to thank you for setting up my security detail. I was shocked at first to think that would ever be necessary, but I've gotten enough angry comments from people to convince me otherwise. Anyway, I've now made friends with all of the security people involved, so their efforts are no longer quite so obtrusive.

"The reason I wanted to talk with you concerns our path forward in helping Earthlings understand the medical effects they are inflicting on themselves from the electromagnetic radiation that surrounds all of us, and especially from their use of electromagnetic devices. This certainly applies to smartphones, but to lots of other wireless and radiation emitting devices as well. My colleagues from the FCC and I have devised a strategy for reaching out to the public. This will involve use of infomercials that will play on TV and on the internet that will first alert Earthlings to the problems with RF radiation, then help them develop ways to mitigate the effects."

Here the President interrupted. "I think I can see where this is going. This is going to cost money, and not just a little of it, if you're going to counter the pro-industry commercials that dominate the airwaves. You have one Earthling who has taken your message seriously: me. My political opponents have received large donations to their election campaigns from telecom companies, and I must admit that most have donated to my campaigns as well. But I have done some research and believe there are ways to make their products and delivery systems a good deal safer. So, I am anxious to help you get your message out to the public."

She shifted a bit in her chair, then continued, "When I undertake projects, I need to announce how much they are going to cost. I am guessing you and your FCC friends don't really have a very good way to estimate the cost yet, and it will probably balloon when you go international, which I'm guessing you will ultimately want to do. At that point, other countries will need to come up with their own money, but from what you've told me about your thoughts, given what I know about the cost of TV and internet ads, this will surely approach one billion dollars, just for the US effort. A small fraction of that could be applied to your international efforts, but if we advertise that aspect of the program, it would just raise hackles from the conservatives in Congress.

"So, let me just say that we'll cover your costs up to one billion dollars over the next three years, but in installments, so that if you achieve your goals before we get to that total, the rest will be saved. If your costs exceed the one billion, we will review the situation, but I would consider more if that were necessary. Does that make sense to you? Would that be acceptable?"

Sensei's mouth was open and her lavender eyes just stared at the President for a moment. Then she was able to respond, "Thank you, Madam President. I'm stunned at your response. I believe the funding level you mention should cover our costs for quite a while. We certainly plan to hire an advertising agency to produce infomercials that will catch people's attention, but we haven't even contacted one of them yet. I'm truly grateful that we can already claim to have cash in hand for this adventure! Given your response, I believe we should also hire an accountant."

The President laughed.

With that, they shook hands, and Sylvie took her leave. As she walked out the President thought, *I obviously caught her by surprise. I'll bet that doesn't happen very often! But this is a very important project, and I'm delighted to support it. Besides, supporting this effort will keep me out of the line of fire from the telecom industry. Once the public becomes aware of the dangers from their devices, they'll demand change, and I can respond to the will of the people. I can take the billion from my discretionary funds and distribute it over several years.*

Before she left Washington, Sylvie contacted Kyle Jeffries, one of the Camitorians who had originally landed in New York but had subsequently moved to Washington. They were able to communicate via slightly amplified brain waves. "Kyle, how are you enjoying living in Washington? Is it more interesting living here than it would have been in New York?"

"Actually, it is. The reason I came to Washington was to be nearer to the source of the action that runs the United States, and I wanted that closeness. I've certainly been able to sample that firsthand. I even got a job as a staff member in one of the government offices, although I had to avoid identifying myself as an alien. Getting a security clearance was really tricky. And I managed to avoid telling them I was one-hundred-forty-seven years old. But my work there has been very exciting."

"Kyle, that's wonderful. If we need to try to understand something concerning the United States government, we certainly know whom to contact."

"I'm not an authority on much about the US government, but if such a situation arises, I'll do my best to help."

With that she wished him well and headed back to the airport. The security people had noticed her responsive expressions from the brain-to-brain communications enough times that it was now becoming commonplace to them.

When Sylvie reported back to Linda and Rob, both were stunned. Rob commented, "I'll bet you're the only person in history to get a commitment of a billion dollars from a President without even asking for it!"

Sylvie, Rob, and Linda contacted the ad agency Rob had mentioned. Its head, John Simpson, was enthusiastic about developing the project, especially when he learned the funding for it already existed. They first got two famous physicists to discuss electromagnetic radiation, how it varies with distance from the source, how its absorption in matter depends on its frequency, and what a Faraday cage is. Then two medical experts discussed the effects RFR can cause in Earthlings bodies, but especially the enhanced problems it can cause in children. Front and center in these discussions were the Council of Europe standards for safe levels. They also cited numerous cases where people, especially children, developed symptoms of RFR effects immediately after a RFR emitter was installed near their home or school.

Then they became more specific. The next series of spots for TV and the internet showed the problems that could be encountered with cell phones and cordless telephones. They first indicated some wavy lines representing the radiation lines surrounding, but not penetrating, a Faraday cage, with the background voice explaining that the cage provided near total protection from the RFR coming from the outside. Then they showed what happens when the source of the radiation, the cordless phone or the cell phone, is inside the Faraday cage, as the RFR is then trapped and reflected back and forth between the walls, floor, and ceiling, greatly enhancing its intensity. They explained that this is what occurs if one is inside a metal home or vehicle using a wireless device. Then they had a sonorous voice intoning the lesson learned: "If you live in a metal home, get a wired landline and hardwire your internet connections. Cordless phones are as dangerous as cell phones inside any metallic or shielded structure. And if you wish to make a call from your metal vehicle, don't! Go outside to make the call."

The next target was smartphones. The spot showed people walking with their phones in a hip or breast pocket, with the RFR field lines being emitted outward, and into their bodies. Then it showed someone holding the phone next to their ear, again with the RFR being emitted both outward and into the person's brain. A graph in the corner of the spot showed typical radiation levels into the body and brain, along with indicated Council of Europe maximum levels. The lesson to the audience: "If you're not protecting yourself from the RFR from your smartphone, you are probably experiencing dangerous levels. And this is a ticking time bomb; the effects are cumulative. When using the phone, use speaker mode whenever possible. Turn it off or switch it to airplane mode as much as possible. And never hold it right up against your ear."

Sensei had another thought, which she shared with Rob and Linda in phone calls, "Are we making a mistake by not including in our effort some of the other devices that emit horrendous levels of RFR? I am thinking specifically of microwave ovens, but I will bet there are lots of other equally dangerous devices."

Linda interjected, "Yes, those will also include pulsed radiation from the Smart Meters the energy companies are using. And there are also baby monitors and smart watches, both of which have become popular."

Rob replied, "You're correct to worry about the other devices. But perhaps we should save those for another day. We don't want to overwhelm the people we're trying to convince."

Sylvie acknowledged, "Ah, TMI as the texters say."

The Camitorians in leadership positions, except the two in Moscow and Beijing, were pressed into service to turn the spots into international service messages. While many Camitorians were still trying to conceal the fact that they were aliens, a fair number in each city had either been outed, in many cases by their children, or simply had given up trying to disguise themselves. In most cases, enough was now known about them that their opinions were usually taken seriously.

In order to get the infomercials into the languages of the cities in which Camitorians had landed, Sylvie translated them from English to Camitorian, then sent the video and her translation to each Camitorian leader to translate into their local language. This allowed them to include nuances inherent to their specific cities.

Sensei had tried to play a minimal role in these spots, but her fame made it essential that she appear in some role even in the international spots. Needless to say, she began to get more death threats from the lunatic fringe members in the United States, and also from those in other countries. Extreme right wingers everywhere didn't want her messing with their smartphone freedoms, even if her motivation was their wellbeing.

None the less, Sensei was the darling of the media. She was smart, very engaging, beautiful, and gave great interviews. And to top it off, she was an alien! Suddenly every talk show host on the planet wanted her on their show. She rapidly learned the pitfalls of being a media sensation. She could no longer leave her apartment without being recognized, usually with friendly "Hi Sylvie" greetings, but occasionally with something like "Why the hell don't you go back to your own goddamned planet?"

And, of course, there were the paparazzi, camped outside her apartment building hoping for a sighting of her. She found it difficult to go anywhere without being blinded by flashbulbs or the flashes from smartphones.

In recognition of the death threats, some of which had to be taken seriously, the US government had increased her security detail to include, in addition to her transporting detail, more security guards around her apartment building, and at least one more on her floor.

Some of the other residents of Sylvie's building were uneasy about all the uniformed security personnel hovering around their homes, although many realized they were necessary, since Sylvie was a rather high-profile person. Of course, there was the redeeming quality of sharing an apartment building with an international celebrity.

Linda, Rob, and Sylvie decided to show the TV spots first in the cities in which Camitorians had landed, excluding Beijing and Moscow, to test their effectiveness. The plan was to fine tune them after getting some feedback. Initial comments indicated they were useful, at least for those who paid any attention to them. People were becoming aware that their electronic appliances and devices could be made safer with very little effort, and were grateful to Sensei for bringing the necessary information to their attention. This was producing a philosophical change in how some of the consumers in those cities regarded their electronic toys.

But they also commented that the videos were too formal. Maybe even boring. And the ones appearing on the internet weren't getting shared very often.

The trio got together again in Sylvie's apartment. After Rob had studied a few dozen of the critiques, "Linda, can't we get those serious physicists to be less formal? Or maybe we need some physicists who are used to doing public presentations."

"Yeah, Rob. You've got a point there. Well, we can make changes like that on our next generation videos."

Chapter 14. Disinformation

A few days later, the main article in Breitbart News charged,

SENSEI FOUND TO BE A FAKE,
Alien Woman Is Demented Earthling.

Sources report that Sylvie Sensei, an alleged alien, is actually an Earthling who is trying to capitalize on the recent alien landings to further her own cause, whatever that might be. Her features that appear to make her different from Earthlings, her light green skin and lavender eyes, are the result of some skin coloring and contact lenses.

Sensei has risen to fame by promoting the discredited notion that the radiofrequency radiation that is essential for communications, high-speed data transfer, self-driving cars, gaming, and many other essential activities, is dangerous. This, despite the careful attention given to that question by the United States Federal Communications Commission. The FCC guidelines, established decades ago and reviewed in 2019, established the safety of this 'electromagnetic nectar from the Gods,' as noted by well-known scientist Raymond Sketchovich.

Sensei has had the temerity to suggest that the FCC's limits are much too high, and that research has shown these levels to be dangerous. This questionable research was duplicated at the behest of the FCC and found to be wrong.

Of course, the 'sources' the article referred to were in the social media, which had been sprinkled liberally with the fake news. It had spread exponentially before Breitbart News picked it up.

Sylvie was immediately besieged by mainline news people, her phone ringing off the hook for several hours after the fake news hit the internet. As soon as she got a break, she placed a call to Rob. Before he could even say hello, she gushed, "Rob, the news media are claiming I'm a fake, that I'm really an Earthling with artificial skin coloring and contact lenses. This can easily be disproved, but I'm afraid the questions raised could set our whole RFR lowering effort back to square one, as you Earthlings say, while we're wasting time refuting the misinformation."

Before she could say any more, Rob countered, "Oh Sylvie, I can understand how upsetting this is for you, but I don't think this will be a particularly serious problem. I had assumed you'd be besieged with calls from reporters as soon as I heard the report, and that you'd call as soon as you were able to get off the phone. So, in the meantime I called a friend of yours. While I wasn't able to talk with her directly, I'm guessing she'll have an announcement about this matter soon."

"Rob, I could have a DNA test done to prove that I'm not an Earthling. Would that be a good thing to do?"

"That's a good idea, except that I don't think it would have any effect. The people who already believe you would accept the test, and those who don't would claim it was faked. I suggest that you tune in to the evening news. I think there will be a definitive statement about your honesty."

He was right. At her afternoon press conference, the President was asked by several reporters whether she thought Sensei was a fake. After the hubbub died down, she replied, "Ms. Sensei is as real an alien as you and I are Earthlings. To suggest that she is artificially colored green is absurd. Furthermore, the restrictions she has been advocating on radiofrequency radiation are based on medical research that has been vetted and reproduced. I completely support her work and the mitigation efforts she's been advocating."

Mack was sipping on his second martini as he made his next conference call to his other three telecom CEOs. He said, "Well, our initial bit of disinformation didn't quite work out as planned. In fact, it would be best characterized as a colossal failure. Only the usual spate of conspiracy believers accepts our story. So, we need to come up with an addendum."

Matt Barkem, working on his scotch on the rocks chimed in, "How about if we work on a conspiracy theory where the President is being held hostage in some way by a group that Sensei is a part of. The President's 'captors' are telling her what to say. Of course, they forced her to defend Sensei."

The other three thought that would be a splendid idea. Thus, word went out the social media as to the new developments on the story.

Unfortunately, polls taken a week after the new theory indicated that less than twenty-five percent of the population believed it. Sensei's popularity was so strong that only the most devoted conspiracy theory lovers believed the fake news stories.

Mack summarized the situation for the other three CEOs, "Our disinformation campaign has made us about as popular as a massage therapist with a hangnail. Given the results, I don't think we have much of a chance of improving our result beyond the truly dedicated conspiracy advocates and alien haters.

"We'll have to stick with assassination. At least the twenty-five percent won't think of her as a martyr."

Chapter 15. The Opposition

The four telecom CEOs were meeting again at Mack's office building. After they had all seated themselves in the elegant meeting room, he began, "My friends, a terrible thing has happened while we've been developing our disinformation campaign and waiting for our assassin to do his job. Ms. Sensei has become a worldwide rock star. Her popularity is greater than that of any politician, and she's changing minds in ways that I believe are a grave threat to our bottom lines. We're being flooded with lawsuits regarding many medical issues the plaintiffs are claiming were caused by radiation from our transmission towers. Furthermore, many local governments are taking steps to remove some of our towers and small cells in critical areas, even finding legal ways to break our permit agreements.

"Finally, we're being pressured to use the funds we've collected from our customers through the years allegedly to provide fiber optics networks, as opposed to wireless broadband, directly to the homes of millions of customers for their designated purpose. Not spending these funds for what they were intended is causing a public relations debacle, not to mention litigation. This in turn is causing serious concerns among our shareholders, since our stocks are suffering as a direct result.

"Why are we concerned about Sensei? She continues to travel worldwide, is received by heads of state and adoring throngs wherever she goes and looks too goddamn healthy to me. Also, gorgeous. Seems awful to assassinate such a beautiful woman, but we do have to remain focused on our priorities. What the hell is taking our takeout artist so long? Curson, have we been scammed for sixty million dollars? This is beginning to look like larceny of an enormous magnitude."

Curson squirmed in his seat a bit, then replied, "Well, I can't say what's taking so long, and I have no way to get ahold of The Russian, except perhaps to hang out in Sam's Bar and Grill. I've tried several times to call the son of a bitch, but he doesn't pick up. He obviously doesn't want to talk to me. If any of you would like to spend some evenings at Sam's to try to contact him, you're welcome to take over for me. I sure as hell don't fancy sitting there night after night trying to look like one of the thugs. And I don't even know if he ever goes there anyway except for meetings with clients. Any volunteers?"

There weren't any. From what Curson had reported to them, no one had the guts to venture anywhere near Sam's.

Striker was on the phone with The Russian, "Goddammit, Russian, I've been stalkin' that alien bitch for two weeks now, and the only thing that's clear is that it's goin' to be harder'n hell to wipe her out. She's always surrounded by security, and they're large dudes, obviously packin' heat. But you told me this had to be different from what we usually do anyway. We don't want to be identified just because we can't change our usual mode of attack."

"Come on, Striker, you're supposed to be a clever guy. Well, at least not too stupid. You've been tryin' to convince me that Carlos the Jackal had nothin' on you. Sorry to tell you, but you definitely ain't in his league, or even anywhere near it. He'd a had this job done by now. So, since you're so goddamn clever, tell me some ways you've been thinkin' you could make her go away."

"She's in motorcades once in a while but tryin' to shoot out one of the cars in a line with gunfire would be suicidal for the hit man. Can't find someone who is willin' to do that for any price. Couldn't sell anybody on the benefits to their wife and kids. Like life insurance: your net worth skyrockets as soon as you're dead. But that's not an easy sell. If we had the resources of the US government, we could get a missile to take out her car, and I've been lookin' into that. But it's goin' to be difficult—actually impossible—to get the goods for that. Maybe a blast with her and her security dudes as they're leavin' some place, but then one has to arrange for the explosives, and the timin' would be difficult. Poison? I have been tryin' to figure out how to mess up her food supply, but I don't see a way to do that without poisonin' a whole goddamn grocery store. Even if I did that, I couldn't be sure it would poison *her*. Like I said, this is complicated! Maybe blowin' up her car when she's goin' somewhere; that may turn out to be the best option."

"Well, keep me up to speed, Striker. We can talk over some specifics when you get to somethin' that looks like it might work. At least I don't think our clients are likely to go to the cops to try to get their money back."

The two of them laughed heartily at that possibility.

"Jeezus, Russian, I might be done by now if I could just shoot her. But, even if you'd let me do that, I can't ever get in range of her. She has no regular schedule, and I sure as hell don't have a way to find out where and when she's supposed to be."

"I told ya' I don't want this to look like a mob job. However, maybe you could shoot her, and spin it to make it look like some loner nut case just wanted to kill a high-profile alien—some racist thing—doesn't like green skin. In fact, I found there are a number of hate sites already on the internet that don't like these green weirdos, no doubt come to take over our planet. I can start postin' comments with one of my aliases and see where that goes."

"All right, all right."

Buzz, the head of Sensei's security, was shifting his weight from left to right while talking to his boss, who was seated behind his office desk. The office décor could be described, perhaps too generously, as cinder block functional. "I'm really uneasy about protecting her. We've heard no rumblings of plots against her, but that seems too good to be true. She's an incredibly high-profile target worldwide, and she's certainly made some enemies in the telecom community. And that doesn't begin to count the right-wing nut cases who think they'd be promoting patriotism, or some damn thing, by executing aliens. She has certainly gotten hate mail. By the boatload. A few of those nut cases undoubtedly exist in the US military, and they might have access to some pretty daunting weapons. How hard would it be to take out one car in our two-car caravan? The US took out an Irani general from thousands of miles away with a goddamn drone!"

"How sure are you of her security when you're transferring her from her apartment to her limo? We've put a lot of manpower into that."

"Yeah, that's not the part that worries me. It's the two-car caravan. All it would take is an IED, an improvised explosive device like the locals used in Iraq. "

"Right. The way that was countered in Iraq was to beef up the shielding of the vehicles. We do have a limo that was used to transport presidents, a so-called Beast. It could be the limo that carries her. And maybe we should go to a three-car caravan with that Beast in the middle."

"Okay, that would make me feel better. I keep running possible scenarios in my brain that the evils might use to do her in. The Beast should take care of the IED concern. But I'll check out some more potential attack modes with the new configuration."

Chapter 16. Attack

Sylvie's infomercials and the talk show interviews were causing her national and international reputation to explode, and her picture appeared on the covers of many magazines, both in the US and abroad. Furthermore, her message about the dangers of RFR were spreading around the globe. Thus, she began to receive invitations to address political bodies in different countries. Since her Earthling language was English, she decided Great Britain would be the next easiest place for her to visit, and thus the first request she would accept.

She was surprised to see that her convoy for her trip to the airport now consisted of three limousines, and she was ushered to the middle one. The first and third cars had, in addition to the driver, two people who seemed to be armed with weapons she didn't recognize, but which she was certain could deliver a lot of firepower, at least by Earthling standards. *Well, okay, I guess the Earthlings feel I'm more secure with all these armed people protecting me. I'm sure this isn't really necessary.*

However, the horrific explosion that occurred two minutes later along one of the streets, only a short distance from her apartment, changed her thinking about security. It also commanded the attention of everyone else involved with protecting her.

"Hey, Russian, I got her. I fuckin' blew her to kingdom come or whatever heaven those goddamn aliens believe in. I had my lookout tell me when her convoy left her apartment. They always go down the same street, then turn at the same corner. My scopin' out of that alien woman's situation had her in the first car of a two-car convoy on every trip. The second car had all the riflemen who were protectin' her, so all I had to do was blow up

123

the first car. No mob job, just a good old fashioned explodin' assassination. I used an IED. I learned all the details, and there ain't many, from a guy in Iraq. The second car was just turnin' the corner when the bomb blew the first one up. What a beautiful explosion. You can hit those rich sons of bitches up for the other half of the payment. How much did you say that was?"

"Never said."

"Well, how much did you say I'm gettin' out of this?"

"Plenty. You'll net two million if you really did the job. But take it easy, Striker. I'll watch the news to make sure you got her. Your enthusiasm about your deeds hasn't always been such a good match with reality."

The lead story in the evening news:
"ASSASSINATION ATTEMPT ON SYLVIE SENSEI
Alien Woman Shaken but Unharmed"

Goddamn that idiot Striker, he botched another job. And this one will undoubtedly make any subsequent attempts that much harder.

As The Russian listened to the newscast, the reporter related what happened, "An abortive attempt was made to assassinate Sylvie Sensei, one of the immigrants from planet Camitor. She is best known for her efforts to improve the health of Earthlings by reducing the electromagnetic radiation to which we are all exposed. Her three-car convoy was headed for the airport when the first car was bombed. The driver and two passengers in that car were killed. She was in the second car, which was damaged slightly, but she and its passengers were unhurt.

No group has stepped forward to claim credit for the bombing, although the police are searching the remains of the car that was bombed for clues.

Curson answered his phone reluctantly. "Jesus Christ, Curson, was that the work of the person we've hired for sixty million as the down payment to kill Sensei? Or was that some other bunch of idiots with the same goal in mind? How could anyone have fucked up so badly? Maybe we should demand refund of our sixty million and see if we can hire someone with brains."

"Shit, Mack, that must have been our boys. I don't have a way to get in touch with The Russian. Like I said, I've tried his phone, but he's not picking up.

"I'll do what I can, but I wouldn't assume very much if I were you."

So Curson put on his seediest clothes, the ones he wore when he worked on the lawn at his Hamptons estate and went to hang out at Sam's Bar and Grill. He parked his old Ford a block away and walked the last block but was shaking with nervousness by the time he got to the bar. Of course, his disguise wasn't very effective. He looked like a rich guy wearing his yard working clothes. *Jeezus, that was some altercation. It nearly ended in a fight. With knives! I was only spared when that other guy, undoubtedly more of a challenge than I was, distracted the tough who was harassing me. And my pocket was picked twice. But no sign of The Russian.* Following the third night, he decided not to risk his life with further visits to Sam's.

Sensei was shocked and horrified by the whole event. *Such a situation would never have occurred on Camitor. I guess we were warned about the violent attitudes of some Earthlings, but somehow I didn't expect to encounter them in such a personal way. I feel horrible about the men in the car that was bombed. I've gotten to know all my security people, and those three all had families who will be mourning their loss. I'll have to get their addresses so I can write them a note of condolence.*

She received communications from several of the Camitorian leaders, asking if the attack signaled that it was time to invoke the retaliation plan. To each one she replied, "I don't believe this was an attack on Camitorians. I believe it was aimed at me. In any event, we need to be patient. The result of our retaliation plan, billions of Earthling deaths, would be so horrible that I wouldn't want to go that route unless we were absolutely sure we were being attacked as a group. The planet would be essentially unhabitable, even for us.

Rob called as soon as he heard the news. His voice was panicky, "Sylvie, what happened? Who on Earth would want to assassinate you? I can't believe what's happened. Are you okay?"

She had a chance for her nerves to settle a bit, "Yes, Rob, I'm okay. I do appreciate your concern. I've known that Earthlings could be violent, and I certainly have gotten some nasty mail, so I guess we should assume that something like this is just a natural part of the Camitorian transition to Earth. But I didn't expect it to happen so quickly. I'm still shaking from the experience, but what happened to me doesn't compare to what happened to the men who were killed. I feel terrible that they died guarding me."

"I can understand that, just knowing the sort of person you are. I'll get to New York as soon as I can. We need to spend time together."

"I agree, Rob. Please come. That would really help me get over this."

When news of the assassination attempt hit the world's information services, Sylvie began to get messages from all the thousands of those who had made the trip to Earth when she did. Also, e-mails from many of her Earthling friends and admirers.

The Camitorians' brains could only handle one message at a time without having them interfere. Thus, their ear device set out a 'busy' signal to an electronic module many Camitorians had when a conversation was in progress, This signal blocked an incoming call, but asked the caller if they wished to leave their three frequency intensity coordinates so their call could be returned.

It took Sylvie several days to respond to the many messages of love and support she received from both Camitorians and Earthlings.

"Striker, you fuckin' idiot. How the hell could you not have known there were three cars, and your target was in the middle one? Why the hell did you bomb the first car?"

"Jeezus, Russian, give me a goddamn break. They'd been usin' just two cars in her convoy for every trip until this one. Don't know why the fuck they decided to go to three, but couldn't see the third car, so had to assume she was in the first one."

"Well, I'm hopin' that our clients assume that someone else was tryin' to kill her. I'm not contactin' them for now. If I did contact them, they'd probably want their money back. No way is that goin' to happen. It's already deposited in a Caribbean bank. I'll just let them think whatever they want to think."

The Russian's anger at Striker was still simmering when a call on his smartphone suddenly put him on the defense, "Russian, what the hell are you doing? I can't believe anyone could be so inept. I assume that was your guy who fucked up."

"Jeez, Mr. Cambrioni, we hadn't talked about this, but I'm not surprised to learn you have some skin in this game. Anyway, the bitch's security detail had made a change in how they transported her, and my guy didn't know about it. He definitely fucked up, although his plan wasn't a bad one."

"Correction; it was a bad plan. If it doesn't succeed, it's a BAD plan."

"Got it, boss. I've given the guy hell. He's workin' on another plan."

"Not sure if he's the guy we should have doing a second try. Her security detail will be much stronger after the fuckup.

"Don't screw up again!"

So, Cambrioni not only recommended me, now I'm sure he'll demand a cut of the loot. He's never done nothin' for free.

Chapter 17. Another Enemy

One of the CIA analysts was reporting to his boss seated behind his desk in his boring, but functional, office, "General Ogden, we have a serious problem. We've had the telecom folks installing all these wireless transmission facilities, especially the new 5G ones, to optimize our data collection. That has been working like a lawyer trying to make partner, but suddenly it's not. The FCC has forced the telecom companies to cut down the outputs of their facilities throughout the US by a factor of one hundred.

"Some other countries of the world were already at that level or close to it. But this certainly changes the situation in the US and has appeased many involved in the anti-RF radiation groups. They seem to think the change has made their headaches go away. I suspect their problem was really psychosomatic since our telecom friends actually cut the outputs of most of the transmitters by more like a factor of three than one hundred. But even that is having a bad effect for us, since now our data collection effort is not as robust as it used to be. I don't think we can get the FCC to raise the limit again; they seem to have gotten their balls in a vice because of the RF radiation limits they think keep human beings safe. All because of that damned alien woman."

Ogden was the head of the Central Intelligence Agency. He had served in the Army since he graduated, with honors, from West Point, up until he was appointed head of the CIA.

"That's a pisser. Have you heard anything from the National Security Agency?"

"Haven't, but let me check with a friend there." He headed for his office, rather, his cubicle.

Ten minutes later he called, "General, same result from NSA, and they are also blaming the alien woman. I think you'd better call Clayton Berring and see how we can fix the problem. Our satellite networks and global monitoring expansion are not proceeding as planned. All kinds of things will fall apart if we can't correct the problem. Just as self-driving cars were beginning to take off, people will have to learn to drive their own damn cars again, among other things. Just try to imagine what that will do to death rates on the highways. But that's nothing compared to what this is doing to our citizen monitoring efforts. Worst of all, we're going to have to reevaluate our electronic warfare efforts."

"Yeah, I'll call Berring and see what the NSA hierarchy wants to do."

"Berring, Ogden here."

"Yeah, I'd recognize your voice even if I didn't have caller ID. You always sound like a General. Can't escape your past."

"Oh come on, Clayton. I don't want to get into the civilian-military arguments again. We've already wasted far too much time on that over the years."

Berring had received his law degree from Stanford, after doing his undergraduate work at Harvard. He had quickly gone into politics from his home state of California, finally having been elected and reelected six times for the US House of Representatives. His service on several important committees had been responsible for his being appointed head of the NSA.

He and Ogden interacted frequently, often sharing banter about their military/civilian pasts.

Ogden continued, "I actually have something more serious to talk about. Our data collection has suddenly gone on the blink, and I gather yours has too. It's because the FCC has forced the telecom people to lower the power of their transmission facilities, most likely in response to an appeal by that alien women, Sensei. And this is not just in the US; other

129

countries are adopting the new US limits. Any suggestions on what to do? Without the capability we had up until very recently, we'll have to let the citizens of the world go about their way without our knowing what the hell they're up to. That's a scary thought!"

Berring replied, "Yeah, that would be serious. So why not have the President order the FCC to restore the previous limits?"

Ogden added, "Unfortunately, the misguided civilians, of which you're one, have been complaining about headaches and other maladies ever since we got the transmission facility outputs raised, and now they're thrilled about them being lowered. So, the President has a political problem. You know, votes."

"Oh shit, hadn't worried about things like that for several years. What a nuisance. Is there anything we can do to achieve the same result, but not involve her?"

Now Berring's tension had him sitting on the edge of his chair, "How about just getting rid of the alien woman? We've got people around who do that sort of thing all the time."

"Interesting idea. But would that solve the problem?"

"It'd certainly be a good place to start. My black ops people or yours?"

"You did the last one, Clayton, I'll take care of this one."

After a short pause, Ogden mused, "Wait a minute, didn't somebody already try to take her out? I don't think that was one of my folks, Clayton. And from what you're saying, it doesn't sound like it was one of yours. Maybe we should just be patient and see if someone else can get her."

Now Clayton was leaning back in his chair, "Sounds good. Obviously, the other guys aren't as professional as ours, they screwed up royally. But they're at a disadvantage, after all. Our guys can use just about any form of weapon, and they and we are immune from prosecution. What about a directed energy weapon? We've had some success with those in the past. But I agree that we should give the amateurs another chance. It'll keep the Congressional watchdogs off our backs."

Chapter 18. Excuses

Striker was on the phone with his lookout. "Why the hell didn't you tell me there were three cars? That totally fucked up the assassination attempt. We're in deep shit for that failure."

"Okay, boss, I'll get it right next time. I'll tell you which car she gets into, what she's wearin', what color shoes she has on. Anything else you'd like to know? Color of her panties, maybe?"

"Smart ass. Just get it right."

"Must say, boss, that I'm enjoyin' hangin' out in this apartment overlookin' her buildin'. This is a classy part of town. Wonder what you have to do to live here. Makes me think maybe I shoulda' finished high school."

"I don't think you coulda' finished high school. That doesn't require all that much intelligence, but it still sets the bar too high for you."

Sylvie and Linda decided to schedule another lunch out. The security detail had replaced the car that had been destroyed, and they were quite confident that the Beast, the bomb proof car in which Sylvie and whomever else she had with her, was essentially indestructible. Linda took an Uber from her law office on New York's east side, where she worked when she wasn't in Washington doing FCC work. When she arrived at Sylvie's apartment, she was met by the security detail, and then both were ushered into the Beast.

"Wow, Sylvie, this is really elegant. Can't say I've ever been in such an amazing vehicle."

"Well, it has a tremendous amount of shielding so that it would be difficult to bomb it. I heard it was used as a limo for presidents."

"Incredible. I doubt if I'd ever feel really comfortable in a vehicle like this. Especially knowing that someone has already made an attempt to bomb your car. I just can't believe anyone would do something like that. To you, of all people. You're trying so hard to improve the lives of Earthlings!"

"Yes, sometimes gratitude gets expressed in strange ways. Apparently, the bombers didn't think I was trying to improve their lives."

"What a statement. If that's gratitude, I'll be happy to let them skip their thankyous!"

"Hey, boss, here they come. The alien is in the middle car. Send 'em to the moon! Or back to wherever she came from."

Okay, be patient. I know exactly where the bomb is placed. They changed routes since my first attempt, but this new apartment puts me right where the action is. Well, almost there. Ah, there's the first car. And here's the second one. Back to your goddamn planet, bitch! With that he hit the trigger just as Sensei's car was over the IED.

He immediately called, "Russian, I did it. Detonated the goddamn bomb right under the second car. But … wait a minute, there's a problem that I can see now that the smoke is clearin'. All three limos are still movin'. How the fuck could that be happenin'? Boss, this can't be real."

"If they're movin', it's real dumbass. Jeezus, Striker, did you fuck up again? Maybe your IED wasn't as powerful as you thought. This could turn out to be a real problem for you."

"Gimme a break. I made this bomb exactly the same as the first one. That one blew the car to pieces and killed everybody in it. Why the hell didn't this one do the same goddamn thing? Did those fuckers bring in another car, one with more shieldin'? That's the only thing I can think of."

"Well, Striker, let's give up on the car bombs. Start designin' another way to get rid of the bitch. The guys who are payin' for this are gettin' to be real pains in the ass. My ass. I'm gettin' at least six calls a day, which of course, I'm not answerin'.

"We need to think of a better way. Fast! No more excuses!

"And I'm not sure you even get another chance. You know what that means for you. It won't be pretty!"

"I'm on it. Thinkin'!" Then after a short pause he said, "Sure as hell wish we could get some rocket propelled grenades. Of course, I wouldn't have any idea how to use the damn things."

Linda couldn't suppress the flood of questions as the Beast continued its journey, "Sylvie, was this intended for you? I don't know who'd be trying to kill me. At least they didn't manage to kill anyone, although I'm not sure why. That certainly was a terrible sound, and it shook the hell out of our car. Can't believe we didn't get hurt. It sounded like a bomb. Did someone just try to kill us? Is someone really out to get you? And why?"

"Linda, I'm really sorry this happened. Everyone in the lead and trailing cars seems to be fine. It's a good thing the bomb was supposed to destroy this car. All its extra shielding will make it much harder to damage than the other two cars. But a bomber probably wouldn't know that."

Forrester never did manage to settle her nerves. She spent the entire luncheon sitting on the edge of her chair. "Sylvie, I really want to keep meeting you for lunches, but maybe next time I'll just meet you at the restaurant!"

"Yes, I think that would be good."

The news headlines read:
"SECOND ASSASSINATION ATTEMPT ON SENSEI
Alien woman uninjured
Still no group claiming responsibility"

The Russian thought, S*hit. I guess the security folks are at least one step ahead of Striker, although that ain't too difficult.*

As The Russian listened to the news, he learned that Sensei had been on her way to a luncheon with the Chair of the FCC, Linda Forrester, who was also in the car when the explosion occurred. It also noted no one in any of the three cars was injured.

Curson was becoming more and more reluctant to answer his phone. But his caller ID said it was Mack so, reluctantly, he picked up. Mack began speaking even before Curson had a chance to say hello. "Goddammit, Curson, these guys are the most incompetent people on the planet. They've had two tries to eradicate Sensei and have fucked up both times. And this time they could even have killed Linda Forrester in the same blast. Sweep out two witches with the same broom. But they blew it. They're incredibly inept killers!"

Curson wiped some sweat from his brow, "Yeah, Mack, I find it difficult to believe they could screw up twice. I keep calling The Russian, but he doesn't pick up. As long as he doesn't answer, I don't know how to get ahold of him. I'm not going back to that godforsaken bar again. It's apparently even too shady for The Russian. I guess he doesn't spend much time there either."

"General Ogden, Clayton Berring here. Must say our colleagues in crime have the most incompetent assassins I've ever seen. We certainly won't recruit for our black ops people from these guys. Imagine the opportunity to eliminate both Sensei and Linda Forrester, the FCC head, at the same time. They may never have a chance like that again."

"Right, Clayton. How many more times are we going to let them screw up before we assign our folks to do the job. I guess their only virtue is that they don't cost anything, at least for us, and they certainly won't allow anyone to cast blame on us! Well, the conspiracy theorists probably will anyway, but the accusations obviously won't stick if we are so unfortunate that we get a congressional investigation. Given all that, I guess we shouldn't interfere, at least not yet."

"Agreed."

Sylvie's phone rang. She was seated in one of her elegant chairs, which was next to her landline. "Hello, this is Sylvie Sensei."

Rob's voice sounded panicky, "Sylvie, this is terrible. Two attempts on your life, both with heavy duty explosives. I fear this will keep on until whomever is doing this succeeds. What can we do to get you out of harm's way? Maybe you should continue your efforts in some other country. That might not be any better, but at least that's something to think about."

"Thanks for your concern, Rob. Let's give that some thought. I'm definitely getting tired of these bombs. Camitor was never like this, not for anyone."

Chapter 19. Change of Venue

Sylvie was in deep thought about the dangers she was facing, when the corded landline rang. Distracted, she answered, "Hello, this is Sylvie Sensei."

"Sylvie, I think you should come to Paris for a visit. The French have been in the forefront of the RFR solutions for decades, and I am sure they would love to get to know you. Perhaps it would also be good for you to get out of the US for a while. Maybe the New York Earthlings who are trying to kill you will give up if you're no longer there. Besides, spring is a wonderful time to visit Paris!" The caller, Francois Dupre, was the lead Camitorian in France.

Francois had let it be freely known that he was an alien. During his time in Paris, he had made quite a name for himself, going out of his way to spread the message of RFR mitigation and agreeing to be interviewed many times on French TV. He'd become nearly as famous in France as Sensei had in the US, but absent the death threats and bombs. He was a rugged looking individual, sturdily built with thick dark hair, green eyes, and a well-trimmed beard. And he usually had a pleasant expression, which went over well when he joined with the French Wi-Fi mitigation effort.

He continued, "We could have you address the French people, with me acting as interpreter. You know, you just think your thoughts, I'll receive them, and then speak them in French. That way you wouldn't have to worry about getting your pronunciation correct. That can be a bit tricky in French. And it would be good for me to have you front and center; I wouldn't want the citizens in this country to get tired of me! Maybe you could stay for a few weeks."

She thought for a moment about Francois' comments, "I can't imagine they'd ever tire of you. You've done a wonderful job there. I don't even have to give your invitation any thought; I'll accept. I'd be delighted to get out of the US for a while.

"And, if I give my initial address to the French people it would be perfect to have you serve as interpreter. I'll store thousands of French words in my brain, so I can learn to speak French quickly. I understand that will take a little practice. But we should go with me thinking responses and you being the translator. I bet the French would be intrigued by our means of communication."

She quickly placed another call, "Rob, I'm going to take an extended visit to France. Do you remember me talking about Francois, the Camitorian representative in Paris? He's invited me there so I can address the French about the hazards of RFR. Of course, they have the situation pretty well under control. Their limits were as bad as most of the rest of Europe until they lowered them* in 2022, so it probably is not that important for me to go there for a visit. But I'll be grateful for the change of scene. And perhaps that'll cool off the people who seem intent on killing me. So, I'll not be in New York for a few weeks. I'll miss seeing you; your visits have added a wonderful dimension to my life."

Rob needed no time to respond, "I don't think we need to end our visits together while you're in France. They'll just have to shift to Paris. I think we'd really enjoy continuing to learn about each other in that lovely city." Then he lowered the pitch of his voice, "It's supposed to be very romantic."

Sylvie's expression quickly changed to her brilliant smile. "Rob, I was hoping you'd raise that possibility. I'll make sure I have sufficiently spacious accommodations to house another person: you!"

Rob was definitely warming to the possibility, "Just tell me your dates, and I'll be there. Probably not for all the time, but

*Author's optimism, since this was written in 2021.

137

you never know. With all the interconnectivity we have now I'm guessing I can conduct my business from France. At a low RFR level, of course! And FCC meetings have evolved to being partially conducted via Zoom, so I can do many of those in that mode, and travel back to the States only when it's absolutely necessary."

Sylvie continued to smile at the possibility of sharing Paris with Rob.

Then she placed a second call, "Linda, I'm going to go to Paris for a few weeks, departing ASAP. I'm definitely getting tired of these bombings. Maybe it would be a good thing if I were somewhere else for a while. I'll miss our luncheons, but my not being here might also take you out of the line of fire."

"Sylvie, that's a great idea. I might even come visit you once or twice. Paris is a lovely city; I've had some wonderful experiences there."

"Oh, that would be great!" She ran her hand across her eyes. *Oh, that would be complicated! I guess I can have two visitors. Rob and I are not trying to keep secrets from anyone. But having Linda there also would surely blow the lid off any secrets he and I might have hoped to preserve.*

Chapter 20. Transition and Complications

For her trip to Paris, Sylvie packed only a small bag of personnel items, assuming she would purchase new garments as she needed them. However, she packed larger bags of her research equipment, which she needed to have shipped. But she was concerned that the equipment would arrive safely in Paris.

She discussed the situation with Buzz, the head of her security detail, "Some of this equipment is irreplaceable. Can I be absolutely sure that it will arrive where I intend it to go in Paris and that it will not be damaged?"

Buzz smiled at her concern, "Ms. Sensei, the US government has ways of getting things shipped around the world with total confidence for its safety. The stuff is always under the watchful eyes of government employees. I'm totally confident everything will arrive in Paris safely. Even quickly!"

"Thank you, Buzz. I appreciate your reassurance."

She had only brought the pieces she thought might be difficult to obtain on Earth with her from Camitor, but she had added considerably to that in order to create a complete working laboratory.

Francois was delighted to meet Sylvie at Charles de Gaulle International Airport, full of both anticipation and concern about the future he and she would have. They shared a somewhat formal hug and kiss, although he was certainly hoping to improve on that in the near future. He hailed a taxi and brought her to the apartment he had acquired for her.

The Camitorian rumor mill had been buzzing with the news that Sylvie had an Earthling boyfriend, so Francois, somewhat reluctantly, had arranged for a spacious place for her in Paris that could accommodate Sylvie, her research equipment, and her friend. That was fortunate, as Rob arrived soon after she did. Francois smiled ruefully to himself as he watched Rob unpack.

After being introduced, Francois stared at Rob's equipment for a few seconds, then asked, "Rob, what are all those devices you have with you?"

"These are what I'll need to maintain communications with my company personnel. Don't worry; I've gone to great lengths to minimize the RFR that all of these gadgets emit, excluding the smartphone, of course. But I keep that turned off most of the time. The other items can all be hard wired."

When Sylvie saw Rob's electronics, she observed, "Rob, these things will create a huge electromagnetic problem, despite the efforts of the French, if they have to run on Wi-Fi. If the connections are hard-wired, though, things should be okay. But, Francois, you probably thought to have the apartment provided with the appropriate connectors. Are we Wi-Fi free?"

After a second's thought, "Good god, Sylvie, I didn't think of that. Let me check to be sure. If not, we'll have the wiring done for the entire apartment building."

A few minutes later he reported back, "The building manager intended to have the internet hard-wired in your building, but it didn't get done. He thought Wi-Fi would be okay. I told him that was unacceptable. So, he promised to get everything hard-wired. That should be done by the end of the week."

Sylvie replied, "Merci, Francois. We'll just be without connectivity until then, but we can survive for that length of time in Earthling twentieth century mode. I also noticed that the telephone was wireless, but fortunately I brought my corded landline with me. So, we should be all set very soon."

Rob interjected, "That'll be fine Sylvie. I can go to an internet café to conduct my most urgent business communications for a few days. And, of course, the stuff I downloaded to my computer before I came will take care of most of what I need."

Sylvie asked, "Rob, what are the most urgent issues you're working on?"

"Oh, we're trying to develop some software that we think will improve the sensitivity of our electronic devices, which of course means they will be able to operate at lower RFR levels. I think we're at a point where we're going to have to make some decisions. That's what most of the calls will be about."

"Okay, this sounds important. I will want to hear more about your project as it develops."

Then Rob observed, "Sylvie, this apartment is lovely, and is beautifully furnished. I guess I wouldn't have expected anything less from what the French would do for a famous visitor, but even so I'm blown away. Your furniture is all elegant French Provincial, only even fancier than in your New York apartment, and the draperies, all done in a soft blue with a bit of red trim, are absolutely beautiful. And you have a wonderful view of a park outside your living room window, complete with mothers pushing infant strollers. I see it even has a playground, with swings, climbing bars, and a sandbox for the youngest kids. "

"Yes, Rob, this really is nice. We can get to know each other better in an even lovelier setting than we had in New York."

"Sounds good to me!"

For a few days, they managed to leave their apartment for jaunts around their Paris locale, enjoying French pastries and coffee, walks along the Seine, even shopping for clothes. Sylvie loved the fashions displayed in the shops which they passed. Rob was fascinated by her questions, and just seeing what excited her.

The Parisians didn't disturb them much, apparently not yet having realized that the famous Sylvie Sensei was in their midst. And the gendarmes hadn't yet realized the potential for disaster that an attack on her would provoke. So, they got to enjoy their time together in solitude, at least for a little while.

Sylvie couldn't get enough of the store windows. "Rob, is that not a beautiful dress? Do you think it would look good on me? I'm not sure my natural green complexion would go with the soft orange colors in the dress, though. Oh, is that what Earthlings call peach?""

"Yes, peach. And there's only one way to find out how it would look on you. You must try it on."

Minutes later, "Oh, that's wonderful. I think I should buy it for you."

"Oh no, Rob, it is much too expensive. I wouldn't even buy it for myself."

"All the more reason for me to buy it!"

She wore it when they went out for dinner that evening. And it did go beautifully with her light green skin.

A week later, "Sylvie, this is Linda. I'm coming to visit you in Paris. Please get me an apartment for a week."

"Uh, … hi Linda, I'm delighted that you are coming to visit. I will have Francois arrange a room for you in a hotel, since you will only be here for a week."

A week later, Linda arrived at Charles de Gaulle International Airport, where she was greeted by Sylvie and Rob. *Aha, now I understand why Sylvie hesitated a bit when I told her I was coming to Paris. She already has an FCC representative on site!*

The three of them spent most of the week touring Paris, as well as some of the nearby towns, consuming some spectacular French food and wine, and generally just enjoying being together. Their group often was a foursome, as Francois was happy to serve as tour guide, and to expand on his own experiences in France. Sylvie was able to feel some peace of mind, following her harrowing experiences in New York, and began to think most Earthlings were more like Camitorians than the savages she was beginning to suspect inhabited New York City. In fact, she was enjoying herself so much in Paris that she began to give serious thought to moving there and turning her New York apartment over to Jason Becker, the Camitorian who was her second in command.

She gave him a call, "Jason, it's Sylvie. How are things going for you in New York?"

A call from Sylvie wasn't unusual, so Jason wasn't surprised, "Fine, Sylvie. All your TV and internet spots are running smoothly, and there's a flood of positive letters to the editors in most of the mainstream papers. The positives even include most of the letters to The Wall Street Journal.

"And there's still no one claiming responsibility for the bombings of your cars, and no police reports indicating they are getting close to identifying the culprits. But nothing of that level of hostility has happened since you left."

"Actually, Jason, I was wondering more about your reactions to your tasks. And might you be comfortable taking over as head of the New York office? I'm concerned that my identification as the leader there has had negative results, and that perhaps it would be advantageous for our long-range plans of integrating with Earthlings to have someone else in charge of the New York effort. What would you think of that?"

That wasn't a complete surprise to Jason, but he donned his diplomat hat, "I'd be happy with whatever you decide. I think we've enough known Camitorians in New York that the effort will continue. We'd certainly miss you here, but I believe things could run much as you've set them in motion. If you put me in charge, I'd continue the policies we've established without change.

"But you may be right that things might settle down here if you were to stay in France. And I suspect, you might be safer!"

"Okay, Jason, thank you for your reassurances. I haven't made a final decision yet, but I'm certainly giving it serious thought. If I do stay here, you could take over my apartment. "

Of course, he had seen her apartment, "Wow; that would be fantastic!"

Sylvie popped into Francois' office, "Suppose I remained in France. I wouldn't want to usurp your duties as leader of the French contingent of Camitorians, but would you feel awkward having me here?"

Francois wasn't surprised by the question, given how happy Sylvie and Rob seemed to be in Paris. "Oh no, Sylvie. If you stay you will become leader of the Camitorians in France."

"No, let me stop you there. That wouldn't be the case. I could remain overall leader of the Camitorians on Earth but resign my position as leader of the United States group. I would just be stationed in Paris instead of New York. That separation of duties may be something that should be done anyway."

Francois was beginning to sense a real opportunity, and it wasn't related to his status among the Camitorian hierarchy. He had been an admirer of Sensei even before they left Camitor. Being in the same place together and working closely with her seemed like a dream come true. "Sylvie, I certainly wouldn't object to sharing some responsibilities. That might make both the national and international operations more efficient."

"Francois, I think that's an excellent suggestion. We can pursue the details of that later.

"I believe you've helped me make up my mind. Would you be so good as to help me with my pronunciations in French?"

"Of course. I'd be delighted to."

Later that same day, Sylvie announced to the Camitorian hierarchy that she would be shifting her home to Paris, although she would remain as overall leader of the Camitorians on Earth. And that Jason Becker would be the new head of the US mission.

The CEOs of the telecom companies weren't included on the announcement, of course, but they did notice that there had been some changes. They met again in Tom Mack's office.

"Colleagues," Mack began, "something strange has happened. The number one evil witch we've been trying to eliminate seems to have vanished from our sights. Rumor has it that she's transferred her efforts to France, and at least the part about her vacating New York seems to be confirmed by the fact that some new alien named Jason Becker has identified himself as one of the Camitorians and seems to be issuing all the information coming from them now.

"Of course, that raises the question, what should we do about our plan to eliminate her? She's already had a huge negative effect on public opinion regarding our efforts to connect the entire world's inhabitants to all the 5G small cells, the larger transmission towers, and the thousands of satellites, but that's not likely to change now whether she's dead or alive. So, is there any point in continuing to pursue her elimination?"

Matt Barkem needed no time to think about it, "I propose that we call off the effort. We're not murderers, at least not in the usual sense. Rather, this was a business transaction. And now that she's left New York, I don't see any point in having our killers follow her to France. We were, after all, taking a risk getting involved in this business anyway, and abandoning it would just get us out of the game."

"But" Jack Rathbone noted, "we are out sixty million of our hard-earned dollars. What the hell are we going to do about that? Curson, you keep telling us that you have no way to contact The Russian, but it would sure as hell be nice to get our sixty million back. They didn't earn a goddamned penny of it!"

Curson's smile hardened before he replied, "Well, if any of you have a suggestion as to how I might try to contact the thugs, I'd love to hear them. Or if you'd like to see if you can find these guys, I'd be happy to bow out of that effort.

"But I should observe that our killers might well have had an effect. Their efforts may be what persuaded Sensei to move to France. So perhaps we did actually get something for our money."

Rathbone countered, "It sounds as if you're telling each of us that you're sorry, but we're out fifteen million. Is that right?"

"Fuck you. As I said, you're welcome to try to contact The Russian. Maybe you'd like to spend a few nights in Sam's Bar and Grill and see if he shows up. I might previously have thought that for fifteen million I'd do that, but upon further reflection I've concluded my life is worth more than that."

"Easy, guys," Mack enjoined, "cool down. Jim has said what we all agree with, namely, that none of us is willing to risk our lives for a paltry fifteen million. I guess we have to regard that as the price of the education we just received. Although it really galls me to say this, perhaps we should view calling off our anti-Sensei effort as a way to save the second sixty million."

Rathbone ended the discussion, "Regardless, that sure as hell is a high price for tuition!"

The General's secretary indicated there was a call on his secure line. He picked up the phone, "General Ogden, Clayton Berring here. We need to discuss the situation with respect to the alien woman. She has badly compromised our ability to monitor both US citizens and those in other countries, as well as the capabilities of the recently optimized 5G network. Actually, it could be worse except, my sources tell me, that our telecom friends are continuing to play things to their advantage. When the FCC set dangerously high-power limits on their devices, that was fine with them, and they claimed they were just abiding by the legal issuances from the FCC.

"Of course, the FCC has been somewhat of a paper tiger. Initially its decrees didn't have any force of law. They gained some teeth when Congress passed measures to require compliance with the standards they set for devices. But they do no testing, so who's ever to know if there's been any compliance.

But when our favorite alien woman got the FCC to lower the limits, the telecom folks suddenly claimed that the new FCC's rulings were no more enforceable than those of the previous one, and they would just stick with the old rulings. In the few cases where they got challenged, though, they've capitulated. And they apparently did lower the outputs of their emitters somewhat, hoping to avoid further litigation."

"Right on all counts, Clayton. That brings us back to the primary issue; what to do about our least favorite alien. We had been acceding to some group of bad guys to do her in, but they have obviously failed miserably. We were sure our black ops folks could take her out, but we held back on that. My contacts tell me she's moved to Paris. Maybe the thugs have succeeded at some level by scaring her out of the US. Now our telecom friends can probably do whatever they want without worrying about consequences. Of course, that assumes the new FCC won't be able to come down very hard on enforcement. If that's the case, that means our monitoring of US civilians will be in good shape, and I would suggest we should forget about eliminating her.

Ogden continued, "Of course, that ignores the fact that what she's been pushing for could mess up our ability to monitor foreigners of all types: civilian and military. Many foreign countries had limits in place on their radiation emitters that were close to what the US had before Sensei inflicted her changes, although they had considerably lower limits for the radiation levels in schools. But the damned Italians have much lower limits; they're about what Sensei has inflicted on the US. That's really made our lives difficult. And other European countries, Poland, and Switzerland, Russia, and others, have followed Italy's lead. So, although our capabilities aren't as good as we'd like, I fear that political inertia is heading the RF levels to something like the new FCC limits. So, there's not much to be gained internationally by getting rid of her.

"God, I'm glad we're not back in 2020. We've put up tens of thousands of transmission satellites since then, and this orbital infrastructure has given us reasonable capability to monitor everyone on the globe, even with the new limits. Sensei or not! So, I propose that we put her assassination on the back burner and wait to see how things develop. Are we agreed on that approach, at least for the present?"

Berring developed a contented smile, "Sounds good to me, General. Murder has always made me uneasy."

Chapter 21. A Case Study

Sylvie's peace of mind was shattered by an interaction she had with Gerald Jackson, a young American man. He had requested a meeting with her, indicating that he was suffering from cancer he believed was induced by excessive use of his smartphone. He further mentioned that the one place he had wanted to visit dating back to his boyhood was Paris and had decided to do so before time ran out. Since he was going to be in Paris anyway, he asked if he might meet with her.

She wasn't sure where this meeting would go, but she felt sorry for Gerald, so she acquiesced. French Security had decided by now that they needed to be concerned about her safety, so they had ramped up her protectors. Thus, after the usual spate of background checks, now being conducted by the French gendarmes, Gerald was ushered up to her apartment, where she asked him to be seated, and offered him tea and homemade biscuits.

"Yes, thank you. That would be wonderful."

As he focused on his teacup, she had a moment to study him. He seemed to be about twenty-five years old, was of average height and build, but had a rudely distinguishing feature: a strange distortion around his right eye socket that made the eye appear oddly large.

He began the discussion, "Ms. Sensei, I came to see you because I wanted to thank you for what you've done, not just for me, but for everyone on the planet. You see this really weird looking eye? Of course you do; it's hard to miss. I believe it's directly related to the use of my smartphone. I've been a very active user for about a decade. Let me rephrase that: I was totally addicted to it and used it almost continuously from sunup to when I went to bed at night. Mostly talking to my friends. I was also texting and playing a lot of games on it. At first I had a Galaxy, but then I got an iPhone.

"When my right eye began to be distorted, and that's right where I held my iPhone, I also began to suffer headaches, blurry vision, and general pain around my eye. I tried to ignore the problem until it began to strongly affect the eye's appearance.

"After some X-rays, my family doctor concluded I had glioblastoma, the kind of brain cancer that both Edward Kennedy and John McCain died from. Obviously, mine wasn't as advanced as theirs at that point. Now the doctors are recommending surgery to remove the tumor but seem to be ignoring the cause of the problem: my smartphone. I've been checking the internet and have learned that glioblastomas can happen to people who are heavy smartphone users, like I was.

"Had I been more aware of what's been affecting me for the past ten years, and what you've been trying to tell the world about, perhaps I might've avoided the cancer in the first place before it got to this stage. I just wanted to acknowledge that you've probably spared many people from ending up like me, and to thank you for that."

Sylvie was stunned that someone would make the effort to express their gratitude for having warned them about the hazards of RFR devices. She smiled.

He continued, "Ms. Sensei, I now realize that my real problem is one that many people suffer from, namely, their addiction to smartphones. And you've certainly given all of us the instructions we need to prevent the most extreme effects of that addiction, such as simply reducing usage, keeping the phones on airplane mode as much as possible, and, especially, not holding our phones right up against our heads. And to put it on speaker mode whenever possible. I'm doing those things now, hoping that sticking with your recommendations might prevent my cancer from getting worse.

"But it requires great discipline on my part. I now also turn my phone off at night, or at least keep it as far away from where I sleep as possible. I know the smartphone manufacturers recommend keeping phones at least an inch away from one's ear, but who ever does that? So, I especially appreciated your suggestion of putting two fingers between my phone and my head. Finally, perhaps the most difficult part, I must cut back on the use of my smartphone. Some of my friends are actually being more careful with their phones because of what I'm going through.

"Ms. Sensei, just spending time with you has given me hope for some possibility of recovery. I need to go ahead with the surgery, but measures beyond that will be up to me, and won't involve my doctors. They tell me I won't make it if I don't have the surgery. Of course, that may still be the case. But I'll do my best to practice the safety rules you recommended.

"And thank you for agreeing to meet with me."

It took Sylvie a few seconds to collect herself, "Gerald, I appreciate you coming to deliver your thank you in person. It sounds as if you've mastered all the things you need to do to insure the best possible result for yourself.

"Good luck, Gerald."

As he rose and left the room, Sensei thought to herself, *it sounds as if Gerald has a realistic view on his prospects. But his tumor has really distorted his eye. I don't know how large or invasive it can become before there's no hope for recovery, but at least he's applying the rules for smartphone safety, and will continue to do so. And maybe they'll help. I certainly hope so.*

Two weeks later, Gerald's mother sent Sylvie a note indicating that he had undergone surgery for the tumor. The ultimate prognosis was yet to be determined. But that was the last communication she received about him. Given the absence of further news, she assumed the outcome was not good. *Gerald's situation makes me sad every time I think about it. Surely he would have informed me of his progress if the operation had been a success.*

Chapter 22. RF Radiation Mitigation in Europe*

Sylvie wasn't aware that her potential killers had called off their efforts, but she did feel a newfound freedom in France. Although the French authorities had taken a hint from those in the United States, concluding that she needed a security detail, the gendarmes were, for the most part, willing to let her proceed as she wished. When she and Francois, and sometimes Rob, took their weekly walks there were only two gendarmes trailing behind at a respectful distance. Furthermore, the Parisians seemed quite friendly. She'd heard they could be somewhat hostile to foreigners, but perhaps having Francois with her most of the time was helping.

After Sylvie had gotten comfortably settled into her new French abode, she was able to pursue what was certainly a major passion all along: limiting the RFR in schools. From a plethora of medical studies, she was well aware that children were more likely to suffer ill effects from excessive RFR than adults, and she wanted to spare Earthling children, and of course any Camitorian children that had already been born, or who might come along in the future, from the harm RFR could cause.

On their weekly walks, Sylvie and Francois would lapse into their silent conversations where their minds were engaged in their brain wave communications. "Sylvie," Francois observed, "I presume you're aware of the many Earthling medical studies that have been performed showing the harmful effects of RFR on children. Perhaps you're less familiar with the measures France has put into place in response to those data to limit the amount of radiation that's allowed in schools. In 2015 the French National Assembly passed a law to limit exposure to RFR from Wi-Fi-enabled devices, paying special attention to children."

*See additional information in the Appendix.

Now he was on a roll, extolling the French virtues in response to RFR. "This legislation included completely barring Wi-Fi in nursery schools, minimizing Wi-Fi in schools for children up to eleven years of age, and requiring that the Management Board of Schools be informed of any new tech equipment being installed in schools. In addition, the law emphasized equipment reducing smartphone radiation exposure to the heads of children less than fourteen years old.

"Then, following the earlier measures, in 2018 France banned smartphones in schools.

"There were also directives aimed at general protections, requiring that citizens must have access to environmental/cell tower radiation measurements near their homes. Cell antennae locations must be mapped for the entire country, with that information being made available to the public. In addition, Wi-Fi hotspots are all labelled and marked with a pictogram." He was well aware of the international situation, especially that in the US. "Measures such as these also exist in the US. Because the telecom giants must apply for authority to install such emitters, the locations of all such devices can be found on the internet. The locations of hot spots are also available there.

"As you probably know, Earthlings have defined a unit, the Specific Absorption Rate, or SAR, which is the rate at which energy is absorbed per unit mass by a human body when exposed to RFR. This is what is biologically relevant, although RFR's damaging effects can be quite different in different parts of the body. This has spawned another feature in the French law, that SAR Radiation labelling must be indicated on smartphone packages. Furthermore, information on procedures for reducing exposures is mandatory in the smartphone manuals included with smartphone packages. Of course, that assumes people read the instructions, but that requirement at least emphasizes that the French authorities do recognize RFR hazards."

"Yes, Francois, I am aware of some of these things, but thank you for the review. Apparently, France has met the challenge of excessive RFR to children, although the French politicians didn't lower the general RFR levels* until 2022. But then they reduced their allowed levels by a factor of fifty, bringing them into agreement with the levels the US FCC allowed, and the most progressive countries in Europe had chosen earlier. Anyway, the new regulations should be acceptable to most users, and they certainly don't eliminate use of Wi-Fi devices."

"I agree. When the French Parliament devised the law for schools, they believed it represented a bold step forward, and could serve as an example for other nations for reducing the dangers from RFR. It was also a call to action for the governments across the world to undertake such protective legislation. Although international response always seems to be slow, the trend is at least in the right direction." He then noted, "Happily, the United States, with the new FCC, has led much of the world to lower general levels."

Sylvie asked, "Has France passed any more RFR directed legislation since then?"

"Well, the previous laws are still intact, but maintaining their intent has required the French to provide shielding, especially in the schools, to maintain the intended low RFR levels to their children. The worldwide telecom industry has tried to increase the world's RFR levels by a lot since 2020, thanks especially to the myriad of satellites orbiting the Earth, designed to facilitate 5G."

"Francois, I learned while I was in New York that Russia has also made some determined progress toward reducing RFR dangers. Do you have information about that?"

"I can show you the information." At that point he pulled his smartphone from his jacket pocket, removed its shielding pouch, and turned it on. Then he got a sheepish expression on his face, "Sometimes these gadgets really are useful! I have the information downloaded in a file so I don't need to take the phone off airplane mode. Here's some information; let me read it to you.

*More author optimism.

'In, 2020, the Russian Ministry of Health recommended banning Wi-Fi and smart phones in elementary schools.'

"This action by the Russians followed an effort by the Ministry of Health to encourage the reduction of children's exposure to wireless devices. In March, 2020, following the outbreak of Covid, the Department of Health, together with the Scientific Research Institute of Hygiene, published 'Safety Recommendations for Children Who Use Digital Technologies to Study at Home.' This strongly encouraged internet users to do so via hard-wired connections rather than Wi-Fi.

"Russia has also moved to the forefront of lowering RFR levels to the general public. Their level is currently the same as that of Italy."

"Russia's efforts follow those of some other countries that took action even earlier to reduce the levels of RFR in schools and protect the health of children. In 2013, Israel became the first country in the world to adopt limitations on the use of Wi-Fi in schools. It banned Wi-Fi in kindergartens and limited the use of Wi-Fi in elementary schools to three hours per week in the first and second grades and six hours per week for the third grade. But what is needed here is a standard that specifies radiation levels, not just exposure times, since the levels have increased in the general environment since the requirements were initiated.

"Cyprus has also been a leader in recognizing the dangers of Wi-Fi. In 2017, it banned Wi-Fi in kindergartens and halted its deployment in elementary schools. In addition, The Cyprus National Committee on Environment and Child Health initiated a nationwide campaign to raise awareness about smartphone and Wi-Fi exposures to children.

"Finally, I note that Italy adopted one of the lowest RFR levels of any country, now at the same level as Russia, years in advance of the new RFR levels in the US.

"All of these mitigation strategies followed a report issued by a Council of Europe panel in 2011, which recommended banning mobile phones and Wi-Fi in schools. The

Council has no legislative authority, but it represents forty-seven European nations, as well as Russia, Turkey, and several other countries. The Council was concerned about potentially harmful effects on humans, but especially on 'young and still developing brains.' They ended up recommending lowering thresholds for RFR, establishing thresholds for lifetime exposure, and banning mobile phones and wireless networks altogether in schools."

At this point, Francois paused to catch his breath, and Sylvie interjected, "What you've told me apparently doesn't prohibit hard-wired devices, such as land-line telephones and hard-wired computers, anywhere."

"Correct. There are no limitations on hard-wired devices, since they pose almost no threat. The Council report also urged smartphone users to keep them on speaker mode, or to use a headset (not Bluetooth) whenever possible."

Sylvie added, "So it appears that Europe has been on board with some aspects of RFR safety, most notably, with respect to children, for more than a decade, and I presume even more countries will adopt the precautions that have now been set forth, in France and Russia, and most recently, in the United States."

"But" Francois noted, "this is in constant battle with the US telecom giants. The US lagged in acknowledging the dangers of excessive RFR because of their influence. Of course, with the newly constituted FCC, the necessary regulations are in place, and can certainly be extended to produce new limitations in countries that haven't yet acknowledged them. There are apparently some difficult political decisions needed for this to happen."

He continued, "It seems that the telecom industry in the US has enough influence, or maybe the issue is really money, to persuade the US public to ignore the new limits most of the world is adopting. It will be interesting to see if the newly constituted FCC can change that if given enough time."

Chapter 23. Ménage a Trois?

Francois had arranged for an office for Sylvie, complete with all the basic trappings: desk, file cabinets, a worktable, and two storage cabinets. There was also a computer, hard-wired, of course.

Soon after she arrived in Paris, Francois popped into her office one morning, with furrowed brow, stammering several times as he attempted to start a brain-to-brain discussion, and finally succeeding, "Sylvie I've a difficult issue to discuss with you. I have been losing sleep over this. I've tried to get the answer to my question just from careful observation but wasn't learning what I needed to know. Or perhaps what I wanted to know. I finally decided to simply broach the subject directly."

Sylvie, with a very concerned look, "Francois, what could be troubling you so? Please think the thoughts that will tell me."

Shifting back and forth, left foot to right foot, he took a deep breath and let out a sigh, "You see, I find you very attractive. I knew that to be the case even before we left Camitor, and was sorry that we had to spend three decades apart while our space craft were in transit. Now, for the first time in our lives, we are together in Paris. But I also find that you seem to have a suitor, and that you're living with him. I certainly don't want to denigrate Rob; he seems like quite a fine man. But he's an Earthling, while you and I are Camitorians.

"Well, I'm muttering, but what I'm asking is whether you and I could develop a deeper relationship. It seems more natural to me than the one you apparently have with Rob, especially given that our life expectancies are considerably longer than Rob's, and our genes are undoubtedly more similar than yours and his. I don't know if you've given thought to having children, but that must surely be an important factor in your deciding who your ultimate partner will be.

"Oh, Mon Dieu, I must apologize; this has become much more rambling, and far more personal, than I intended. Please forgive me."

Sylvie had been listening intently, folding and unfolding her hands, finally smiling to herself at Francois' stammering. She turned off her brain's transmission while she organized her thoughts in her mind, then sent her thoughts to him all the while looking into his soft brown eyes. "Francois, I'm honored and flattered that you've taken such an interest in me. I hadn't been aware of your feelings, but I guess that was easy to overlook, since we were separated during our trip to Earth, and we both had a lot to deal with on our respective spaceships. As for my relationship with Rob, we are obviously good friends. We enjoy each other's company very much. We're not married and have made no formal agreements; we just haven't gotten to that subject. Rob is quite aware that our genes are different, although my research has shown that they're not as different as one might expect.

"I'm a bit uneasy discussing things like procreation between Earthlings and Camitorians, at least in the context of our present discussion. But I was curious enough about that possibility to consider it in my research. The answer to that question is that without modifications to the DNA of either the Camitorian or Earthling, conceiving children would not be possible. However, I don't believe the modifications that would allow cross species breeding are beyond our capability.

"But that doesn't address the question you began with, namely, could you and I develop a deeper relationship. That would presumably roust Rob from his present favored male friend status, since I don't want to be in a ménage a trois. And I don't think you were asking about that either, threesomes being rare, maybe even nonexistent, for Camitorians."

He smiled, lightening the moment, "Ah, Sylvie, I see that you have learned some French!"

She smiled at his comment, then continued, "This is an exceedingly difficult question for me to even consider at this time, but I'll do my best. Could I see myself breaking my relationship with Rob? I surely don't want to do that, since we do have a wonderful time together, and I respect him immensely. But I don't really want to destroy your and my friendship either, even though it's in its infancy. I have to tell you that my attempt to reply to your question simply shows me that I don't really know how to respond. Perhaps once we get to know each other more deeply I'll have a better understanding of where my relationships with both you and Rob are going. But at this stage, I'd ask that we just let our relationship continue to develop naturally."

"Thank you, Sylvie. That was probably a more heartfelt answer than I could have ever hoped for, given my rather bumbling attempt to have this discussion. I will certainly honor your request to just find out where our friendship might lead."

She touched his arm, hoping that would convey her strong feeling of friendship for him.

Wow! I didn't see this coming. Francois and Rob are both fine men, and I guess I'll soon enjoy Francois' company almost as much as I do Rob's. But how do I select either of them? It'll be terribly painful, given what that'll do to the other. I'll just have to overlook that implication and let both relationships develop. I can't possibly entertain having intimate relationships with both of them.

Chapter 24. Presentations and Complications

Sylvie had been invited to give a presentation to a group of educators in Great Britain, so she flew to London for the event. Rob and Francois both went with her, the former because he thought he was her paramour, and the latter because he wished he was. Neither was essential to her interactions with the British. French Security insisted they be taken to the airport in a three-car caravan of limos. They had no choice in the matter.

The primary interest of the educators focused on the effects of Wi-Fi on children of various ages.

The presentation was held in a small auditorium, and Sylvie used a microphone that clipped to her collar and was, of course, wireless. She winced at that realization but figured it would only last for a short time. It did allow her to walk around on the stage, though, and to exude her confidence.

After discussing the medical evidence for health-related effects of RF radiation on Earthlings in general, with special emphasis on the data relating to children, she concluded with, "I hope I've convinced you that it's critical to limit children's exposure to RF radiation, especially young children. This should involve, first of all, eliminating Wi-Fi to as large an extent as can be achieved. This can be done by hard-wiring computers and as many other electronic devices as possible. But it might also involve restricting the times that children can have access to any electronic devices in school, although that raises complexities about the use of tablets in your curriculum. However, as educators, you're the experts, and will have to decide for yourselves what's necessary. But banning the use of smartphones altogether in school is incontestably important. Children of all ages don't need smartphones in school. In fact, I'd have thought educators would have banned them long ago for completely independent reasons!"

After the laughter died down, she continued, "The limitation on time spent on wireless electronic devices should be especially tight for young children, since their brains are developing rapidly at those ages, and RF radiation has definitely been shown to have the greatest negative impact when the individual is at an age of rapid brain growth. This might include devices other than smartphones and computers. Wide screen TVs in classrooms can also be a source of dangerous RF radiation.

"I should note that France has established an excellent model for how these limits should be implemented."

Francois winced, and the comment precipitated some grumbling, which Sylvie detected, immediately recalling to her a comment from Francois that the British don't generally feel the need to have the French telling them what to do. However, they do relax that when it comes to making wine.

She overlooked the grumbling, "Before I close, though, I want to mention that it's important to limit Wi-Fi exposure even to adults. I'm not so unrealistic as to think you might give up your smartphones. But it's dangerous for adults to be addicted to them. There are obvious ways to just limit your exposure to the RF radiation they emit without giving them up altogether."

She itemized those in case they were unaware of them.

"In any event, I thank you for the chance to discuss the potential effects of RF radiation with you."

There were many questions following her talk, but they mostly involved reiteration or expansion of the points she had made. None of the questions challenged her assertions. She had made her case so well, and the scientific studies were so convincing, that there could be no doubt of the validity of her message. In any event, they were impressed by the capabilities of this alien woman.

Following the questions, a dozen people, including Sylvie, Rob, and Francois, went out to dinner. She got the usual questions about what Camitorians ate. Sylvie found some vegan offerings on the menu, but after having spent some time in France, she found the food in Great Britain to finish a poor second. Of course, she avoided making any comparisons to French cuisine. She had already dipped her toes into the pool of French-British rivalries and had quickly realized that was not a good place to go.

She and Rob returned to their hotel. As they were getting ready for bed, he asked, "Sylvie, you seem distracted of late. Is there something bothering you? Have I done something that upset you?"

She paused for a second, then replied, "Goodness no, Rob. I guess my mind has been absorbed in these presentations. I want them to go well, and I have been concentrating on that."

But Rob noticed the one second pause. *What's she not telling me? I guess I'll just have to be patient.*

When should I tell Rob about the interaction I had, and am continuing to have, with Francois? Should I tell him at all? I don't want him to be upset, but that is surely the effect it would have on him. I guess I'll postpone that discussion until some other time.

She kissed him passionately. "Anyway, I'm looking forward to sleeping with you, starting right now."

But he noted that the snuggling didn't seem as genuine, or natural, as it usually was. And soon she was asleep.

The following morning at breakfast, Francois arrived a few minutes after Sylvie and Rob. He had learned the ways of the French during his time in Paris, so he gave Sylvie a hug and a kiss on her hand that lasted a bit longer than it should have. Sylvie barely responded to the kiss; the look on her face was one of great discomfort. Rob definitely noticed what had happened and observed that Francois seemed to put his whole heart into the action. He also noted that the entire interaction apparently was one Sylvie would have preferred to avoid.

Breakfast was a rather quiet affair, each of the three in their own thoughts.

What an incredible woman. What'll I have to do to win her hand?

I'll have to keep my eyes open; that was certainly a revealing moment when Francois joined us. I need to pay close attention to situations where he and Sylvie are together. I do find it odd that he seems to accompany us damn near everywhere. Except in bed, thank god.

How am I going to handle future situations like this? I can't bear to have many more threefold interactions like the one that just occurred.

Chapter 25. Procreation

Sylvie had taken the time to confirm that all her genetics research equipment had arrived safely, but she hadn't yet had a chance to reassemble the pieces and get back to using it. *I do want to have children. That's certainly possible with Francois, but I'm not sure it would be with Rob. If it isn't, then I'll have to develop my relationship with Francois. Assuming that does flourish, then I'd end up choosing him for my mate. But if my research shows it's also possible with Rob, then I'll still have to deal with my dilemma.*

She had found that Earthlings and Camitorians had the same number of chromosomes. That was pretty basic, but beyond that, things got murkier. They also both had about thirty thousand genes distributed among those chromosomes, but not all pieces of the genomes were common to the two races, nor did all Earthlings even share the same thirty thousand, and similarly for Camitorians. Not surprisingly, the functionality of some of the genome's components could exhibit greater differences between the two races than between members of the same race. Furthermore, since multiple genomic pieces can affect a single bodily function, Sylvie had to be sure to identify every component that could affect conception, and then those that would affect the development of the child throughout its life.

Since she was doing these studies for her own edification, she couldn't let them interfere with the things she needed to do as the head of the Camitorians on Earth. Thus, most of her research work was done after she had been left alone for the day. Since the beings of the world, both Earthling and Camitorian, occupied most of her daytime hours, she often ended up doing her research at night.

And to complicate things further, Rob was living with her. So, in the nights when she was actually able to accomplish some research, she had to put him to bed, kiss him goodnight, tell him that she needed to do some DNA investigations, and to leave it at that. She certainly didn't tell him her investigations were on the possibility of Earthling-Camitorian procreation. Fortunately, Rob was an early to bed type, so that did leave her some time to work.

After several weeks she arrived at a conclusion. An Earthling and a Camitorian could conceive a child, although it would require some modification of the genome of one or the other person. The genetic modifications developed by the most advanced Earthling geneticists seemed rudimentary to the Camitorians. But Sylvie was absolutely certain she knew how to modify her genome to make conception possible.

I'm glad that turned out to be the case. I'd have been very sad if I had to break things off with Rob just because he and I couldn't have children. I suppose we could have adopted, but I really do want to pass on my Camitorian genes.

However, her conclusion was complicated by Francois the day after she reached her result. He had also been a geneticist before he left Camitor and had also brought the most critical components of his research laboratory with him to Earth. The first thing he said to her after popping into her office and greeting her in the morning, smiling broadly and bubbling with enthusiasm, was "Sylvie, guess what I learned. I've been studying Earthling and Camitorian genomes and have come to the conclusion that it would be extremely difficult for two beings from the two species to conceive a child. Huge changes in the Earthling's genome would be necessary to make that happen. I'm still working to figure out how much of an effect these changes would have on the child's life after birth, but those could also be enormous."

Sylvie thought for a second, then replied, "Francois, that's very interesting. But what exactly did you mean by 'huge changes,' and do you think a Camitorian geneticist would know how to make them without endangering the life of the Earthling?

I think it'd be irresponsible to undertake something like that if it would place the Earthling's life in jeopardy."

That comment led Francois to think things were definitely going his way. His smile was increasing in breadth. "I don't know the answer for sure, but it's quite possible that the changes could be dangerous. I certainly would not want to undertake them."

She shifted slightly in her chair, but her expression didn't seem to indicate as much concern as Francois would have liked. "Well, thanks for the information, Francois. But did you consider the other possibility, that of modifying the genome of the Camitorian? Would the changes there be as large? Or dangerous?"

He paused for a moment, his smile becoming less broad, "No, I didn't consider that possibility. I didn't think a Camitorian would want to modify her genome, given that our genes are so superior to those of the Earthlings."

Sensei noticed his reference to modifying 'her' genome.

"Sylvie, I believe it would be most difficult for you to conceive a child with Rob. The whole reason I began my studies was to see if I could answer that question."

"Thank you, Francois. I'll take your information to heart."

Hmm. That wasn't exactly the response I was hoping for. And why do I sense that she knows more about this issue than she's letting on? Her question suggests that she's considering modifying HER genome.

I'm not at all sure I can accept Francois' conclusions. I perceive that he wasn't acting as a completely objective scientist in his study!

Chapter 26. Plots Resume

"General Ogden, this is Clayton Berring."

"Yeah, my caller ID indicated it was you. What's up?"

"Well, my NSA agents have indicated to me that we're having difficulty obtaining information from our monitoring operations in Europe and elsewhere. Italy, Israel, and Russia have been especially problematic, since they've had tight upper limits on RF radiation levels for many years, but we've been able to monitor the calls between those countries and the less restricted ones, and that allowed us to get most of the information we needed. Thank god for France and Germany, as they are involved in a lot of those calls, and their limits were as high as those in the US. But since that goddamned alien woman, Sensei, has moved to Europe, she's convinced most of those other countries, most notably, France and Germany, to adopt the more rigid standards that the US FCC recently imposed. Now essentially all of Europe's RFR levels are the same as those in Italy. And that's making it damned near impossible to monitor the communications between any of the European countries.

"Of course, things in the US have also become more difficult since Sensei got the FCC reconstituted. Fortunately, our telecom friends, in violation of the newly mandated FCC levels, have managed to keep most of the RF radiation levels high enough that we're still doing pretty well here."

Ogden leaned back in his chair, glancing out his office window, marshalling his thoughts, "Actually I was about to give you a call. Same problem, as reported from my CIA agents. So, the question is, what do we do about it?

"But, before we go further, is this a secure line?"

"Yeah, sure, General. Can't imagine I'd call you on anything else."

"Okay, we'd tabled the idea of doing a hit on her a couple of months back. Do we need to reconsider that initiative? And would it do any good? I'm fearful that she's institutionalized the low radiation levels. And we have the additional problem of her popularity; the disinformation campaign pushed by her other set of enemies was a huge flop."

Ogden continued, "And, another thought. I guess those unknown assassins have given up, following Sensei's move to Paris. Haven't heard a peep from them, or a blast, since she left. I'm assuming they'd have international connections, and it wouldn't be that difficult for them to find someone in France to blow her up. But maybe they've decided she won't do them any harm from there."

"Right; I think we're on our own now. But you raise a good question. With regard to increasing what has now become virtually international RF radiation standards, I think we would need to get rid of Sensei first, and then figure out how to get those countries to abandon their new standards. Given the capabilities of our black ops people, I think the second thing will be more difficult to pull off than the first. Political persuasion on diplomats isn't always so easy. And without the second there isn't much reason for doing the first."

Ogden paused for a moment, "Yeah, you have a point. There would be no motivation for eliminating her if it wouldn't have any effect on the RF levels. As a goal, though, we need the other countries to increase their limits at least a factor of ten to get us back to our previous capabilities."

"Correct. Let me think a bit about how to pull both efforts off and discuss it with my some of my NSA people. Only the most trusted ones, of course. Can't have any leaks on this!"

"Right, Clayton. I'll look forward to your next call. In the meantime, I'll talk this over with my CIA confidants also."

A few days later, "General, Clayton here. I've squeezed in a couple of meetings with a few of my favorite NSA associates, and we've batted around some thoughts with regard to increasing

167

RF radiation levels that I wanted to mention to you. In the past, we've left the big telecom companies to control the FCC. But that's obviously no longer workable, so we'll have to take charge. One of the issues we discussed was what would happen if most of the countries of the world decided to abandon wireless communications in favor of hard wiring their devices. I don't think we need to worry too much about that. Even if many people do go for cabling in their homes or workplaces, they're frequently on the move, and then they need their wireless devices either for phoning or texting. And as far as installing new infrastructure, we decided that all the transmission towers, small cells, and satellites we'd ever need are already in place.

"We also discussed the impact that the fairly recent coronavirus has had on RF radiation levels. Our guess is that it's forced more people to rely on their electromagnetic toys and wireless devices, and that has just enhanced people's addiction to them. However, this has also boosted fiber optic communications, so it's not clear what the net result is. However, it's becoming obvious that fiber optics will be the winner here, resulting in an additional complication to our monitoring efforts.

"Thus, our group has devised a tentative plan. It obviously would need to be fleshed out, but here's the basic idea. Rub out Sensei. Then communicate, through third party diplomatic channels, that certain European government officials who are resistant to boosting the RF radiation limits back up to our acceptable levels could be in danger. That could work, although we may need to assassinate another one or two others if they didn't get the message from the Sensei assassination. But we could just do the alien, and then see how things develop. Death threats can be excellent motivators, especially because there will always be a few weak-kneed links in any group of, need I say, Earthlings. I don't think it would be too difficult to identify those who would be most likely to capitulate. Our friends over in the State Department would probably have their favorite cave-in candidates."

"Interesting, Clayton. We'll have to figure out the details of the diplomatic maneuvers, but at least we can leave those involving Sensei to our black ops experts. As far as identifying the government officials most likely to capitulate, I'm pretty sure those involved will figure out that a single assassination might spawn others. So, I suspect that the crying from the most cowardly will be evident immediately after the Sensei deed is done, even if State can't come up with appropriate candidates. But we can leave that open for the moment."

"Okay, General. I'll put my black ops people onto their mission. We can be looking into the possibility of diplomatic maneuvers while they're doing their planning."

"The Colonel here."

"Hi, Colonel. I don't know your real name, but I guess that's the nature of your business and our interactions. I need your organization to carry out an assassination. This is, as usual, a matter of national security."

"Yeah? Aren't they all?"

Berring always had difficulty talking with the Colonel. He suspected he couldn't carry on a conversation with his wife. Or more likely, he wasn't married. Maybe he wasn't even a person. A robot, maybe?

"The person we need assassinated is Sylvie Sensei. I presume you've heard of her."

"Yeah. Is this a one-shot mission, so to speak, or are we trying to stop an alien invasion?"

"No, there aren't enough aliens on Earth to carry out an invasion, so it's just her."

"Shouldn't be too difficult. She's in France, right?"

"Right."

"Okay, I'll take care of it."

"Thanks." But Berring was pretty sure the Colonel had terminated the conversation before he managed to thank him.

A telephone rang in Paris. "Jacques Noir here. This must be the Colonel. Nobody else calls on this secure line."

"Right, Jacques. I have a job for you, and I'm calling you for two reasons. First, this is going to be an incredibly high-profile assassination, and you're our most proficient assassin. Secondly, it will take place in France, probably Paris, and I think that's where you live. Of course, I'm never sure where you really are. But that probably doesn't matter."

"I live everywhere, but Paris is nice. Who's the target? Some head of state? I've done a few of those before. I really enjoy challenges like that."

"No, even more high profile than that. Sylvie Sensei."

"Jeezus, I see what you mean. Well, what's in it for me?"

"More than we've ever paid you before. Ten million Euros."

"C'mon. I need a whole lot more than that for this job. How about fifty million? This is a particularly difficult task, and it will require a lot of surveillance and planning."

"Shit, who do you think I am? The goddamn United States government?"

"Yeah, Colonel, you ARE the goddamn United States government."

"How about a compromise. Twenty million Euros?"

"Fifty."

"Thirty?"

"Fifty. Or the job don't get done."

"I can see you're not going to compromise. But this is an unusual case. Okay, fifty million. And our usual deal: twenty-five up front, and the rest when you've finished the job."

"That's how we work."

Chapter 27. Meeting with the Children

On a late spring morning, Francois called Sylvie with a question, "We received an invitation from a secondary school that wondered if you could address their student assembly next Tuesday. Might you be available any time that day?"

"Let me check my calendar. Ah, that morning is clear. Please say I'd be delighted to visit and ask them if ten-thirty is okay. That would give a natural break at noontime so the meeting wouldn't last too long."

They had both made many trips to schools, allegedly inspecting the campuses to be sure their RFR levels were below allowed values. But they always were; the French government had been meticulous about enforcing the limits they had set.

What Sylvie enjoyed most about these visits was the chance to interact with the French children. She insisted that should occur on every one of her visits. Francois had been working with her on pronunciation, and she had become proficient enough to talk with the French kids without generating comments about her funny accent. Of course, it helped that her Camitorian brain was able to store a vocabulary that was undoubtedly vastly larger than what any of the children could have in their brains.

When Tuesday arrived, French Security escorts drove Sylvie and Francois to their destination, where they were greeted warmly by the administrators and many teachers. The principal gave Sylvie an enthusiastic woman to woman hug.

After Sylvie was introduced to the students by the principal, she went through her standard talk, which lasted for ten minutes, and followed that with time for the students to ask questions. Her talk gave some basic facts, namely, she was from a planet called Camitor, it was about five light-years from Earth, and it took the group making the flight about thirty years to get from Camitor to Earth. She also noted that there were other Camitorians in Paris, and the students might recognize them from their light green skin color.

And then the barrage of questions began.

"If it took you thirty hears to make the trip, does that mean you spent a lot of your life going from your planet to ours?"

"No, as it turns out. The people from my planet tend to live a lot longer than people from Earth. Earthlings do not usually live past one hundred years, but Camitorians typically live several hundred years."

"You're very pretty. You don't look so old. So how old are you?"

Sylvie generally got a serious look for this response, "On my next birthday I'll be two hundred eighteen years old."

That was always met with gasps.

"Do you have any children?"

"No, I've been too busy with my duties involving the trip to Earth, and the things I had to do once I got here. But I want to have children sometime."

"Do you miss your old planet?"

"Yes, I certainly do. Camitor has many features that are like those on Earth: grass, trees, lakes, rivers, mountains and plains, but the lifestyle of the Camitorians is quite different from that of Earthlings."

"How is that different from what we have on Earth?"

"Camitorians are usually gentler with each other than I have observed Earthlings to be. We don't like to fight wars, so nothing like that has occurred for nearly two hundred thousand years."

"Did you have to leave your family there?"

"Yes, I did. And I do miss them. But they might be making the trip to Earth before too long."

"Are you able to stay in touch with them?"

"That's not so easy. Being five light-years distant means that any communications sent from Earth to Camitor take five years to get there. And then their signals back would take another five years. So, we do send each other news items, but it's impossible to have a conversation."

"Are there animals like we have on Earth? Are there monkeys and lions?"

"There is a wide variety of life forms, just as there is on Earth. We do have animals that resemble your monkeys and lions, but they don't look exactly like the ones you have here."

"Did you have pets when you lived on Camitor?"

"Many people do have pets, although they are usually small, like small dogs and cats. But of course, they don't look very much like your dogs and cats."

And often, "I heard that there might be lots of you here. How many are here?"

And Sylvie gave her well-rehearsed answer, "It's difficult to know, since we're distributed throughout many cities on Earth, and Camitorians have died and others have been born since we left our planet, and even since we arrived on Earth. So, I'm sorry I can't answer your question very well. But there were one billion of us on Camitor before we left."

That was followed with, "How many people are left on Camitor?"

"There are still about one billion."

"Why did you leave Camitor?"

"In many years, our planet will be consumed by its sun. It'll take a long time to transport everyone from the planet before that happens."

"Are all of them going to come to Earth? That'll be a lot of new Earthlings!"

Sylvie didn't really want to answer that question, knowing it would raise hackles in some Earthlings, "Well that'll be a long time in the future, many thousands of years, so I can't really say if all of them will be moving to Earth. Some of them might even find another planet to move to."

"My Mom said she heard you had a boyfriend who's an Earthling. She wanted me to ask you if that's true."

Sylvie had to pause for a moment before replying. She knew that there had been gossip in Voici magazine, so the rumor mill was running at full throttle. "Well, I have lots of friends, both male and female, who are Earthlings. As you and your mom undoubtedly know, the newspapers and magazines love to make up stories, especially about friendships between men and women. So, I'm guessing your mom got her information from some magazine story."

But the student persisted, "She said she saw you one afternoon walking along the Seine with a man who wasn't green, so was probably an Earthling. And she said you were holding hands."

"Well, I do have a very good friend who is both a man and an Earthling. But I'm not sure I would say he is my boyfriend." *I think I won't mention that we have been sleeping together for several months.*

At that point the teacher rescued Sylvie, explaining to the students that she was very busy, and needed to get back to her work.

Francois sat in an inconspicuous spot in each of the rooms Sylvie visited. When they left the last one for the day, he looked her in the eyes and inquired, "Sylvie, given how much you love kids, surely the possibility that you can have kids of your own someday has to be important to you. Furthermore, for you not to have kids would be depriving the Universe of an incredible gene set, that is, yours."

Sylvie laughed to avoid the implications of his question, "Well thank you for the genetic compliment, Francois. You're right about my wanting to eventually have kids. But I can't see that happening for a few more years. There's just too much that needs to be done before, as the Earthlings say, I can go down that road."

Damn, she just evaded a perfect attempt to say that our relationship would be the obvious solution for her to have kids. Well, I heard before we left Camitor that she had lots of men chasing her, and she clearly has had plenty of practice circumventing attempts to lure her into partnerships. I'll have to create more elegant verbal traps!

Once or twice a week, Sylvie would have a block of time in which she had no meetings with officials or school children scheduled. She jealously guarded those few hour segments so she could do some serious genetics research. One of the things she was most interested in understanding was the connection between the headaches, brain fog, and other brain related symptoms Earthlings felt from the RFR fog in the atmosphere and the organ failures that occurred. This necessitated that she correlate every organ's connection to every piece of the genome that might also involve the brain. Even with the lowered thresholds, different proximities to emitters made it impossible to avoid high RFR everywhere all the time. Thus, this research was crucial for understanding the effects of high intensity RFR on humans.

Rob knew that he must not bother her when she was working with her research equipment. The intensity of her expression made it obvious she couldn't be disturbed. But he always looked forward to an update on what she had learned in the evenings.

Of course, she didn't tell him about what she had learned either from her studies or those of Francois regarding their possible procreation.

Chapter 28. Off to Russia

Sylvie knew that sooner or later she would have to visit Russia and China, the countries that tended to be most hostile to the Camitorians, at least as perceived by the heads of the missions there. She decided that Russia would be the safer of the two for the moment, since they had been trying to mitigate their RFR for some time. That at least put them on the same side as she on that issue, although China wasn't far behind.

Igor Vivanovich, the Camitorian who had led their contingent to Moscow, was far more concerned about how the Russian leaders would respond to the more than one thousand aliens in their city than he was about their efforts to minimize RFR. As he had said soon after the Camitorians landed on Earth, he worried that the Russians might view their presence as the beginnings of an invasion, and would simply attempt to round them all up and execute them. So not even he had let it be known that he was an alien.

But the Russian leaders must have known there were aliens in Moscow; their landing was sufficiently dramatic that it had been observed by many in their country. Igor was well aware of this, but after losing a lot of sleep over it, he concluded that the authorities had enough on their plates that they weren't bothering to identify the Camitorians. At least not yet.

Still, after a lengthy discussion with Sylvie, he decided to remain in his alien closet. He was concerned that his conversations with the other Camitorians in Moscow were being monitored, but was quite sure the electronic spies could not possibly understand any of what they heard. The Camitorian language was rich, with many different ways to say the same things, so he was not concerned about their messages being deciphered. But the difference between that language and any other language on Earth would identify the speakers as aliens. Of course, the brain-to-brain communications made surveillance of those messages more of a challenge than the usual electronic intercepts, but in many cases the waves were out there, and therefore could be detected.

Of course, Sylvie had become such an international presence that her visit to Moscow could hardly be disguised. Furthermore, she realized she could use her meetings with Russian officials to praise their mitigation efforts of RFR, especially in schools, and this could only be viewed by the rest of the world in a positive light. That would surely please the Russians.

But she either needed an English to Russian or French to Russian tutor to provide a crash course in pronouncing the thousands of Russian words she had stored in her brain a week prior to her trip. So, she hired a native Russian speaker for the task who was living in Paris. She knew Igor would also help, although he had to be circumspect about providing language lessons for an alien. When he met her at Putin (previously Pushkin) International Airport, he continued to extend her tutorial on the way to her hotel. The Russian official who accompanied the two of them was duly impressed at how rapidly her communication skills evolved over the two-hour car ride.

The following morning, she was met by the Minister of Education, the official who would accompany her on her tours of Russian schools. "Ms. Sensei, I wasn't aware that you were fluent in Russian."

"Actually, I was not until last week."

"But … but how could you possibly achieve fluency so quickly?"

She explained, "Camitorian brains can store an entire vocabulary. Then we just have to practice pronunciation. I have a Russian friend who met me at the airport and worked with me on my pronunciation on the way to my hotel. I am pleased that you find the effort to have been acceptable."

"Yes, we know about your friend Vivanovich."

Oh, that sounds ominous.

"But" he continued, "your efforts to master the Russian language can only be characterized as stunning, I must say. The school children will think you're a Russian."

I wonder what exactly he does know about Vivanovich?

She always had her RFR meter with her. Upon visiting two schools, she was pleased to find that the levels she was observing were well within the international guidelines set by the BioInitiative 2020 report, and that the Wi-Fi was turned on only for restricted times. Those were especially short for the youngest children.

When she met with the children, she got the usual spate of "Are you really from another planet?" questions. She was asked to describe some of the details of the trip from Camitor to Earth, and the students were duly impressed. They were especially fascinated when she described the farms that existed on the spacecraft to supply the travelers with their food. Then they asked all the questions that she had learned to anticipate from her visits to the French schools. However, they missed one important bit of information: *No questions about my Earthling boyfriend? This group let me off easy! Of course, they could not have observed me holding Rob's hand as we walked along the Seine.*

Then she met with the Minister of Education. "Comrade Kolznitsky, I'm pleased to learn what you've done to mitigate the potentially destructive effects of electromagnetic radiation for children. I find it to be especially impressive that you've gone to such lengths to limit Wi-Fi use, especially through both the thresholds you have imposed in schools, and in the time limits you have set for Wi-Fi usage. But I'm also impressed with the limits you've set for the general public."

To Sylvie's relief, he seemed pleasant enough, "Da, I'm happy to see that you've recognized what we've achieved. This is especially important in the international context. Our greatest adversary, Although the United States authorities have recently attempted to lower their limits, the telecommunication giants still seem hell bent on increasing exposure to electromagnetic radiation of their entire populations. Furthermore, they've done very little to limit the exposures to children in schools. We can be patient. We predict that in a few years the numbers of deaths due to RF radiation poisoning will begin to increase sharply, and that it cannot be corrected by any measure they might impose once it begins.

"We will undoubtedly witness their destruction by their own hands! We will have won our largest international conflict by just being patient!"

"Well, I hope they come to their senses before the deaths you predict happen on a large scale, but I agree that will require some changes."

Suddenly Kolznitsky's demeanor changed as he looked into Sylvie's lavender eyes. "The sources of RF radiation are everywhere, due primarily to the tens of thousands of RF emitting satellites now in orbit. We can no longer escape their effects entirely but must institute standards for our children and general population to mitigate them as much as possible.

"Allowing private industry to control both the dangerous proliferation of RF devices as well as the damage they can cause may irreparably harm our planet. We are extremely concerned."

"I agree, Comrade Kolznitsky. I am concerned too. We must do what we can to make people aware of the potential problems with their devices, and to show them a better way."

Chapter 29. Progress and Tragedy

"Colonel, Jacques here on our super-secure line. Just thought I'd give you a progress report."

The Colonel answered in his usual gruff voice, "I suppose that's good, but I've not heard anything on the news, so I presume she's not dead yet."

"Right. But I've spent the past two weeks scoping out her activities. She leads a complicated irregular life, has many people coming and going to her apartment, and doesn't seem to have any sort of consistent repetitive schedule that I've been able to figure out. That complicates my planning, but just means I'll have to be on the lookout much of the time and take the opportunity to shoot when it arises. But it also means that it might be difficult to take my usual precautions."

"You called just to tell me that she has a complicated life? Is that supposed to get me excited?"

"I know how anxious you get sometimes, so I was just calling to reassure you that I was working on this project."

"Next time you call have something to report. This line can probably be tapped like any other, even though that's not supposed to be the case."

"She's even gone to Russia. I couldn't do anything about her when she's in Moscow."

"I knew that too. Next time, real progress."

The line could not be tapped, but it's activity could be monitored with extremely sophisticated equipment. The French intelligence people knew about both Jacques Noir and the Colonel, although they didn't know who the Colonel actually was, nor had they ever identified Noir. However, they routinely kept tabs on their conversations as well as they could. And when those two were talking to each other, the antennae of the intelligence staff were especially attuned to them. Although they couldn't have known if Sensei was discussed in their conversations, their suspicions, correlated with Sensei's activities, made it pretty clear who was the subject of their discussions was.

Inspector Gaudet was standing before his superior, wringing his hands together, "Chief Inspector, this is serious. We can't let the United States' black ops people take out Sylvie Sensei. Or anybody else, for that matter, but especially her. It would be a terrible blow to France's standing in the world if she were killed on French soil. Furthermore, she's just trying to help, even though some humans—okay, Earthlings, and apparently especially Americans—don't seem to appreciate it."

Chief Inspector Perrier agreed, "Oui, we must prevent whatever they're planning. I suppose we can strengthen the guard we have accompanying her everywhere, but even that wouldn't be perfect. Besides, we already have our best people surrounding her all the time. None the less, I'll add six more of my men, two more per shift, to her protective group and instruct them to be fully attentive all the time. I'll emphasize that we believe a threat is imminent.

"I don't think we have to worry about bombs; that's not Noir's modus operandi. But we need to be especially on the lookout for a rifleman whenever she is outside. Of course, she needs to keep her blinds pulled in her apartment so as not to be a target when she's inside. She won't like that, but we must insist. We did check out her apartment before she moved in, and one side overlooks a park. I think we could allow the blinds on that side to be open during daylight times. A gunman in the park would be too obvious a location for Noir. He never does his deeds out in the open."

"Good, I'll draft a memorandum to her explaining our concern and our logic. She'll certainly want to know why we have to institute all these new precautions. She seems to question everything we do. Nicely, but she wants to know."

Upon studying the list, "Oh Rob, look at these new restrictions. I wonder why I need to go along with all this. Of course, I will, but I have sensed no problems."

Rob was also perusing the list. "I think we have to trust what French Security is doing. They certainly have capabilities to be aware of things we don't know about, and I do believe they're looking out for our, actually your, best interests."

"I guess so. It just seems so unnecessary. The whole protection effort offends my Camitorian sense of decency and faith in my fellow Camitorians or Earthlings. Maybe that doesn't apply to all Earthlings."

Francois had arranged for the three of them, along with three armed gendarmes, to take a walk of a few blocks to one of his favorite patisseries, where they could enjoy some croissants and coffee. Her apartment building had a front entryway that was flanked by two large bushes. As the group emerged from between the bushes, Noir saw his chance. *Things aren't perfect; the sun isn't quite where I would like it to be to best conceal myself. However, this is as good as it's ever going to be.*

Thus, he made two mistakes. The first was that the sun gave a reflection off his rifle, and the second was that he continued to peer through his telescopic sight for about three seconds after he pulled the trigger to see what effect his shot had. The first allowed one of Sensei's guards first to see the glint of light, then to see a wisp of smoke from the shot that was fired. The second allowed the guard to fire a shot of his own back through Noir's telescopic sight, and into the eye socket immediately behind it. The hollow point bullet and the shrapnel from the telescopic sight did their job.

Sensei stood in stunned silence for a moment, then cried out, "Francois, you've been shot!" Her guards had been trained to assist shooting victims, but it was clear that he was beyond help. His green eyes stared blankly at the sky. He had apparently also seen the glint of light from the telescope and had reacted instantly to protect Sensei. He succeeded in that, but as a result, took the bullet himself.

Sensei sobbed and choked out her words as she realized what had just happened. "Rob, ... Francois saved my life, but he did so ... at the sacrifice of his own. This is horrible. I have never had to deal ... with anything like this before. This would never have happened ... on Camitor. I don't even know how to react."

Rob's face reflected his shock. "Sylvie, let's get back inside quickly. The gendarmes will take care of the situation here."

"Okay." But before leaving, she bent over and kissed Francois' lifeless face.

Once they were inside, she sobbed, "I know I need to do some things now, like let people know what to do with Francois' body. Everything else, including naming his successor, can wait until tomorrow.

Rob thought to himself, *I certainly never imagined that the competition Francois and I had for Sylvie's heart would end like this. I'd never have wanted him to die. What an incredible tragedy.*

In what seemed like an eternity, tomorrow did arrive. Then Sensei managed to pull herself together enough to send a note around to the other Camitorian leaders.

Camitorian leaders, with great sadness I have to inform you of the death of Francois Dupre, the leader of our French delegation. Francois died as he lived, giving of himself in every way to further our cause. In this instance, he dived in front of me and intercepted a bullet that was intended for me. Words cannot express my feeling for his heroic act. I ask that you join me in mourning his death. (signed) Sylvie Sensei.

The Camitorian who had been Francois' second in command, Philippe Dumand, succeeded him as leader of the

Camitorians in France. Sylvie had a brief conversation with him, "Philippe, I'm sure this is as much of a shock to you as it is to me. You've let it be known for some time now that you're a Camitorian, so that'll make your public persona easy for the French to accept. I'm sure you'll do a wonderful job of taking over for Francois."

"Thank you, Sylvie. This is a shock for all of us, but every one of our ten outposts on Earth has had to be ready for a contingency such as this. I'll do my best!"

When the head of French Security learned of the events of the day, he immediately called Chief Inspector Perrier, "Mon Dieu, but this was a terrible event. However, I can't think of any person more deserving of a bullet into his eye than Jacques Noir. At least I guess that was Jacques Noir, judging from the telephone intercepts we'd gotten and the killer's style. But his body had no ID, and his disguises have always been so effective that we were never able to even figure out what he looked like.

"Well, if that's who he was, his death should spare a lot of important lives! The world should be damned grateful to us. But thank god he didn't succeed in killing Sensei.

"None the less, this surely emphasizes the necessity of her security detail!"

Chapter 30. End of Collaborations

The headlines screamed,
FRENCH ATTEMPT ON SENSEI'S LIFE FAILS
Camitorian Francois Dupre Murdered

When he got the news, Berring immediately called General Ogden, "Jeezus, General, this goddamn woman lives a charmed life. Is she part cat? In which case she has six more lives to go. That's more lives than I have competent assassins. I suppose the first two tries to kill her weren't damaging to the assassins, although if they were mob related that may not be the case. I'm not normally superstitious, but I'm wondering if maybe I should be when it comes to her?

"At least the newspapers seem to be blaming this on the French. Well, I guess that was sort of the case; the news wires are speculating that the assassin was French. But no one knows for sure who the hell he was. They're just guessing it was Jacques Noir, and I'm sure a lot of potential assassin victims around the world are breathing easier."

Ogden was at his desk, pondering the news that was just coming to him, "Yeah, Berring. All true. But perhaps it doesn't matter so much now. I presume your folks have been working on improved ways to make the existing Earthly bath of RF radiation satisfy our needs. Mine have, and apparently believe they've made progress on that front."

Berring responded "And that's a damn good thing, since we just lost the guy who was probably our best hope to eliminate Sensei. The news items just said he'd been killed but didn't say how he screwed up. We'll probably never know, not that it really matters.

"So, I suggest we just give our technical people all the encouragement, including money, they need to get things to work the way we want, but with the existing thresholds in place. I don't see an obvious way to get them increased, Sensei or not. Certainly not at this moment."

"Right, General. I agree."

"Colonel, this is Clayton Berring."

"Yeah, I know."

"I've had a discussion with General Ogden, and we decided that we'd not pursue the assassination of Sensei further. I'm sorry about your assassin, but she seems to be impervious to danger, and we don't want to risk any more assets. We'll try to solve the problem another way."

"WHAT THE FUCK? You've just cost me my most skilled assassin, and now you're telling me that it wasn't even necessary? Why the hell should I work with you anymore. Don't ever call me again. I'm done!"

"Colonel, wait." But the line had gone dead.

The French Minister for Education, Marcel Andrade, came equipped with an ego that was much too large for his job, or any job for that matter. He decided to impose his will but needed to enlist Sensei in his effort. So, he called her.

"Ms. Sensei, this is Minister of Education Marcel Andrade." He said his title slowly to give her every opportunity to appreciate its importance. "I believe we can improve our RF radiation safety more by imposing stricter regulations on the communications towers. This might even spark a radiation mitigating revolution in the rest of the world. The world's governments would be following my, or rather our, lead. The French government reduced the allowed levels of RF radiation in the atmosphere by a factor of fifty in 2022, and I am going to propose that we reduce the thresholds by another factor of ten. And to implement this immediately. If you'll support this effort, I believe we can make it happen."

She paused a moment, wiping her hand across her brow to get the swatch of hair in place, as she often did when she needed an extra second to think, then replied, "Dr. Andrade, I'm uneasy about your proposal. In principle, I always like to hear of officials trying to reduce the thresholds for the communications towers and other radiating devices, but I'm guessing the suddenness of this will impact people's lives, as well as worldwide business operations, in rather negative ways. If you were to propose giving the telecom companies time to adjust, and supplying some government support to aid their conversion to fiber optic cables to every residence, that would definitely make your proposal vastly more palatable.

"But this proposal by itself ignores the most dangerous aspect of RF radiation in people's lives, most notably, what their personal devices do to the levels in their homes. You might want to announce your proposal along with an educational program to make citizens aware of the dangers of Wi-Fi, and what's needed to mitigate them.

"There is another problem with your proposal as it is; it may cost you the support of many of the people who have gone along with your efforts in the past."

"Ms. Sensei, I'm sure you'll see that this is for the best. And my proposal is for this to take effect immediately. The President authorized me to proceed with the press conference to see how the public would react."

Hmm, I'm not sure he's telling me all that's behind this effort.

Berring placed another call, "General Ogden, great news. My technical folks just delivered a document to me that describes new devices that'll increase the sensitivity of our intercepts by nearly the orders of magnitude we lost to the radiation mitigators. That means we can maintain our worldwide surveillance capability even with the wireless transmission thresholds in place in Italy for several years, and more recently in France and

Germany. Of course, that assumes they won't lower the thresholds again."

"That's good news indeed, Clayton. I just received a memo with a title that appears to confirm the study to which you refer. But, as you note, that assumes no one will place more stringent limits on our radiation emitters.

"If they did, I'd assume Ms. Sensei would support the new limits. So, we're not necessarily out of the assassination business forever, although I'd hate to risk another high-quality assassin."

"Right, General. That's just as well. With Noir dead, I'm not sure we have the assassination capability we used to have."

Chapter 31. Restructured Alliances

Marcel Andrade, flush with delusions of grandeur, proceeded with a press conference to announce his new restrictions on communication tower and small cell emissions in France. As soon as he'd finished his announcement, a reporter asked what must have been the most obvious question to everyone there, "Dr. Andrade, how does the rest of the world view this new mandate? Specifically, does Sylvie Sensei support this?"

He responded, "Well, we did discuss this effort. I'm not certain she's on board yet, but I'm sure she will in the near future."

Of course, that created a flood of queries directed to her, asking if she was supporting Andrade. She wasn't surprised that she would be asked about his proposal, so she had prepared a response. "Minister Andrade and I did discuss his proposal. I'm unable to support it at this time. A small percentage of the population is reactive to even tiny amounts of RF radiation in the environment, and the needs of such people must be accommodated. However, simply reducing the levels beyond where they already are with no thought for the consequences may create huge problems. Certainly, such efforts must be completed only after viable alternatives are in place for personal and business communications. Fiber optic or wired connection infrastructure to every home would be essential to avoid disastrous consequences from Minister Andrade's proposal."

That pretty much shot it down.

This flurry of French activity regarding Andrade's proposal certainly got the attention of the people in the US.

189

In particular, Clayton Berring couldn't wait to share the news with his confidant, "General Ogden, I presume you've heard the news from France about the attempt to lower the RF radiation levels from the transmission towers and small cells. The stunning thing is that the proposal met resistance from a totally unexpected source: Sylvie Sensei. She made it clear, well, pretty clear, that she opposes the new limits.

"General, we have a new ally!"

They both laughed for several seconds over that.

When the General could speak again, "Well, Clayton, I guess that really does take us out of the assassination business, at least in the context of RF radiation. I'm sure new issues will arise, but it looks to me as if Sensei is safe for the moment. I'd hate like hell to kill off one of our allies."

"Yep!"

Tom Mack called a meeting of the telecom industry CEOs who had previously discussed the crisis they attributed to Sensei. After gathering in his conference room, "Gentlemen," he began, "we thought our problem with the outputs of our communication devices was over when Sensei went to France, and our emitters just kept spitting out their good old unrestricted radiation. Of course, we were able to ignore the new limits after Sensei's allies on the FCC interfered as long as no one complained. Well, we have a problem: more and more people ARE complaining, and that's forcing the radiation emitters' outputs to be attenuated so they're in compliance. As you've probably found also, consumer groups have devised a shroud that can be put over the small cell emitters that brings their output down to FCC levels. This is complicating our strategy of blanketing the world, at least the United States, with the RF radiation levels we want. What's even worse is the name they've given the shroud: telecondom!"

Jack Rathbone, another CEO, commented, "Offensive, very offensive. But, of greater concern, I heard that the numbers of letters to the editors and Op-Ed pieces in newspapers have been increasing exponentially, and even primetime newscasts are airing stories of people claiming negative effects of small cells near their houses. Citizen groups and opposition websites are springing up like poisonous mushrooms. It seems like every damned city and state has its own SafeTech activity group now. People complain about the headaches, brain fog, nausea, and other ailments this radiation gives them if they're too close."

Jim Curson, leaning back in his chair, added an essential feature to the conversation, "Well, we'd given up on taking out Sylvie Sensei. Should we try another attempt on her? But I really doubt if that would make any difference. And the efforts of the world's assassins in that regard have been notably unsuccessful!"

Rathbone shifted the conversation, "I have an important piece of information, which I got from a contact in the Central Intelligence Agency. That is, that some nutcase minister in France proposed lowering their already ridiculously low RF radiation thresholds another order of magnitude."

Mack and Curson, almost in unison, "Oh my god; that would ruin us if it spread worldwide."

"Wait," Rathbone said, "let me finish the story. When this French idiot proposed his new standard, the reporters immediately flocked to Sylvie Sensei to see what she thought of it. She immediately opposed it, saying she could anticipate huge economic and sociological problems if the proposed thresholds were put in place without any viable alternatives. Of course, by that she meant communications wired to all premises. My contact says, since the proposed reduction isn't going to happen. He thinks the proposal is dead, largely because of her opposition."

After pondering that for a few seconds, Matt Barkem, expressed his relief, "That means Sensei is on our side. Well, partly, anyway. But there's no reason any longer to assassinate her."

Mack offered, with a smirk, "Well, I suppose we could give her a medal or something, but the real question is whether or not we can survive with the RF radiation level restrictions that France imposed in 2022. Italy had even somewhat lower limits for years, and those gave us immense grief. But, if we can survive with those levels, we should just let them stay there, as the citizenry has been demanding, at least in every situation in which we got sued."

"Tom," Curson replied, "I think we can live with those levels, although we do need to keep all the emitters in place. Going to 5G waves of course was the way of the future: self-driving cars, higher speed data transmission, new gaming possibilities, and so forth. The RFR of higher frequencies is more readily absorbed, so we needed a small cell emitter every few city blocks in order to enable all those 5G-enabled effects. And now advancing to even higher frequencies of 6G will require new equipment, that is, more emitters, although we haven't told the public about that yet.

"Unfortunately, there were a lot of folks who objected to the towers and small cells, claiming they were cluttering their neighborhoods, and were just plain ugly, especially if they found one stuck in the lot next to their house, fifty feet from their bedroom. But as far as communications, our technological capabilities have improved enough in the past year that we can live with the new limits. And reduction of the outputs will alleviate the symptoms we've been hassled about, and which I'm forced to admit are real, since we put the new emitters in place and launched the tens of thousands of satellites.

"In fact, I've been suffering from headaches and brain fog since a new emitter was put up a quarter mile from my house. And they went away when the emission level was reduced! I must confess that it also helped when I turned off my Wi-Fi at night."

Mack observed, "Holy shit, you mean we let somebody put an emitter up close to one of your houses? That was a huge mistake! But I guess that, along with the improvement when you shut off your Wi-Fi, does confirm what the allegedly electrosensitive citizens of the US have been telling us. But I sure as hell wouldn't want news about your nightly Wi-Fi shutdown to get out!

"As Matt pointed out, though, this leaves us in the astonishing position of being on the same side as Sylvie Sensei. Well, as long as it doesn't affect our profits, so be it. We might even use her in our advertising. Perhaps we can replace our disastrous disinformation program with a new one touting her virtues."

After choking for a few seconds, Rathbone asked, "Do you think she'll let us use her in our advertising?"

"Well, we can just go ahead and use some of her quotes in our ads, and then see if we get sued. Remember all those lawyers on our payroll; we need to keep them busy."

Chapter 32. New Projects

Sylvie and Rob were still both reeling from the death of Francois, but in different and complicated ways.

I valued Francois as a friend, even though we were competitors for Sylvie's attention. He certainly had the inner track, just because he was a Camitorian. On the other hand, she was living and sleeping with me, so it would appear I was leading the competition. But that's just because I got there first. Sylvie often gave Francois admiring, maybe even loving, looks, and he certainly returned them. I was never sure I'd ultimately win her hand. And her response when he was shot: it looked like heartbroken love to me.

Either Rob or Francois would have made a husband with whom I could forever be happy. But, as Francois pointed out, there would be no question whether he and I could conceive children. On the other hand, my studies do indicate that Rob and I could also conceive, albeit with a few changes in my DNA. So perhaps the fates have directed me to do what must rank as one of the most interesting biological experiments of all time. Can Rob's and my DNA be made compatible?

But she also worried about the life expectancy issue. *Francois and I would most likely have spent many more years together than Rob and I could. But I wonder if a few genetic changes could extend Rob's life beyond what would be expected for an Earthling. I'll have to look into that.*

In any event, Rob decided the best way for them to get over their mourning would be to launch into new projects. He invited Linda to fly to Paris as soon as possible so they could have a face-to-face meeting in Sylvie's apartment and discuss some new ideas. She agreed enthusiastically.

As soon as she arrived and they greeted each other with hugs, Linda said, "Sylvie, I was so saddened to hear about Francois' death. I know he was an extremely valuable member of your Camitorian team, and a good friend of yours as well. I'm sure he'll be missed."

Sylvie replied, "Thank you, Linda. I had known Francois for more than fifty years, first as a geneticist, then as a fellow traveler to Earth. His contributions to the Camitorian effort on Earth were huge. Yes, he will be greatly missed. But" and she had to take a breath before she could continue, "Philippe Dumand will take over for him, and I'm sure he will do a superb job."

They took the gendarme-provided limo to Sylvie's apartment. There was very little conversation; all three were deep in their own thoughts. But the mood improved when they got to Sylvie's apartment. Linda was happy to settle into one of Sylvie's soft chairs and enjoy her oolong tea and homemade Camitorian cookies.

After an awkward silence, Linda inquired, "Sylvie, you've been serving us oolong tea pretty consistently. That's fine with me; I love it. But I was wondering how you came to know about it." She smiled, "And you've apparently developed an addiction to it."

"That's correct. I first learned about it in New York City. My first passion upon arriving on planet Earth was to light roast coffee, but the tea supplanted that. And I think I have become addicted!"

As Linda glanced around the apartment, she commented, "I see you have some unusual looking devices over on the table. Is that more of your genetics lab equipment?"

"That's equipment that Francois had in his apartment, and yes, I do plan to use it in my genetics experiments. As I mentioned, Francois was also a geneticist before he made the transition to Earth. Although I had much of the same equipment, he did have a few pieces that will provide some additional capability to my research effort. But I'll also be able to continue the work he was doing before his death."

"Was that similar to your work?"

"Some of it was, but his main interest dealt with reproduction in plants. I hope to extend his work in that area."

The room again fell silent for a minute. Rob, in particular, wrestled with some mixed feelings, ranging from regret that he didn't get to know Francois as a friend to some level of relief that the competition for Sylvie had ended.

He cleared his throat, "I'm sure you both remember when we did the video describing RFR problems with metal motor homes, recreational vehicles, and vehicles in general. By the way, are motor homes and RVs something that Camitorians might ever have utilized?" *Maybe that question will reorient our minds away from Francois.*

Sylvie replied, "No for the Camitorians, but yes, I remember the videos we did. RVs and motor homes are pretty ubiquitous on American highways. I've also seen them in other countries I've visited, but they appear to be much less prevalent than in the United States."

Linda added some thoughts, "Of course our videos pointed out some of the good and bad points with metal and shielded enclosures, and hopefully made the point about what Faraday cages can do with internal and external RFR. That provided the background for the discussions of smartphones and wireless telephones. But I'm not sure those videos focused on the most important subjects. I'm thinking we need to look at all vehicles, since most of them are metallic enclosures.

"Furthermore, our previous videos were given exposure to a limited audience in order to get some feedback on our efforts. I believe the new videos could be shown more broadly in the US and in other countries after they undergo some redirection.

"But" she added, "as I recall, we did get some feedback, and it indicated that the videos were a bit stuffy, and maybe too technical for the wider audiences we'd ultimately like to reach. Perhaps the runs we made with them were just the beta tests. The feedback we got should make it possible for us to get them ready for show time."

Sylvie asked, "Beta testing? I don't understand."

Rob replied, "That's the test stage of some development that is past the preliminary one, denoted as the alpha stage, but probably not where it is ready for general distribution."

Sylvie commented, "Ah, got it. Alpha, beta, … . But when does one reach gamma testing?"

Rob and Linda didn't have an answer for that.

Sylvie continued, "Linda, I think you're suggesting that we generalize our video to deal with vehicles of all types that have metal bodies. And I think that's almost all cars, SUVs, minivans, vans, and many of the RVs. This might even get the motor vehicle industry to modify their products to make them safer."

"Yes, Sylvie, I think we're on the same track," Linda said. "However, customer demand is also important. If we educate consumers about the potentially high RFR levels inside their vehicles, they would certainly pressure the manufacturers to accommodate their concerns. I think we should direct our video to both audiences."

Rob glanced at his watch. "This has been a productive discussion. The cookies were wonderful, Sylvie, but I'm wondering, Linda, how you're holding up."

"Oh, I'm managing to stay alert, Rob, as long as the discussion continues to be so stimulating."

Rob suggested, "Ah, since it's roughly noon, why don't we continue our discussion at a nearby patisserie. Linda, if you don't need sleep, I'm sure you could use some sustenance."

"Thank you, Rob. Great idea!"

They walked the two blocks, gendarmes in tow. Once they were seated and had ordered some baked goods and coffee, Rob continued, "Since we want to do new videos anyway, I'm wondering if we could involve the motor vehicle industry in creating them. Are you both up for that? It could prove to be interesting."

Linda replied, "Sounds like a possibility, Rob, but I fear it's overly optimistic. Let's contact our ad agency again to see what we can do to improve our videos. Once we have the new ones, we can try to convince the manufacturers to go along with us!

"But I'm definitely beginning to fade. I didn't get much sleep on the flight over. Can we continue tomorrow?"

That met with sympathetic approval.

Since the ad agency was in New York, Sylvie, Rob, and Linda were able to initiate a conference call there in the late Paris afternoon. She explained to John Simpson what they were trying to demonstrate.

John's smile indicated his delight at hearing her voice, "Why yes, Ms. Sensei, I think we can come up with a new video that'll show exactly what you're trying to tell people, but we can definitely introduce more pizazz. I've given that some thought.

"For starters, how about having you in it as a major participant, since that's guaranteed to get everyone's attention? First you can be interviewing some cartoon character of a world-famous physicist, I'm thinking an Einstein cartoon look-alike that could replace the somewhat stuffy real-life scientists we used previously. We could have our Einstein cartoon character explain what a Faraday cage is, and why a metal enclosure either prevents external radiation from getting inside it or traps radiation originating within. I could also imagine some little fuzz-balls bouncing off the sides of the cage, illustrating this effect.

"Then we could have you making some measurements inside, say, a minivan and a sedan. You could show the RFR that exists inside the metallic enclosures when you get a call on your cell phone and also when the phone is just sitting there turned on, but not in use. I can also imagine showing what happens to RFR levels when you have a minivan with two parents and four kids, everyone doing something electronic, like calling, texting, gaming, with their smartphones and tablets, that should really light up your meter.

"Finally, you could show what the RFR levels do when you turn your phone into a hotspot, whether it's inside your car or not. That should peg your meter! But you should be the narrator in all of these situations. I think the personal touch here would reduce the formality."

John paused for a moment to catch his breath, while Sylvie, Rob, and Linda nodded approvingly to each other. "And I had an additional thought that would allow us to apply the discussion of metal enclosures most generally. I remember that there used to be metal mobile homes that were never intended for travel. In fact, I know someone who lives in one. Most of those homes are now made with other materials, as are some RVs, so our messages wouldn't apply to the nonmetallic versions. But some older ones had metal exteriors and were transported to trailer parks where they were expected to stay forever. For the benefit of the owners of those, it might be useful if you showed the measurements of cell phones inside those metal sided homes. We should also include measurements of cordless phones that have plug-in base stations; I remember you saying that RFR from those devices is as bad as for cell phones.

"Does this appeal to you? Did I miss anything important?"

Sylvie swished her swatch of hair into its proper place, laughed lightly, and responded, "My goodness, John, that sounds like a complete program. I like your ideas very much, and they would certainly illustrate the principles we're trying to demonstrate. But I think we need to add one more feature in order to avoid having me gain another enemy, the executives of the motor vehicle industry. That would require a bit of work, but I think it might be important. In fact, we could offer a solution to the problem for them. It would involve installing all wireless receiving and emitting technology, that is, antennas, external to a metal enclosure. They would then be hardwired to all the communication devices inside the vehicles. This would produce the same effect as a corded landline and a wired Ethernet connection for a laptop or tablet. I'm sure the effect would be dramatic and would certainly give the manufacturers something to work on. Of course, smartphones would have to be modified to couple to the external antennae via cables, although I don't believe this would require much modification."

"Got it," John replied. But before we end this call, I should give you an update on your finances. I'm obviously in regular contact with your accountant, so he occasionally lets me know how we're doing spending your resources. As of yesterday, you're in great shape. You've spent only a small fraction of your budget on costs for creating the videos and on paying to run them."

Linda replied, "Thanks for the update on that, John. Since Sylvie moved to Paris, I've inherited the role of point person for our finances. I keep forgetting to ask you for updates, but you're certainly keeping track! As is our accountant, of course."

As soon as the video began to be shown, the executives involved in the manufacture of nearly all of the world's vehicles indulged in a collective gulp. But they also realized that Sylvie had offered a plan for them that would allow their customers to use their electronic devices while riding in their vehicles.

Late one Paris afternoon, as Sylvie was deep in concentration on a genetics issue that she was working on, her phone rang. "Ms. Sensei, this is Brad Fletcher, the CEO of the largest manufacturer of recreational vehicles in the world. Since most of our vehicles have external aluminum, we've been watching your new videos with alarm, seeing how it might affect our sales."

She sat bolt upright in her chair in surprise at her caller, but quickly regained her composure. "Hello, Mr. Fletcher. We realized that might be the case. But I presume you noted that the video also shows how much the radiation levels inside the vehicles are decreased if the owners install a shielded external antenna with wired connections, and make sure they keep their cellphones on airplane mode while inside. In the absence of the couplings to external antennas, calls should be made outside the vehicle. We weren't trying to put you out of business. Rather we were trying to offer a helpful suggestion."

He replied, "Thank you. We recognized that you were trying to be helpful. And we've responded."

"We're well into a design for the antennas, and we're working on the wiring now. Furthermore, we're collaborating with a cell phone manufacturer to accommodate our antennas for calling, texting, and connecting to the internet. These will be standard equipment on all our new models and could be installed at a small cost in those that already exist. We've also gone a step further. We're developing a near transparent metallic shielding into our tempered glass windows to further protect the occupants and drivers.

"But to get to my point, we're running a new advertising campaign in which we urge our potential and existing owners of our vehicles to use only use antenna-coupled devices. We were wondering if you'd be willing to appear in our ads to emphasize how important that would be to their health."

Now her discomfort had taken a different tack: thinking through the guarantees she'd need before agreeing to his request. "I'd be happy to appear in your ads, provided it's in the sense of a public service appearance. I wouldn't want to appear to be supporting your product over that of the other manufacturers. Perhaps the ad could indicate that your company was sponsoring it, but that its message would apply to an owner of any metal vehicle."

"I understand your concern. This isn't quite the way we were thinking the ad would run, but I'm sure we can accommodate your wishes."

Sylvie had learned how the business world works. So, she responded, "Excellent. Of course, I'll need to see the ad before it runs."

"Yes, of course."

Sylvie added, "I might also mention that there's a benefit to having a metal vehicle, provided one does not use a wireless device, such as a tablet or a smartphone, inside it. The metal enclosure offers some shielding to its occupants from the deluge of electromagnetic radiation that pervades the world outside the metal enclosure."

"Thanks for pointing that out. I hadn't thought of the benefit of living in a Faraday cage; we'll include a comment to that effect in our ad."

When the ad finally ran, executives from several other RV producing companies called Sensei to thank her for insisting on objectivity.

Back in their apartment one evening, Sylvie commented, "Rob, I think we've really had an impact on the safety of Earthlings. I presume you're personally grateful."

I do believe she's teasing me. I like it!

"Sylvie, since I've begun to spend most of my time around you, I'm guessing I'm about the safest Earthling on the planet, at least electromagnetically."

"But Rob, I'm not sure that applies in all other ways! Remember the bullets."

"Ah yes, the bullets. I'm ignoring those. Anyway, Sylvie, I agree that we may have greatly improved the safety for just about every other Earthling. All they have to do is pay attention to our messages."

Chapter 33. DNA Modifications

Sylvie and Rob were back in their Paris apartment one evening after a hard day of meeting with various French government officials. Rob had already taken off his shoes.

Sylvie was comfortably settled on the sofa, her feet propped up on the coffee table. "Rob, why don't we cook something easy this evening. We can enjoy a nice glass of wine while we're preparing dinner, and then have more with dinner. I'm too pooped to even do my part of the cooking tonight. I like that word by the way: it's funny."

It didn't take him long to respond, "I agree with half of that, but let me suggest that we take our bottle to the bistro down the street and order our dinner there."

"Sounds good to me."

"I'll put my shoes back on. And I agree about the funny word."

It had now been more than two months since Francois was killed, and they both continued to struggle with their loss. At the same time, their relationship was growing unhindered, and they were grateful for that, even as they mourned Francois' death.

The bistro was dimly it and smelled of wonderful French dishes. They sat down at their table, and the waitress opened their wine. After Rob sampled it and gave his approval, the waitress poured a glass for each of them. They sat quietly for a few minutes, mostly gazing into each other's eyes, sipping their wine. Gradually the bistro's ambience helped their ongoing concerns about Francois melt away under the warmth of their feelings for each other.

Finally, Rob cleared his throat, rubbed his hands together a couple of times, and said, "Sylvie, I've been wondering if we could consider making our relationship more permanent. I'd propose marriage to you, but there are some huge issues involved with that, and we need to discuss them before making such a momentous decision. For one, I've seen you interacting with kids, and I'd be greatly surprised if you didn't want to have children of your own. But I have no idea if it would be possible for you and me to conceive babies."

Sylvie had been sitting on the edge of her chair, anticipating where Rob's question was going, "Actually, Rob, I've also been thinking about how our relationship might evolve. You're right about my wanting to have children. So, I did a little research in my laboratory, spanning many nights after you were asleep, to see if it would be possible for a Camitorian and an Earthling to conceive. Of course, I also had to be sure the child could grow without any hindrance from its DNA. I'm quite sure the answer is yes. It would require some modifications to my DNA, but I believe I know how to make those changes. Then I would need to let things settle for a few months before checking my DNA again to be sure the changes went as I intended."

Now Rob was sitting on the edge of his chair, "Oh my god, Sylvie, I'm stunned that your thinking about this has gotten to the stage where you even asked that question, let alone answered it. But what if you modified my DNA? Would that also be possible? Or even easier?"

"I didn't investigate that possibility, although Francois did. I'm not sure I trust his results, since he was determined to get the ones he wanted." She smiled, then continued, "He didn't describe them in detail, but he seemed to think it would be much more involved than changing mine. So, I would prefer not to change yours."

"But that raises another question, Sylvie. I know you're an incredibly talented geneticist, and it would surely be an interesting experiment for you to see if an Earthling and a Camitorian could conceive. So, I need for you to give me some assessment of the fraction of your interest being in our creating babies and how much in just an extraordinary genetics experiment. To what extent am I serving as a guinea pig?"

"Oh Rob, one of those is one hundred percent and the other is zero. You're the winner. I did my studies to see how it would affect us. I didn't even consider the 'extraordinary genetics experiment' aspect of my work until you just now raised the question."

She smiled, "And anyway, how could I think of you as a guinea pig?"

Then she developed a sly smile, "Now that you mention it, though, it could lead to an extraordinary research paper. We could be co-authors. Would that not be fun? Actually, your DNA would be a co-author with me."

Rob's expression had evolved from furrowed brow to a happy smile, then to a laugh from her banter. "Thank you, Sylvie, you've put my mind completely at ease with your answer."

The waitress was becoming impatient, so they looked at their menus and gave her their orders. Given the discussion, food was not the highest priority for either of them, so the waitress left a bit disgruntled at the small orders and the fact that they wouldn't even be ordering wine. Not much profit there. And probably a pretty small tip.

Rob wasn't quite done with his questions, "But there's one other major issue we need to deal with: the difference in our life expectancies. Would you even consider marrying someone who would only give you another forty or fifty years, when you might well live two hundred more years? There have been times in the past year when I wasn't at all sure you'd outlive me but, I note with some uneasiness, the threats seem to have disappeared. Or maybe your protectors have just become so proficient that those who would do you harm have given up."

"Rob, if I can share forty to fifty years with a man I love as much as I love you, I can't imagine I could ask for any more from life."

God, I wish I could think to say things as beautiful as that. What an incredible woman.

"Sylvie, that makes me very happy. Perhaps we should give serious thought to marriage. The French don't seem to have any problems with us living together, so I think it just boils down to what we want to do. But I would be happy to formalize our commitment to each other."

"Oh Rob, that thought makes me incredibly happy."

And what you could not possibly know is that I also have some ideas for how to modify your DNA so you could live longer.

And as they were leaving and he was holding the door for her, she said, "Rob, I'm convinced I know how to modify my DNA to make conception possible between us. So, I believe I'll proceed with the DNA modifications."

"Oh my god, Sylvie, that's incredible. How soon will we know if what you did worked?"

"Well, I'll be able to monitor my DNA, but I'm guessing then it would be three or four months before I can be sure. Then it'll be nine more months before we can be absolutely certain."

Rob looked puzzled.

"Gestation periods are the same for Camitorians as they are for Earthlings, and I expect to be fertile in about three months."

The security team had to just stand there looking awkward while Rob and Sylvie kissed.

They were sitting at their breakfast table the following morning, with the sun shining brightly through the window that overlooked the park. They hadn't organized themselves yet for the day; they were dressed in bathrobes, hair completely untended. Rob asked, "Sylvie, are you thinking about rearranging the furniture in the living room? I like it pretty much as it is, but I'm open to suggestion."

Sylvie sat for a moment with a stunned expression on her face, "How did you know I was considering rearranging the furniture? I don't think I ever said anything about that to you. Have you been reading my brain waves?"

"I'm not sure how I knew that. Maybe I was sensing your thoughts. Is that possible? I didn't think that was possible for Earthlings."

She got up and gave him a hug, "I think you've just received my thoughts through brain waves. I'd also thought that was impossible for Earthlings, but I now believe I was wrong. I've been pretty sure at times I was 'hearing' your brain waves, but this is the first time, to my knowledge, that communications have gone the other way. Let's try some more communications."

Of course, Sylvie was sending and receiving in broadcast mode, that is, with the same intensities on all three of her natural communication frequencies. Rob, of course, was only able to communicate on a single frequency.

"Ah," he said, "I believe you are thinking we could start a class for Earthlings to learn how to communicate through their brain waves. But you're wondering how we would select the students. You'd want only those with the best developed brains, or they wouldn't have a chance."

"Rob, that's incredible. That's exactly what I was thinking.

She continued thinking her thoughts to him, "So maybe we should start a class. We could give it a try to see if there was any hope for anyone not named Rob Thompson."

"I'm liking this idea. It should be fun! Okay, I must be a reasonably smart guy, or you wouldn't have had any interest in me. But I'll bet there are other Earthlings whose brains would allow the sort of communication we just did.

"Sylvie, let's find out!"

Oh shit, I guess this means that I need to be very careful what I'm thinking about. Sylvie can 'hear' everything that goes through my brain.

He immediately got a message back, "That's correct, Rob. But the reverse isn't true; my brain automatically shuts off communications if I want to keep my thoughts to myself.

"But I don't want to scare you. We can communicate via brain-to-brain all the time now, at least when we're close. But I'll have to get you a Camitorian earpiece so we can talk over longer distances. Oh, and if I pick up some thoughts I suspect you didn't want to communicate to me, I'll just ignore them."

He replied, "I guess that's the best I can hope for, short of brain surgery. But that aside, if we did brain-to-brain all the time I'd be deprived of hearing your wonderfully musical voice. We must use vocal communications some of the time."

"Okay, Rob. If you insist!"

Chapter 34. RF Radiation in Vehicles

The next morning Rob and Sylvie were having yet another breakfast table discussion, "Sylvie, I'm not sure we succeeded in making people aware that ordinary cars can also act as Faraday cages. Not very well enclosed ones, but they can still amplify any RFR that originates within them by a lot. We got enough comments from RV manufacturers to suggest that they at least paid attention to our video. But we heard nothing from the major manufacturers of cars."

Sylvie responded, "They must be aware that a potential problem exists. And there are other RFR effects that need to be considered. For example, self-driving cars, which have become very popular in the past couple of years, rely on the Global Positioning System but are very dependent on communications with the 5G radiation from small cells, which have become nearly ubiquitous. And the vehicles that have crash prevention systems, whether self-driving or not, use radar, which produces more RFR. So there has to be a lot of that floating around the roads. A typical car, SUV, minivan, or RV, Faraday cage or not, will not prevent all of that from getting to the passengers."

"Shall we do another video?"

"Sounds good to me, Rob. I'll call John Simpson, our favorite ad agency Earthling, when the sun is up in New York."

John was happy to pick up his phone when his caller ID indicated who it was; he always found it interesting talking with Sylvie. "John, we need you to do another video for us. Are you up to that?"

"Yep, be happy to. What's it about?"

So, Sylvie and Rob went over the discussion they just had with John.

"Use of smartphones in vehicles, with an emphasis on cars, huh? I guess we start with a discussion of Faraday cages similar to what we did before. That was an excellent intro, but I think we should change it a bit so viewers don't become bored. Then we could film you, Sylvie, riding in a car driven by Rob, and just show what happens to your RFR meter reading when you turn on your smartphone.

"We could do this both in a sedan and an SUV. Wouldn't hurt to include a minivan again. Perhaps this might emphasize the message from the last video."

Sylvie replied, "That all sounds good. Actually, I don't think we'll have any difficulty getting an impressive result in all those situations; we've made simple measurements that suggest the levels can increase up to a factor of ten, or even more, when the phone is on, depending on where it's placed. We can also show how little the effect is mitigated when you go to speaker mode. The phone seems to have to work harder when it's partially shielded. And, as we showed in the last video, but should repeat, the RFR increases with multiple phones and other electronic devices."

"Factor of ten? For just one phone? Holy crap! This is becoming personal. I'm really going to have to change my errant ways!"

For the moment, the discussion became one between Sylvie and Rob, as they discussed the pervasive radiation they had discussed over breakfast from 5G small cells and anti-collision radar. John just listened in. Each vehicle did mitigate the radiation created external to it, but that RFR was still contributing significantly to the levels within each one.

Sylvie asked, "Rob, would it be possible for car manufacturers to improve the shielding in cars to block out more of the radiation from radar?"

Rob paused for a moment, "Yeah, but that'll increase the radiation levels in the cars from sources inside them. If we're going down that road, we'll need to encourage the auto companies, and perhaps the window glass companies as well, to improve the shielding. I recall that the RV executive you spoke with recently mentioned using RF shielded glass in some of their new models. Perhaps other vehicle manufacturers would also consider that option. That could really help cut out most of the 5G radiation the self-driving cars rely on, both the higher frequency RFR as well as the lower frequency stuff the small cells also emit. But only if the antennas are external to the automotive Faraday cage. Concurrently, though, drivers and occupants will need to make sure they really don't ever use their smartphones inside their cars. This is a two-edged sword."

Sylvie reoriented her anarchistic swatch of blond hair, "Oh, I like that expression despite its martial implications. Those sorts of words are scary to Camitorians."

Rob chuckled in response, "Oops. Sorry about the combative implications, Sylvie. Anyway, we'll need to be sure drivers are educated well enough about RFR to know how to use all the pieces of the puzzle to their advantage."

Rob continued, "Also, we've focused our attention on RFR, but the magnetic fields, especially in electric cars, can also be a hazard. These are lower frequency, but the levels generated can be far above those considered safe for the electrical operations that occur in the human body, and especially for people with pacemakers. The problem with static magnetic fields is that they penetrate through the entire body, unlike the higher frequency RFRs and especially the 5G waves, so can readily affect all bodily organs.

"Actually, Sylvie, as we're discussing this, I'm thinking we need to talk with the auto manufacturers about the problems and our suggestions to mitigate them. I suspect they'll have to do some tests to determine the best way to go.

"So, John, sorry to waste all your time while Sylvie and I dither."

John reassured them, "No problem, Rob. I found the discussion to be very interesting. Anyway, I think we should just go with the smartphone in the car video for now. That's going to be valid no matter what else we decide. We'll postpone the additional stuff until we've figured out the best way to approach the problem. And perhaps after we've enlisted the help of the manufacturers!"

Linda, Rob and Sylvie gathered representatives of the world's auto companies together in Paris. Mergers over recent years had created multinational companies, so the attempts to include every possible company with their invitations often resulted in multiple contacts to each conglomerate. The invitation simply mentioned that they wanted to study the possibilities for reducing RFR and magnetic fields to safe levels in motor vehicles. Since many of the companies had major offices in the US, the recipients of the invitation from those offices may well have thought there was no problem with RFR in cars, having still been under the influence of the FCC prior to Linda's and Rob's assuming their leadership roles. However, they were aware of recent trends in RFR limits by the current FCC and in many foreign countries, so the manufacturers figured they should attend just to be certain their competitors didn't obtain some sort of public relations advantage on them.

In recognition of the electromagnetic skepticism some of the attendees might have, Linda, Rob, and Sylvie opened the meeting with a review of the enormous amount of medical data regarding harmful effects of RFR and magnetic fields. This part of the program was given by a panel of medical professionals, representing several nations. They did get some questions about the integrity of their data, mostly from the American attendees, but these challenges got little support from representatives from the rest of the world.

Rob and Linda then showed portions of the video on RFR from smartphones in cars, emphasizing that the levels in a closed car would exceed the Council of Europe's stated upper limits by a large factor. American representatives were seen to be squirming a bit in their chairs; they'd begun to realize their opinions were definitely in the minority.

Rob noted, "Although you might think that smartphone produced radiation isn't your problem, what we're going to ask you to do is combine that issue with others that are also associated with, or directly related to, all of your vehicles. Then see what, if anything, can be done to mitigate the effects from all sources of radiation."

Linda then introduced some of the other concerns. Those included police radar, radar from crash prevention systems on cars, 5G radiation from the myriad of small cell antennas used for self-driving cars, and general RFR levels in cars produced by all the electronic devices they might have in their 2024 models. Following Linda's formal presentation, they opened the floor for discussions. She, Rob, and Sylvie realized this back and forth might begin to infringe on the secrecy the companies always maintained with their next year's models, but they hoped that the issue would seem sufficiently important that the companies would overlook that problem.

They were wrong. Nothing matters more to the auto companies than the surprises they can present when they unveil their next year's models, so they were extremely careful not to let those be compromised in any way. However, they were at least willing to consider the effects of the radiation that existed in their current models. That would have to do for now.

But especially contentious was the discussion about 5G radiation because of its necessity for self-driving cars. The manufacturers were obviously hyper-enthusiastic about such cars, due to the huge investment they had made in them, and therefore also about the radiation that permitted them to operate. However, the ubiquity of the radiation from the 5G small cells at the levels the manufacturers thought essential to operate their vehicles raised the hackles of Rob, Linda and Sylvie. This was especially problematic because of all the lower frequency RFR they also emitted, all of which has a greater penetration depth than the higher frequency RFR.

Indeed, one auto company CEO, sporting an angry expression, asserted, "You people are making it damned difficult for us to design safe self-driving cars, which everyone knows is the way of the future. The new radiation limits you three are most responsible for imposing forced us to do an expensive reworking of the receptors we had in those cars so they could still receive the signals they needed from the 5G transmitters. Indeed, the 5G radiation levels we had assumed would be available throughout the world suddenly were more than an order of magnitude lower than we had thought would be the case.

"In fact, we are preparing a lawsuit against the FCC to get those thresholds reversed. This should serve as a heads up to the two of you who are on the FCC. We've also requested the levels be restored to their previous values until the suit is resolved."

There was considerable grumbling from many of the other auto executives in apparent affirmation of the CEO's comments. Linda replied, "I'm sorry that you feel so threatened by the lower thresholds imposed by the FCC. That was not mandated by us, of course, but by the enormous body of medical research that showed that the previous limits set by the FCC would impose dangerous radiation levels on human beings— your customers—and on other living things, including plants and virtually every living creature. The level we set was the highest level that the medical research had suggested would be safe for anyone who didn't get within fifty feet of a small cell emitter.

"We were pleased when we found that the auto industry was able to increase the amplification in their receivers to counteract the reduced radiation thresholds, and we'd like to thank you for responding so quickly to the needed limits."

That response disarmed the recalcitrant executive. Another CEO, this one from a German company, added, "I don't see the reduced limits as a problem, given the plethora of small cells. Certainly, city self-driving is well accommodated in the countries that have chosen to go that route, and driving outside the cities seems to be guided well enough by the warning radar and cameras, and other safety features to keep drivers focused and on track. Following your discussion, what I see as the challenge for those of us who produce cars is figuring out how to shield the occupants of our vehicles from the variety of sources of external radiation, and still have the cars pick up the signals they need for self-driving. But I don't see that as an insurmountable problem. All we have to do is place the receivers outside the car. Cars have had an antenna on their roofs for their radio for many years, but they may have to have several, of different design to accommodate the various frequencies, to detect the radiation that is important to their safety."

That comment seemed to silence the person who was threatening the lawsuit, and even seemed to garner murmurs of support from some of the other executives.

Near the end of the meeting, Brad Fletcher, the executive who had contacted Sylvie soon after their video ran, spoke up, apparently deciding that customer safety out voted new product secrecy. He gave a description of the modifications his company was making to their RVs, which he had described to Sylvie in their phone call, hoping that his company's action might stimulate other companies to follow their path.

Sylvie thanked him profusely for his comments.

Sylvie, Rob, and Linda were discussing the outcome of the meeting afterward in a coffee shop. Linda, sitting forward in her chair, obviously still on edge, observed, "I do think we made some progress. Most of the executives were surprised to see that all the radar floating around could be a problem. When they were just considering crash prevention, the radar seemed to be only a good thing. And I think the last guy to comment on 5G really got the executives thinking in positive ways. Limit the radiation and shield the occupants of the cars.

"Protect the lives of our customers!"

Rob, slouching in his chair and looking much more relaxed than he had during the discussions with the auto executives, added, "I agree. Some of the comments we got did give me hope that the automobile folks will give more thought to the RFR their next year's models will produce. We're happy to let them claim they figured this out all by themselves."

Sylvie sat in silence for a few seconds before summarizing, "This really is a complicated problem for them. Mitigating the effects for the passengers from the different sources of radiation produced both inside and outside should give the manufacturers some serious competing factors to worry about. At least we can hope they'll worry about them!"

Then Rob raised another issue, "I've also begun worrying about truck drivers. They spend large fractions of their time inside the truck's cab, probably getting W-Fi from several sources. The largest trucks even have sleeping accommodations. So, the drivers spend most of every day inside their Faraday cage.

"We could have another meeting with the truck manufacturers, but frankly I'm pretty worn out from what we've already done with motor vehicles. And I suspect the truckers and manufacturers will get the message when they start seeing all the extra antennas on smaller vehicles."

Sylvie and Linda nodded in exhausted affirmation.

Chapter 35. Communications Classes

Sylvie and Rob were having a late morning brainstorming session, along with snacks from their favorite patisserie, on how to attract the students for their class to see if they could teach brain wave communications. Occasionally they would verbalize their thoughts, but most of their communications were brain to brain.

"Sylvie, I anticipate that we'll get a huge number of interested people, but very few will be able to communicate through brain waves. I don't see an obvious way to weed out the people who can't interact that way."

She replied, "I don't think we need to worry about that. The classes will really help those who either have the capability to interact that way, or those who can learn to do so. But I believe the classes will even help those who are never able to communicate via brain waves to develop their communication skills. Even that has to be useful."

At the first evening's class there were initially one-hundred excited Earthlings, limited only by Sylvie's restriction on the number of registrants. She had several others produce compelling stories as to why they should be allowed in the class anyway, with some even sending in lists of their qualifications. Of course, Sylvie let them in.

She was filled with enthusiasm as she began, "Good evening to all potential brain wave communicators. I'm Sylvie Sensei, and I really am an alien. I'm excited to see so many Earthlings who are interested in developing this particular capability. Before we begin, please turn off all your cell phones and smart watches. Not only might they create unpleasant symptoms for some of our more electrosensitive participants, but the radiation they emitted would most likely swamp out the much weaker brain-to-brain signals.

"I should note that not everyone who wishes to communicate this way is able to do so, and sometimes they can be successful with some brains but not others. We've seen this to be the case even for Camitorians; some brain structures just make it difficult for them to send and receive the messages to and from a large number of other brains. In other situations, the Camitorians are able to communicate via brain waves with a small group of friends or family members but can't do so with most other Camitorians. I tell you this so that you'll not feel chagrined if we conclude your brain won't allow you to exchange waves with my brain. You may still be able to send and receive messages with some other Earthlings who, in many instances, also won't be able to communicate with my brain.

"So, all I'm saying is that, if you and I are forced to the verbal communication mode, you might feel disappointed, but should not feel you are deficient! That may change as our classes progress. I should also tell you that Camitorian children often are not capable of brain-to-brain communication initially, but they learn how to do that as they grow older and their brains develop." All one-hundred-four nodded in response.

Sylvie began the class with some simple exercises. She encouraged couples who routinely did brain-to-brain communication to try communicating with someone they didn't know. The group began to try to achieve their goal, first thinking the messages they wanted to send, then talking softly to see if they had succeeded. Occasionally there would be a burst of laughter, but the room remained fairly quiet as everyone worked to see if they could succeed.

After an hour Sylvie announced, "What I need for you to do now is come up to me one by one thinking some thought that you wish to communicate to me. The rest of you should continue working on your brain-to-brain communications until it's your turn to come up. If I tried to communicate with the group as a whole there would be a jumble of messages, mixed in with the omnipresent electromagnetic environmental junk, which would make it impossible for me to determine who was sending me waves. When you come up, please think of something that's not too obvious a thought. I don't want to give you any suggestions or I might be able to anticipate your subsequent message. If, after you've sent me your thoughts, and if I can receive them, I'll send a response to you. After you've received my response, you should repeat it back to me to be sure we are transmitting in both directions.

"However, I'll give you one hint: don't have your thought be something that you generally keep secret. In that case your brain might block your attempt to send the message, and I'd never receive it no matter how successful we might otherwise be.

"So would the first row begin to approach the podium."

As the first person approached her, the room grew silent, since everyone wanted to see what might happen. After a few seconds, Sylvie laughed and shook her head affirmatively, then asked, "What message did I send back to you?"

The woman replied, with a laugh, "Get some flea powder or a flea collar."

Sylvie said enthusiastically, "Fantastic; we succeeded! Your name is …"

She thought her response.

Sylvie then told the group, "This is April Eberhard. The message Ms. Eberhard sent to me was 'My dog has fleas.' So, the flea powder or flea collar was my response." The crowd broke into applause. "And you can see that at least some Camitorians and Earthlings can do brain-to-brain communications."

Rob was sitting in the back of the room, tuning in with his Camitorian earpiece, and smiling. He already knew that. He'd decided to join the class to satisfy his curiosity regarding the frequency that brain-to-brain communications would work for Earthlings. Of course, it also allowed him to watch Sylvie performing in a different venue. It didn't matter what she was doing; he enjoyed watching her in action anywhere.

The next person was another lady, but there was no brain-to-brain communication with her. She claimed she and her husband had been communicating that way for years, and had been continuing to do so in the class. Of course, the next person was her husband, who also was not able to send or receive with Sensei. She tried to explain to them, "I don't doubt that the two of you have been doing brain-to-brain communicating with each other, Your brains are apparently well matched. I suggest that, as you practice, you try exchanging thoughts with someone you don't know as well as your spouse. This may work best, though, if you choose someone who is a friend."

She then added, "Communication can involve much more than interchange of messages, however that takes place. If it is brain-to-brain, that is wonderful. If it is verbal, that may be good, but the voice doesn't always tell everything that's going on inside the brain. Of course, it can also produce misleading information.

"But sensing another's emotional state often requires no message transmission. The expression on one's face as well as their body language can convey a more accurate picture of a person's feelings than might be communicated by exchanging messages. And couples often communicate a great deal by those means."

The next several people also failed to send and receive signals from Sensei. At that point a man in the remaining group spoke up loudly, "I'll bet that first woman was a plant. Either she's a Camitorian or you and she predesigned your sent and received messages." And there was some mumbling among the crowd that suggested others were suspecting there might be some truth to his assertion.

Sensei realized she had a difficult situation on her hands, so she asked Ms. Eberhard if she was an Earthling. She was surprised by the question, but confirmed that she was, and even announced her address. Sensei then asked her if she had prearranged their communication. She said she had absolutely not. Sensei then had an idea, "I'd like for someone in the audience to write a message on a piece of paper and give it to Ms. Eberhard. She will communicate to me by brain-to-brain mode what's on the message, and I'll tell all of you what I received from her brain."

One of the women wrote down a message and handed it to Ms. Eberhard. She read the message to herself, and Sylvie promptly said, "It's a cloudy day but tomorrow is supposed to be sunny."

The woman who had written the message turned to the group with a huge smile and said, "That's exactly what I put on the paper. You had better believe these two people are doing brain-to-brain communication."

The group applauded again. There were no further challenges to Sylvie's abilities. Or Ms. Eberhard's. Sylvie went through the remainder of the group to see if there were others who could communicate as the Camitorians did. Marcel Jacobson, a tall, broad-shouldered, curly-haired young fellow, had an expression on his face that could only be described as mirthful. He generated his thought that was supposed to be communicated to Sylvie, and suddenly her expression registered surprise. One can only imagine what a Camitorian looks like if they blush; in her case her light green suddenly became a darker green with a reddish tint. Rob also picked up the message, "Sylvie Sensei is super sexy." Rob laughed.

There weren't many who found through the three-hour meeting that they were able to do brain wave communication; Sylvie ended up with a total of eleven, including Ms. Eberhard. Many of those who were unable to communicate were frustrated at their failure to do so. Sylvie realized this might happen to many of them, but she encouraged them to keep practicing.

Sylvie hadn't been sure if there would be any Earthlings who could communicate through their brain waves, so she was pleasantly surprised by the results of the first class. Of the eleven successful brain-to-brain communicators, there were four married couples, one of which was same sex. All had been thinking their communications throughout their marriages.

Sylvie realized it was going to be difficult to help the eleven who could communicate brain-to-brain to advance their skills when she had to share her time with those who needed help getting started. It quickly became obvious that she needed to hold advanced classes for those eleven.

But first she had another class for the remaining ninety-three, followed by attempts of those to send and receive messages with her. Five people showed that they had developed brain-to-brain messaging capability from their work in the classes. That brought to sixteen the number who had demonstrated that capability, of which there were five couples.

A week later, the advanced classes began. Sylvie again started by requesting that everyone turn off their smartphones and smartwatches.

Sylvie wondered how capable the members of the five couples would be when they weren't communicating with their spouses. So, she shuffled the members of the group to have them 'talk' with someone who they hadn't previously known. The communications were not as good when the couples were mixed. Often the basic idea of the message was transmitted, but some of it got garbled. Transmission was improved when the senders distanced themselves from other couples as much as possible, concentrated intently on the message being sent, and the receivers closed their eyes to shut out distractions. Communications seemed to work best when the sender and receiver were next to each other; locating them in opposite corners of the room completely shut off their messaging. Indeed, when the greater distances were tried, the messages that were received were garbled random thoughts from other pairs of the group. The Earthlings hadn't yet developed the selective capability the Camitorians used to focus on messaging with a desired individual. This wasn't surprising; the Earthlings, Rob included, hadn't developed the three-frequency carrier wave selectivity by which the Camitorians communicated.

And there was another problem to which Sylvie became aware after a while. She had tried to obtain a meeting room that was somewhat insulated from the environment. That turned out to be a large school recreation room, which had no W-Fi, and was surrounded by playing fields. None the less, there was bound to be some environmental RFR background. But as the second meeting progressed, she became aware that more confusion of signals seemed to occur near one member of the group. Sylvie tried to see if she could identify a problem with that individual. It didn't take her long to spot the smartwatch the woman was wearing. When Sylvie noted the woman's watch, she quickly turned it off, and suddenly all communications improved.

Then there was the Lothario, or Marcel Jacobson, who decided to pursue his teasing of Sensei with another message to her, "I'll bet Sylvie Sensei is a spectacular lover."

However, this time she was ready for him. She sent back to him, "Do keep in mind that I'm old enough to be your great, great, great, great, great grandmother." She would have to wait, though, to see if that had the desired impact. Rob found Jacobson's second attempt less amusing than his first. *Is this guy trying to start something, or is he just playing games for his own amusement?*

In the next advanced class, Sylvie had the students work on using even more focused concentration to enhance communications. But she found when she had them direct their messaging to an individual who wasn't their spouse, the members of each couple tended to send messages to their spouses regardless of who the intended recipient was. Apparently, selectivity was something for which Earthlings needed a few thousand more years of evolution.

In that session, Sylvie asked her sixteen students what messages they had been sending, that is, what form they took. In all cases but two, they were words. She then told them that

Camitorians could send words, but in many cases, sent messages involving symbols, pictures, and whatever else was convenient or came to mind. She asked them first to consider transmitting simple images. For example, in place of the word 'tree,' think of an image of a tree. She noted that this would specify more about the tree than just the word, since the image would indicate what kind of tree the sender had in mind. For this exercise she kept the spouses together and paired the remaining people with others with whom they seemed to be able to communicate well.

The couples were able to communicate with combinations of images and words although, for the most part, not as efficiently as when they were just using words. However, all but one of the pairs began to see results as they continued their efforts. She found that the non-spousal pairings didn't do nearly as well as those that included spouses, which she understood to result from shared experiences lending additional meaning to the images. The improvement with time gave Sylvie reason to believe that including images would work. As the pairs practiced, they began to realize they were communicating more efficiently with the combination of words and images.

One of the husband-wife pairs was a Japanese couple. They noted that they had been communicating with images from the start, and merely improved that capability with the class. As the husband explained to the group, "We recently immigrated to the France from Japan. The Japanese language, obviously our native language, includes both words and images, The Kanji are the image part of the Japanese language. They aren't themselves pictures, but they convey more meaning than a word can. Or even a simple picture. So, we are accustomed to including images in our talking and writing. I think this mode of communication was very natural for us once we formalized the brain-to-brain talking.

"But we were pleased to find that our communications became even more efficient when we included the pictures you suggested along with our Kanji. So, your suggestion even improved the ability to send thoughts to each other beyond just use of the pictographs."

When Sylvie had originally established the pairings of the unpaired six people, two of them, a man and a woman, quickly indicated they wanted to work together. Their communications seemed to be making great progress as they proceeded through Sylvie's exercises. At one point, Sylvie accidently picked up a message that the man, who happened to be Marcel, had sent to the woman, and it was considerably more amorous than they probably would have liked to share with the group. They had apparently developed a relationship and were finding their brain-to-brain interacting to be working extremely well. At that point Sylvie just smiled. She hoped that no one else overheard the message. She decided the couple would need help in becoming more circumspect in their unrestricted interactions.

Sylvie also observed that the husband-wife teams had a definite advantage over those who had not known each other previously. The many shared experiences the couples had over their years together made it possible for them to communicate without specifying every detail they were trying to convey, and in some instances, could transmit entire messages by just sending a picture.

There was one exception, though: the Bickersons. Sylvie noticed that their interactions did not seem as comfortable as those of the other couples, and in between exercises they would tend toward verbal speech that was not very gentle.

"George, I'm sure you're the reason we're not able to communicate as well as these other folks. I'm concentrating as hard as I can to send you a message and you're just not receiving it. I was telling you that I'm becoming extremely frustrated with you."

"Well, maybe if you'd tried to send a nice message, I would have been able to receive it. Your messages always sound as if you're pissed off, and I'm sick and tired of having to deal with your perpetually angry thoughts."

"George let's quit this class. I don't think it's helping us improve our communications. I think Ms. Sensei was overly optimistic."

So, they packed up their things and walked out. From overhearing their interaction, Sylvie concluded that the mutual warmth between the members of a couple could affect their ability to interact. Of course, that probably carried over to all their interactions.

Needless to say, the classes did wonders for the abilities of the remaining fourteen students to communicate, certainly by the brain-to-brain mode with their spouses, but also with other Earthlings with brains that were suited to that form of communication. All of the couples, except for the Bickersons, attested to the improvements in their general ability to interact with each other, much to the improvement of their marriages. Sylvie mused to herself, *these meetings are having unexpected results. I seem to have graduated from language instructor to marriage counselor!*

In their post-meeting coffee shop analysis of the classes, Sylvie posed, "Rob, that incident with the smartwatch made me realize there are probably more devices out there that can produce lots of RFR that we've not addressed. There seem to be new ones coming on the market every week, for example, tracking devices for lost keys and purses, Bluetooth tracking device for pets, and probably lots more I don't even know about."

"Right you are, I'm guessing. I don't think we can produce another video for each of those items, so I wonder if there is a different way we can approach them?"

She thought for a few seconds, then suggested, "Rob, what if the FCC set radiation limits for each device? Before a business could market their device, they would have to get it approved by the FCC."

Rob had to mull that over for a bit, "You've asked an interesting question, Sylvie. The FCC actually has set limits on the radiation from RF emitting devices. If a device emits radiation in excess of the FCC limits, it has the authority to withdraw its approval and pursue enforcement action against the appropriate party. Of course, their limits are so high that devices could be in compliance and still be extremely dangerous.

"Furthermore, we do know that some devices claim to be in compliance with the FCC by quoting average Wi-Fi levels but operate in pulsed mode. They time average their radiation output so they are within FCC limits. This allows them to use much higher peak levels. And, as we learned from our medical experts, the maximum levels may be more medically relevant than the average ones. We might try to get Congress to consider giving the FCC more specificity in our approvals. Of course, we'd then have to set new limits that would probably need to be device specific. But that would allow us to challenge any manufacturers to reduce the radiation from their devices to limits that would be set by realistic needs of living entities.

"However, I think that's a good suggestion, Sylvie. I'll raise it with Linda and see what she thinks. That'll take time, though; Congress moves at glacial speeds!"

Chapter 36. Honesty

Rob and Sylvie were walking beside the Seine late one afternoon to observe the flow and the riffles of the water, just enjoying the scenery and being together. The gendarmes had learned to stay a respectful distance behind them as they walked. They paused by a place where the afternoon sun had warmed a spot between the adjacent shadows. Sylvie looked lovingly into his eyes, and asked, "Rob, you seem deep in thought. Is something bothering you?"

Rob had been struggling with a question and decided this was finally the time to ask it. "Sylvie, since we've tacitly agreed to be totally honest with each other, I have an issue we need to discuss. Before Francois was killed, I recall numerous situations where he devoted extreme attention to you, in his characteristically French way. That's probably not something he learned as a Camitorian, but rather that he picked up watching how Frenchmen woo ladies.

"But in some of those cases you pretty clearly were pleased by his attention, and in others, as far as I could tell, when you suspected I was watching, you seemed embarrassed, perhaps even to the point of wishing that he hadn't been so exuberant.

"But, even after Francois' death, I have to wonder if I'm on the outside looking in. Had he not been killed would you have chosen him over me? If we now get married, will I forever have to wonder if I really was your second choice? Maybe I'm just showing a bit of jealousy, actually that for sure, but this is something that has been troubling me, so we do need to discuss it. I've hesitated bringing this up, just out of fear for what the answer might be"

Sylvie took his hand. "Rob, I'm not even sure how to answer your question, but I've sensed that it's something that's been troubling you. Up to the time Francois was killed, you and I had spent much more time together, and had shared much more of ourselves than Francois and I had. I really was just getting to know Francois, and by that time I thought of him only as a good friend. I am pretty sure he wanted his and my relationship to evolve far beyond that, he even told me so, but there was no way it could have happened within the time we had.

"My relationship with you has evolved to a depth that his and mine could not have possibly gotten to. Rob, I have never met a man, Camitorian or Earthling, that I could possibly love as much as I love you. There's never even been a close second! Nor have I ever met a man I respected as much as I do you. I doubt if Francois could have gotten to that level of respect, but even if he did, I believe the depth of the relationship you and I have would be difficult for any pair of beings to achieve. Obviously, these are things we will never know, but the depth of our love makes it seem unlikely to me that I could ever be in a relationship with a man that I would prefer to you. I just love you too much for that to happen, my wonderful Robert!"

Rob's expression was changing from concern to euphoria as she spoke, "Oh my god Sylvie, thank you for your reassurances. I don't think this question will arise again. I love you more than I ever thought I could love anyone."

They turned around, headed to a bistro near their apartment, had an early dinner with a couple of glasses of wine, and walked back to their apartment. The reassurances did their job.

Chapter 37. The Airlines

Sylvie fully intended to meet with every student in every school at every level in Paris. This daunting task occupied much of her time and attention, but she so loved the kids, big and little, that she devoted as much of her time as she could to it. Aside from enjoying being with the students, she had two more purposes. First, she wanted to share some of her stories as a Camitorian, and to reassure the children that these aliens were friendly, and they had nothing to fear from them. Second, she wanted to educate them about the safe use of RF devices, especially smartphones and laptops.

However, there was another group that needed to know about the dangers of RFR, and what they could do about it. This was the airline industry.

So, she, Rob, and Linda sent out more invitations, this time to the executives of the world's airlines, suggesting that they meet in Paris to discuss the status of RFRs in the world's airplanes, what medical effects they might have, and if there might be mitigation strategies.

They got back mostly positive responses, with several indicating this was a situation with which they were familiar, since they had at one time limited smartphone usage during flights, but were under pressure from passengers to relax the Wi-Fi limits so they could access the internet. In some cases, the airlines had relented, in others the question was still under consideration. Furthermore, exposure to radiation was not a new issue with them, as flight attendants had raised that with their employers. They were concerned about exposure to a different kind of radiation, that resulting from the cosmic rays that are much more intense at altitudes of several miles than at Earth's surface, where they have been attenuated by Earth's atmosphere.

Cosmic rays are an especially dangerous type of radiation, but the radiation from Wi-Fi was a growing concern.

The trio began the meeting with the usual group of medical experts to go over the highlights of the medical evidence, and to justify the limits set by the Council of Europe. Although those RFR limits were considerably lower than that from the International Commission of Non-Ionizing Radiation Protection (ICNIRP), and accepted by the World Health Organization (WHO), the most forward-thinking nations had adopted those from the Council, especially for children. The medical experts noted that the ICNIRP had been overly selective with the data they considered, apparently so they could produce a limit on RFR that was consistent, more or less, with what the international telecom industry wanted, independent of possible medical consequences.

There were very few questions to the presenters, and none of the skepticism that had prevailed when they met with the auto executives. These people knew about Faraday cages, since that's what airplanes are. However, the point was driven home regarding the effect that two hundred smartphones might produce when enclosed inside a long metallic cylinder. The executives had not given much thought to the stunning level of radiation that would produce. Of course, Sylvie, Linda, and Rob had taken measurements on enough flights on many different airlines to know what those levels could be.

So, the three of them took the stage, with each one presenting a few of their readings. When unlimited smartphone usage was allowed, as in most airlines before takeoff and after landing, the intensities were more than an order of magnitude above the Council of Europe danger level of one-thousand microwatts per square meter. The airlines that didn't permit the phones once the flight was in progress definitely showed much lower RFR levels. However, in some cases, tablets and laptops using on-board Wi-Fi were allowed, and then the levels were still higher than the Council of Europe danger level, although they depended on whether the passenger next to you was using the Wi-Fi.

One executive asked, "So if you're going to recommend that we not allow smartphone usage at all, even pre-flight, many of my passengers will shift their allegiance to some rogue airline that will allow pre-flight calls. Unless, of course, you can impose some laws governing usage that would apply internationally."

Linda had anticipated that question, "Well, we'd prefer that the industry regulate itself, if for no other reason than it would be difficult to achieve agreement from the world's politicians on what restrictions to impose."

That generated considerable laughter from the group.

She continued, "Of course, the medical effects depend on both level and time of the exposure, so perhaps pre-flight usage isn't so bad unless that gets extended for some time because of whatever delays might occur. I don't want to leave you with the thought that pre-flight, and of course, post-flight, usages are okay; those levels are far enough above the Council of Europe limits to be dangerous even for short times. So, our preference would be to ask passengers to make their calls before they board and after they get off."

At that point Rob surmised, "This effect is, as you know, a result of the ability of the metallic enclosure to create incredibly high RF radiation levels when the sources are inside. Even for short times those can be painful to electromagnetically sensitive individuals. I guess the question is to what extent you think you can accommodate those people. These levels will definitely cause a panoply of mostly brain related symptoms in some fraction of your customers."

"So," that executive responded, "perhaps what we should do is survey our passengers under the situations that are currently allowed, say for several months, so that we can get a statistically significant number of responses. We need to tell them what we're doing and the reasons for our efforts. We must determine just what fraction of the airline-using population requires us to consider their special needs."

Another executive spoke up, "If this particularly sensitive group turns out to be significant, we could even prepare special places in the plane where we could create sort of a Faraday cage within a Faraday cage. That is, we could create special reduced radiation bubbles for those folks. They might be something that could be installed quickly if there was one or more persons on board that needed it."

That comment seemed to generate a lot of discussion, mostly supportive but in some cases suggesting that such people could consider some other mode of transportation than an airline.

But there was general agreement that the surveys should be conducted. So at least their decisions would be knowledge based.

Then Linda noted, "Of course, high RF radiation levels in airplanes is not a new problem, or one that is unknown to you. I refer to a report of safetechsolutions.org, submitted in 2015, that details some of the concerns of the airline employees. Perhaps some of your restrictions on Wi-Fi use of your passengers is in response to that report, but the levels still must be far higher than the levels the Council of Europe designated as safe."

One of the executives replied, apparently having discussed this situation with others, "You are correct; some of our regulations do address this problem. But I am hopeful that the surveys we're talking about will give us more information, both as to the extent of the problem, and to what our passengers think they can tolerate."

That seemed to generate murmurs of assent.

Sylvie concluded the meeting with some final remarks, "Please don't forget that letting the smartphones operate even for the few minutes the plane is being boarded and again once the plane has landed does produce dangerous levels of RF radiation. Please do give serious consideration to limiting those effects. They affect all your passengers and flight crew, not just whatever fraction is electromagnetically sensitive. People often don't realize they're being harmed by those radiation levels, but as the doctors who led off this meeting showed, tissue damage and other nasty biological effects are occurring. They'll build up with total exposure time and, therefore, will impact health and life expectancy. We're guessing that keeping your passengers and your flight crews healthy and alive is a high priority for you!"

The executives applauded her comments. Rob thought, *that was certainly the appropriate comment on which to end the meeting.*

"Their post meeting analysis took place in a familiar patisserie. Rob, in his usual post-meeting relaxed state, asked, "Did we have an impact?"

Linda, more relaxed than usual for the meeting postmortem, responded, "These folks do recognize the problem, although perhaps the magnitude of the effects of pre-flight smartphones did stun them a bit. That's good; it really might produce some modifications on their procedures."

Sylvie rubbed her hand across her brow, giving up on the wayward swatch of hair, then added, "I guess I'm an optimist, but my sense from the comments was that they really might do some self-regulating, and that could result in increased passenger protections. I don't think the rogue airlines, mentioned by one person, are really a threat. They wouldn't be competing on international or trans-continental routes."

They all agreed there was hope that real mitigation of RFR might occur for airlines passengers, even if they didn't go along with the measures that produced it.

Chapter 38. Yes

Sylvie and Rob continued to share their optimism over their meeting with the airlines' executives. They were sitting in the comfortable living room chairs of their apartment late one afternoon. They could see the sun shining on the trees of the park outside their window, as well as a few kids actively pursuing the potentials of the playground there. They were discussing how the meeting had gone. "Sylvie, I think the airlines may really make some changes. And if the major airlines people agreed, it wouldn't matter much if the rogues didn't agree with any limits they instituted."

"Right. I feel like we really made some progress. Certainly, the contrast with the auto execs was huge. Of course, the problem is less controllable by them than by the airlines industry."

"Yeah, that's right."

But then his expression turned serious, "But what about us, Sylvie. I feel like we've been so busy with our mission that we've neglected to make progress on our relationship."

She moved from her chair to his and snuggled up to him, "I feel like we have made a lot of progress, Rob. What more would you like for us to have accomplished?" She teased, "Am I not sexy enough for you?"

"God, I can't imagine I could ever be so close to anyone sexier. But, more seriously, we could think about getting married."

She was still in her teasing mode, "But Rob, I've studied how this situation is supposed to proceed for Earthlings. You're supposed to get down on your knee, ask me if I'll marry you, and then, if I say 'yes,' give me an engagement ring."

He arose without saying a word, went to his briefcase, returned, got down on one knee, and asked, "Sylvie, I love you so much that I want for us to be together as long as we both shall live. Will you marry me?"

At that point he opened a small box he had been holding and presented the diamond ring he had purchased just for this occasion.

She gulped, choked back a tear or two of joy, and let him put the ring on her finger. "Yes," she whispered, "I will. I've never wanted anything more than I want for us to be husband and wife."

She took a moment to look at the ring, "Rob, it's beautiful. Where did you find such an artistic design? It's much more elegant than the rings with nothing but the diamond fastened to the ring. I love the swirls that encase the main stone."

After they shared a long kiss, he suggested, "Well then, let's go to our favorite bistro for dinner so you can show off your new ring. I want the world to know that we've decided to get married."

"Okay, Rob. Thank you, Darling. That sounds like a wonderful way to start what I'm sure will be an incredible lifelong celebration."

Chapter 39. Smart Meters

The following morning, Rob and Sylvie took a long time getting out of bed. Finally, as they were sitting at their breakfast table gazing into each other's eyes and slowly ingesting their second cup of coffee, Rob said, "I'm reluctant to get back to our RFR mitigation efforts, following our delightful last evening and romantic start this morning, but perhaps we should. We do, after all, have our lifetime together to continue our celebration.

"Anyway, I've been thinking that we need to do another video, this one on Smart Meters. Are you familiar with these things?"

"I know they're a major concern for people who are electrosensitive. But please give me some details. And why are they even necessary?"

"Well, several of the world's companies that deliver gas and electricity to homes decided they could save money by firing some of their meter readers and replacing the old analog meters with ones that would send out their readings frequently via RF signals to a central location. I don't begrudge the companies trying to be more efficient or to save money, but there's one factor they've ignored in their zeal to increase profits. The Smart Meters are contributing to the plethora of RF signals pervading the environment. Furthermore, the signals are both intense and pulsed.

"The pulsing allows the companies using the Smart Meters to adopt the standard strategy for pulsed device purveyors, that is, advertise that their devices produce a rather minimal average amount of RFR. The pulses are typically one or two milliseconds long, but they're emitted thousands of times per day. The average amount of RFR, which is what the power companies quote when they are lauding their meters, is small, but

237

the spikes that occur when the signals are sent are far above safe levels and, as you know, these pulses can produce entirely new medical issues. At the time the devices were introduced a decade or so ago, few studies had been done of the effects of pulsed radiation. But those that were done since have demonstrated that the pulses can be extremely dangerous.

"Oh, I'm probably telling you things you're completely aware of."

Sylvie laughed. She'd been listening intently, her face developing a serious expression, "Is there no way for customers to avoid this new radiation?"

"Actually, there is, at least to some extent. The companies were met with enough objections when they first began to install Smart Meters that they had to allow their customers to opt out of them, and just keep the old analog ones. The installers were pretty aggressive, but if a customer objected, they could keep their old meter and avoid the pulsed radiation. However, they had to pay a penalty charge to do so.

"Of course, even if you've opted out, you're still subject to the pulses from your neighbors' Smart Meters if you live in close proximity to them. So, you can't evade the pulses entirely unless you can convince your neighbors to opt out also."

"Can't the customers fight that?"

Rob slurped a gulp of coffee, "Actually they can. Of course, as I mentioned, if your neighbors got the Smart Meters you can try to convince them to go back to the old meters. But the companies will charge them. If they didn't think the new ones were a problem in the first place, they're not likely to pay a penalty and revert to the old ones. There are other options, though. One can buy sheets of conducting mesh, either wire or cloth, and hang them between you and your closest neighbor's meter. The meters at the more distant houses won't affect you as much. As we both know, distance is your friend when it comes to all sources of RFR. It's also possible to buy smart meter cages, which provide a shield from the RFR. In fact, I have one of these covering my Smart Meter at my San Francisco condo.

Unfortunately, the medical issues with the Meters are not well known, either because people do not investigate that possibility, or they are not concerned about the effects of RFR."

"So, Rob, how do we proceed? I suppose we could produce a video showing the things you just explained, or we might try to convince the energy companies to change their meters so they emit many less pulses. But that's a question: do they need to emit all those pulses? Presumably changing things after they'd installed so many meters would cost significant amounts of money, and they're not likely to do that."

Rob gave a derisive laugh, "And, of course, the energy companies will always oppose anything that'll affect their bottom lines. Or their executives' salaries."

Sylvie continued, "But I suppose we could cast the video to show what people can do if they can't opt out if, say, they're living in a rented apartment or house, to protect themselves. Presumably the same sorts of shielding you described could at least be used to insulate them from the radiation from their own meters."

"Yes, that's certainly true. And that'd probably be an easier shielding situation, since the radiation from the neighbors' Smart Meter, while less intense, would span a broader area, so would require more shielding material."

Rob shifted forward in his chair, "Sylvie, I just had a thought. We could try to get the energy companies to go along with us but, as you noted, that might be a tough fight. Probably a more obvious way would be to get the FCC to issue a limit on the outputs of the Smart Meters. That would affect both the maximum intensity of the pulses and the frequency at which pulses are emitted. "

"That's a great idea. It could be based on the recent studies that have looked at the medical implications of pulsed RFR." She moved her chair closer to his, leaned her head on his shoulder, and said, "I bet we could get my favorite member of the FCC to introduce some measures that they might pass. Or if they already have some Smart Meter regulations, they can certainly be revisited. Of course, you might have to go back to the US to do that in person. But probably only for a few days. Right?"

"That's a good idea, my Sweet Sylvie. I'll send a note to Linda Forrester suggesting that we investigate Smart Meters and impose some new maximum levels and pulse rates."

"But I've another thought. Why don't you come with me? After I've met with the FCC members, we can get back on a plane and continue on to California. I've been wanting to show you around San Francisco ever since we met."

"Rob, that's a wonderful invitation. I accept! But why don't you go ahead and deal with your FCC business, and I'll follow you a couple of days later."

Chapter 40. Smart Meters and the FCC

Before meeting with the FCC, Rob brought Linda up to speed on his discussion with Sylvie regarding Smart Meters. She responded, "I can see that a new regulation is probably the only way to coerce the energy companies to limit the contribution to the RFR fog from their Smart Meters. It would be nice if they'd see the need for limits, but their whole approach to convincing the public that the meters are a benefit and not a problem leads me to believe that won't happen. So, let's see what the FCC thinks."

All members of the FCC were eager to hear the latest on the medical issues from the radiation from Smart Meters. For completeness, Linda had invited two people who led research groups that looked into medical effects from pulsed radiation at frequencies relevant to those from Smart Meters.

Dr. Maroney, the first presenter, was from a well-known medical school. He ran his fingers through his elegant white mane and began, "I want to distinguish between radiation that, although pulsed, would best be described as being emitted in broad irregular bursts, as opposed to sharp narrow pulses at regular intervals. The first is what you can expect from your smartphone, while the second is what comes from Smart Meters. While there are certainly dangerous medical issues that can result from both, today I'll focus on those from sharply pulsed, regularly spaced electromagnetic radiation. Although there are now a lot of data on both types of radiation, most studies are of one type or the other. Thus, it'd be useful if we could infer what the pulsed effects would be from the burst data and vice versa. So, we have to ask, is that possible?"

"Let me answer my rhetorical question. If the medical effects depended only on the time average of the radiation, life would be much simpler. But that's not the case. It's clear that the medical effects from pulsed radiation depend on the maximum intensity of the pulses and on both their width and frequency of occurrence. So, I'm afraid I don't see any obvious way to relate the effects from the pulsed, burst, and especially from non-pulsed radiation. Those of us doing the research on pulsed radiation have become convinced that we need to have separate data sets for the effects from the two forms of radiation, and that the effects need to be specific to the details of the pulses or bursts. An enormous amount of data now exists on radiation of both types in the BioInitiative 2020 report. More data have been obtained since then, especially on effects relevant to Smart Meters.

"As you probably know, the reason the pulsed data are so important is that the companies that use Smart Meters indicate the radiation levels from the meters as a time average. That's completely irrelevant and in fact, is dangerously misleading. The bottom line is that some of the Smart Meters that are in use can produce serious medical effects, especially if one is in close proximity to it. Specifically, the meter should never be close to a bedroom unless it is shielded.

"Let me give you a point of reference to illustrate how irrelevant average radiation is to Smart Meters. You might ask how encouraged a person condemned to the electric chair would be if he were told that the power jolt he was going to get over about two minutes, if averaged over a day, would only be enough to power a small light bulb."

Dr. Hampton, the other speaker from the medical community, was a researcher and professor at an esteemed university. He noted, "I don't have much to add to what Dr. Maroney said, except to second every one of his points. But I should note that pulsed radiation isn't necessarily bad. It's been used for years to treat various medical maladies. However, it's always been directed at a restricted location in the body and kept away from sensitive organs that don't need the radiation. Furthermore, it's always applied for a short time; never twenty-four/seven. So, when the Smart Meter companies claim that these types of pulses have been used for many years to treat medical conditions, that's true, but it is also irrelevant."

Based on Maroney's and Hampton's testimony, the FCC voted to approve new limits on the magnitude of the pulses from Smart Meters. However, they also suggested requirements for the Meters to emit less frequent pulses.

Linda and Rob were excited to discuss the results of the meeting with Sylvie, but they had to await her arrival in New York. They were planning to meet at a local Starbucks after she arrived but decided to first check the RFR levels. After just a few minutes there, Rob said, "I'm sorry, but we'll have to find another place to discuss our meeting. The Wi-Fi signal here is fogging my poor beleaguered brain. I'm certain it will do the same to Sylvie."

Linda led the way to the door. "Oh Rob, I'm sorry that you're suffering from Starbucks syndrome, but it does affect a lot of people. Once Sylvie arrives, I suspect she'll be too tired to do our meeting postmortem anyway. So, you'll just have to bring her up to date when she's ready for it. You can do that during your time together in the next few days."

Once outside, Rob took a deep breath, "Thanks. I'm feeling much better now."

Linda added, "Unfortunately, we can't control what gets emitted inside public places. And Starbucks has encouraged people to do their internet work there for a long time. But that one did seem especially bad. I'll speak to the manager tomorrow."

Chapter 41. San Francisco

As Sylvie was crossing the Atlantic, she was musing to herself, *I know Rob had to take care of FCC business, so I'm glad to give him a couple of days before I arrive in New York. But I still become apprehensive each time I get on an Earthling airplane. Somehow, I don't have the same faith in their engineering I'd have if the plane were Camitorian. But the Earthling airlines do have good safety records, at least the ones we'll be flying on. Anyway, with San Francisco as the ultimate goal, I can put up with a little angst.*

On her Air France flight she received well wishes from most of the other passengers.

She was greeted by Rob at John F. Kennedy International Airport with passionate hugs and kisses. "Sylvie, welcome back to New York. I've arranged for us to stay the night here, then go on to The City tomorrow morning."

She looked him up and down as if she'd never seen him before, "Rob, I am so happy to see you. This should be a wonderful adventure for us. But what is 'The City?' Is that another name for San Francisco?"

Now he had a chance to return the looks, which he did with enthusiasm. Then he replied, "Right. Folks who live in San Francisco believe it's the only significant city in California. Of course, that's a slight insult to people from San Diego or Los Angeles, but San Franciscans would argue that their city is more European than any other in California, or even in the United States, so that makes it more elegant and sophisticated."

Sylvie was listening intently, her eyes bright, "I can't wait to see it."

Rob continued, "I thought it would be fun to sample some of the sights of New York City in our one night together here, but you're probably tired from your trip, and you've seen most of them when you lived by Central Park. Is that correct?"

"Yes, Rob, both are correct. Thank you for being so considerate. I'd prefer to just crawl into bed with you."

As they were settling in for the night, "Sylvie, I've been thinking we should be setting a date for our wedding. Maybe about five months from when we get back to Paris so you could take the chemicals to alter your DNA right then, and we could be thinking about conceiving as soon as we wanted to after we're married. Or at least as soon thereafter when you're fertile. You said that you could be sure if the changes did what you thought necessary about four months after you took them."

She got a mischievous glint in her eyes, "Maybe we should plan our wedding for soon after we get back to Paris. That should give us the window we need."

"Oh, have you shortened your time estimate for the DNA alterations to be verified?"

"No, Rob. I took the chemicals four months ago, and did the checks I needed to confirm that everything had changed the way it needed to right before I came to New York."

Rob had to take a deep breath, "Oh Sylvie, I love you!" Then he had a sudden inspiration, "Maybe we should get married while we're in San Francisco. Would you like that?"

"I'd love that!" Then she feigned a serious look, "But won't it bother you that I look a little bit green in our wedding picture?"

He didn't need time to think up his response, "Maybe I'll see if I can get some light green makeup so we'll match."

They laughed together and settled in for an extremely warm night.

Their flight west was without incident, at least for them. But not for some of the other passengers on the flight. The passenger sitting across the aisle couldn't avoid watching them. They were obviously communicating, but they weren't talking, at least as far as he could tell. Although there were no sounds passing between them, they were gesturing in ways that confirmed they were communicating somehow. Or occasionally one of them would laugh out loud. Then he noticed that the lady's skin had a light green cast.

Sylvie spent much of her time looking at the scenery outside the airplane window. It was early summer, so she wondered about the green circles on the otherwise brown landscape that dotted the plains states' scene. Rob let her guess a bit before he explained what pivotal irrigation systems were. Then she got especially excited as they crossed the Rocky Mountains, then headed west and south into San Francisco International Airport. However, midway through the flight the Captain had announced over the intercom, "Ladies and Gentlemen, I wish to alert you to the fact that we are honored to have an extremely unusual passenger on board today. You probably know her from her worldwide fame as a visitor to Earth from another planet. And it's my understanding that she's now a permanent resident of Earth. I'm speaking, of course, of Sylvie Sensei."

With that, the entire planeload of passengers burst into applause. Sylvie smiled appreciatively and Rob beamed with pride. During the remainder of the flight many passengers paused by her seat to give her greetings, and to thank her for what she had done for Earthlings. And by the time she and Rob got their suitcases from the baggage claim she had been greeted by hundreds more people. Word travels swiftly.

Rob offered, "Sylvie, I think it's wonderful that you've been so appreciated, although I must say I doubt if anyone even noticed that there was someone in the seat beside you. In fact, several of the people on the plane leaned on me as they reached over me to greet you."

"Am I sensing a hint of jealousy?"

He laughed, "No jealousy, although I could have done without the woman leaning on me who had chocolate on her hand. But I wouldn't change our lives for anything. I love things exactly the way they are!"

And Rob completely forgot to tell Sylvie anything about the FCC meeting.

By the time they reached the Uber that was to take them to Rob's condo, she'd been asked for dozens of autographs. Rob noticed something else in her hand, "Sylvie, you seem to be signing your autograph, then stamping the piece of paper just below your signature. What's the stamp?"

She smiled as she stamped the image of a slightly green smiley face on his hand. "That's incredible. Now I see why everyone laughed as they looked at your autograph."

As they traveled from the airport to Rob's condo, Sylvie remarked, "Rob, what are all those metal boxes on the sides of the poles? Are they small cells? And why are there so many of them; they look like huge metallic barnacles. They appear to be all over The City. Have they been there for a long time?"

"That is exactly what they are. A few years back the San Francisco City Council approved a major installation program for the telecom industry to saturate San Francisco with small cells. The reason you were unsure what they are is that they come in all shapes and sizes. They're also mounted on sides of poles, tops of poles, walls of buildings, and about anywhere else you can think of. As you well know, the goal of the telecom industry is to vastly increase the electromagnetic coverage of the world at the highest 5G frequencies, as well as the lower frequency RFR that is also emitted by those devices, to facilitate much faster data transfer. I know you've seen a variety of the small cells in Paris and New York. Sometimes they're hard to recognize.

"However, there was such an outcry that the closest distance was increased, but many citizens were still being affected. Unfortunately, many of the devices had already been installed, and would later be moved or have their signals turned off or attenuated with a shroud only if the company was sued. But when the FCC lowered the maximum output levels, the telecom companies tried to increase the number of the emitters to compensate. I'm sure you remember the situation with regard to the emitter installed near my place. In some cases, the telecom company that owned it was forced to provide shielding for the home nearest to the RFR device. But, of course, they didn't volunteer that; it only happened if they were sued.

"This whole endeavor has generated considerably more anger than wisdom and has made many enemies out of former friends. It's become pretty ugly."

"That's really tragic, Rob. Especially when what the telecom people are pushing for is really unnecessary. Except to enable things that are also unnecessary!"

But their attitudes became more focused on this issue when, upon entering the condo complex, they discovered that a small committee of Rob's neighbors had formed. One of his friends looked after his condo in his absence, so he had told her when he would be returning, and that Sylvie would be with him. Thus, word had spread that Sylvie Sensei was in town, and the neighbors wanted to enlist her support for their efforts to limit the number of small cells throughout The City. Sylvie was about to say "yes" to whatever they wanted her to do, but Rob interceded, "Folks, Sylvie and I are planning on getting married while we're here, so we wonder if she might make a statement that you could use in promoting your cause instead of becoming as actively involved as you and she might want."

"Oh, how incredibly exciting; congratulations," one of the leaders of the group said. "That would be fine." But now the cat was out of the bag.

Sylvie and Rob interviewed the group members for a few minutes, then she gave them a quote with specifics of what they were trying to accomplish, albeit with some moderation. That was to get all the small cells removed, and Sylvie's statement specified a density of the devices, definitely less than what already existed, but greater than zero. Rob had done his homework from the FCC meeting and knew exactly what the telecom companies needed to get connectivity for basic coverages.

After that interlude, "Okay, Sylvie, let's get unpacked and make our plans to get married!"

"I can go along with that!"

Rob located a Justice of the Peace and made an appointment for the following afternoon. They didn't need any witnesses; they could always be found around the JP's office, so they were assured two such Earthlings could be supplied.

Rob called one of his favorite restaurants for a reservation for that evening. They didn't really have room, but because Rob was such a frequent customer, they created a space for them.

They took a few minutes to appreciate the view from Rob's condo. It was high on one of San Francisco's hills, and overlooked the Bay, which was replete with sailboats. The condo was decorated with paintings of modern art, and the furniture was basic IKEA. But the view from the window was so stunning that it would dominate anyone's perception of the place. Rob sat on a sofa that faced the window, and she snuggled next to him, as they enjoyed the view and sipped a glass of wine. Sylvie commented, "I believe I could stay like this forever. This is the most beautiful setting I've seen since I left Camitor. It may even be even more lovely than anything I ever experienced in my pre-Earthling life."

Rob replied, "I bought this place just because the view out the window was so incredible. But it was never so beautiful as it is now that you're a part of it.

They kissed, then slowly rose and headed to the restaurant for dinner. It definitely met expectations. Their romantic dinner ended all too soon, even though they were one of the last diners to leave. As they headed back to the condo for a much-needed night's sleep, Rob grasped Sylvie's hand, "This is our last night together as unmarried man and woman."

When their heads hit their pillows, both fell into a deep sleep, punctuated by occasional celestial dreams.

As they were having what little breakfast Rob could offer, Sylvie commented, "Rob, I find that the radiation levels in your condo are extremely good. Apparently, the shielding you had installed really helped. What exactly did you do?"

"I'm pleased you noticed the effect. I found that shielding paint that would knock out about ninety percent of the radiation that hits it. It's black, so it doesn't make for a very pretty paint job, but one can cover all the walls and ceiling with it, then paint over that with whatever color you want. Of course, you need to remove all Wi-Fi devices, or the shielding will make things much worse!"

"Wow—that's terrific. I didn't know about that, although I suppose I should have realized that some clever Earthling would figure out how to create shielding paint."

The following morning, they dressed quickly and headed for Rob's favorite jewelry store. They needed to buy wedding rings. The jeweler was stunned when he realized who he was providing wedding rings for. They grabbed lunch at a deli, then headed back to the condo to dress for their wedding. Rob called for an Uber, and they headed for the JP's office. Sylvie wore the peach-colored dress Rob had bought for her in Paris, and he wore a suit. And a peach-colored tie to match Sylvie's dress. Rob had made the reservation under his name, but when he and Sylvie showed up, there were immediately dozens of volunteers to be their witnesses, virtually everyone on that floor of the building. So, their wedding ended up being attended by a far greater crowd than they intended. Indeed, it overflowed the JP's meeting room.

The JP began the ceremony by asking for Sensei's autograph and laughed when she also applied her smiley face. Then he read through the required lines. At the end, Rob and Sylvie kissed and exchange their rings, amid cheers from everyone there. And the onlookers provided far more signatures crowding on the line for witnesses than usually occurs. The number of selfies taken surely exceeded whatever the previous record was. Probably by a huge factor.

But then the JP ordered everyone back to work, and told Sylvie and Rob that he hoped they could find a quiet place to spend the rest of the day. Rob had anticipated the interest in Sylvie Sensei's wedding, so had arranged for a caterer to bring their dinner to them in a secluded spot in Golden Gate Park. Sylvie put on a shawl to cover her head as well as possible, and they commandeered an Uber to take them there. The driver kept looking in the rear-view mirror, and as they exited his car, he gave his well wishes to Sylvie Sensei. Rob tipped him one-hundred dollars and asked him not to tell anyone where he had taken them.

All went well, with champagne, filet mignon for Rob and a stuffed portobello mushroom for Sylvie, and a Rockpile zinfandel, until a teenaged couple showed up, obviously well aware of the secluded spot. They said, almost in unison, "Yo, you're Sylvie Sensei? We've heard of you. What an incredible bit of luck to find you in like our favorite place in the park."

That was the end of the social banter. The discussion quickly evolved to "How much longer will you be here?"

Rob said, quietly, to Sylvie, "I think that is our invitation to leave!"

He answered, "Just long enough for an Uber to get here."

As they walked to their Uber, the young couple was already settling into their evening's endeavors.

But once back in Rob's condo they could shut out the rest of the world. And they did.

The next morning they lounged in bed for much longer than usual, each enjoying the other's newly married body. Finally, they dressed, got a quick breakfast from Rob's sparsely supplied kitchen, got into his car, and headed north.

Sylvie exclaimed, "So this is the Golden Gate Bridge. I've seen many pictures of it, but it's far more beautiful than I could ever have imagined." They drove up to Mount Tamalpais and enjoyed the scenery from its peak. Their meager breakfasts had left them quite hungry, so Rob drove back to Marin where they grabbed a lunch.

Sylvie could hardly contain her excitement at all the sites, but she wanted more. "Rob, I'd like to see all of San Francisco." So, he drove them around The City, down to Fisherman's Wharf, walking out on one of the piers to see the sea lions. Sylvie's eyes were wide with wonder, "Oh, what are those fat, sleek creatures? I've never seen anything like them before."

"Those are sea lions, and they're a staple of this wharf." She continued to walk around for a better view but was continuously interrupted as she was recognized by virtually everyone there. They finally went back to the car to tour some of the major buildings. Rob had made an early dinner reservation, so they settled down for an evening of wining and dining.

"I remember that you really liked the Pouilly Fuisse we had in New York, but you must try a California chardonnay. Our state produces some outstanding wines, as good as any in the world. So, I've ordered one from Hartford Winery, an exclusive California vintners, for you to compare to the Pouilly Fuisse."

She tried a few sips of the Pouilly Fuisse, which produced her wonderful smile. "But you mustn't drink the whole bottle before you try this one." He asked the waiter for a second glass for her and poured a generous taste of the Hartford chardonnay into it. Rob made an effort to see which wine produced a wider smile but was unable to do so. She drank all of that glass, then asked him to pour a bit more of the French wine.

"Rob, I simply can't tell which one I like better. They're both wonderful. I believe I'll just alternate sips of them all evening." She giggled, "They won't make me tipsy, will they?"

Chapter 42. Celebrations

Sylvie and Rob had planned to have their own private wedding celebration, which would continue through the next two weeks, since Rob had then planned for them to honeymoon in France. But the first part of that plan was not to be. San Francisco was not likely to let as auspicious an event as the Earth's first interplanetary wedding go uncelebrated, regardless of what the happy couple wanted. Somehow word had gotten out that the outdoor celebration would begin around five o'clock. Despite the total absence of advance planning, thousands of celebrants lined the street in front of Rob's condo, snarling traffic for blocks. A band had volunteered its services, and several area vintners quickly arranged booths to sell their products, despite their lack of licenses to do so there. Local brewers also managed to set up booths for those more inclined to beer than wine.

The celebrants had forgotten one item: to inform the police that there was going to be a huge traffic blockage. When the event began, the Chief of Police was heard to mutter, "We should arrest all of them, but where the hell would we put ten thousand people. We could just arrest the people selling booze, but I doubt if the local citizenry would let us get anywhere near the booths to enforce the law. If we tried to do that, we could have a revolution on our hands.

"Oh, what the hell. Enjoy the party. It isn't every day that an Earthling-alien wedding occurs anywhere, let alone San Francisco."

Sylvie and Rob appeared on the balcony of their condo and were greeted with a roar from the crowd. To shouts of "KISS HER," Rob obliged. Sylvie was a bit shocked, but quickly concluded that she shouldn't try to circumvent Earthling customs, so she kissed him back. The crowd screamed its approval.

Having achieved such success, everyone went back to their partying. Party animals have their priorities, after all.

After they were back inside, Rob cautioned, "I'm sure that the Parisians are going to want to celebrate our wedding also. And I don't think they will let the San Franciscans out do them."

"I don't see how they could create any better celebration than the one we just had."

"Trust me; they'll certainly give it their best shot."

When they arrived at Charles de Gaulle International airport the next day, Rob had planned to take a train into Paris, and then to their apartment. That was not going to happen. They were met at the luggage claim by several people dressed in festive clothes, who handed them glasses of champagne, and instructed them to get into their limo as soon as they got their luggage. That was not the only limo, however. It was one of ten that took them into the city in a parade, two of which even contained gendarmes. Then, of course, down the Champs Elysees, amid thousands of cheering Parisians.

Sylvie, with a huge smile, asked, "Rob, are these people cheering for us? Why? We just got married. Lots of people do that. Why are they making such a big deal out of this just for us?"

Rob, also bearing a smile, "Sylvie, I must inform you that this isn't for 'us.' It's for you, my darling wife. Well, perhaps I played a minor role to create the festive mood, having stood in to become your husband, but I could have married anyone else in the world to considerably less fanfare. I repeat, this is for you!"

"Oh, Rob, I love you. These past few days have been absolutely incredible."

Despite their exhaustion, they were taken to a park that had a huge tent with thousands more celebrants milling about, all consuming champagne, and every so often taking up chants of Sylvie, Sylvie. And they undoubtedly shattered the record of the number of selfies set just a couple of days earlier.

Rob noted to her, "See? No chants of Rob, Rob. This party has been designed because of you. And maybe just a little bit, because you chose to marry an Earthling, my Love! But I'm surely not complaining. You've made your Earthling very happy!"

Finally, they were allowed to go back to their apartment, where both collapsed from exhaustion and the considerable amount of champagne they had consumed. Indeed, it was several days before they really became fully functional again. Then they embarked on a week-long tour of the French countryside, staying at wonderful out of the way spots Rob had arranged.

But not so out of the way that they weren't recognized; that wouldn't have been possible!

Chapter 43. Sensei to Russia

Sylvie had been dreading what she knew she must face: outing the Camitorians in Beijing and Moscow. She had been receiving many messages from Igor Vivanovich, the leader of the Moscow group, and Bai Xinyang, the leader in Beijing, describing the pressure the Camitorians in both cities were receiving from their children to make it known they were aliens. That meant they were tired of having to paint themselves to hide their greenness. The concern, of course, was the risk all of the Camitorians might face if their heritage became known.

So, one morning after three cups of coffee, she began the discussion. "Rob, I'm not sure how to proceed. I guess I need to visit Moscow again, and then Beijing, with hope that I can influence their respective government's feelings toward Camitorians. I'm not sure how much influence I can have. Even if that's a possibility, will it be enough to mitigate the two governments' potential negativities toward our Camitorians in those places?"

She smiled, "By the way, I presume you noticed that I'm referring to 'our' Camitorians in such a way as to include you. You're now a Camitorian by marriage."

Rob smiled, "I'll happily accept my dual citizenship!" He ran his fingers through his not yet combed hair, "But you raise an interesting question, and it's difficult to know the answer in either case. At the same time, though, I think you underrate the influence you might have. For example, you've told me that Francois discussed with you how, in Russia, the government has imposed strict limits on the amount of RFR exposure to their children, and more recently, on the populace in general. And you confirmed that with your previous visit. They surely know where you stand on these matters, and you might even be able to help them support their newest legislative efforts.

"Given that the general attitudes with regard to RFR in Russia are apparently better aligned with yours, I would suggest you revisit that country, then go to Beijing."

"Sounds like a plan, Rob. I'll write a letter to Comrade Kolznitsky, the Russian Minister of Education, to propose a visit, and perhaps even suggest some things I might do to support their efforts. I met with him before when I visited Moscow, and he was reasonably civil. But at that time not even Igor Vivanovich had been outed, although I suspected Kolznitsky knew he, and probably a lot of others, were aliens."

"It could be a problem when the existence of the aliens becomes official. Will you be okay? Do you want me to go with you?"

"No, Rob, not this time. I think I can handle this myself. I know you have your hands full with your company's projects and your upcoming FCC meeting."

"Okay. It's taken longer than I had hoped to make a decision on our next effort, so I guess it would be best if I stayed in easy communication with my managers. And the FCC is starting to consider requests from the telecoms for 6G authorizations. This should be interesting!

"But good luck with the Russians!"

Dr. Kolznitsky stood before Vladimir Putin in his office, shifting from foot to foot, with beads of sweat forming on his forehead, "Comrade Putin, I have a letter here from Sylvie Sensei, the leader of a group of aliens, and she is proposing to visit Moscow, and to give a TV address. That there may be many thousands like her inhabiting Earth is in itself worrisome, especially because there appear to be about one thousand of them living in Moscow. You recall nearly two years ago there was a landing of two alien spaceships in Moscow, as well as in some other cities on the planet. It wasn't clear how many aliens actually landed in Moscow at that time, but we've been able to intercept their communications and, from those, we've arrived at the one thousand number. Presumably there are a comparable number living in the other nine cities in which their spaceships landed. They appear to be living peacefully among our people, and don't, as far as we can tell, have any nefarious aims.

"However, that's uncertain because they don't talk to each other using any language we've ever heard before. I guess that's not surprising, but what's unusual is they appear to communicate with each other via their brain waves. Since the signals from these communications are faint, we've not been able to intercept all of them. Furthermore, we haven't been able to make any sense of the signals we've gotten from them. Deciphering is not yet possible.

"I should note that they're all trying to masquerade as Earthlings. Apparently, judging from the appearance of Sensei, their skin is light green, which would immediately identify them. However, maybe some have a paler version of green, or perhaps it's even a greenish tan. After all, humans' skin varies greatly from country to country. In any event, they are not easily identifiable."

Putin, always able to come up with a practical solution, fixed his steely smile on Kolznitsky and asked, "Maybe they're hiding their true nature because they're planning something threatening to Earthlings, but just haven't gotten around to attacking us yet. Can't we just round them up and make them disappear? Certainly, one thousand less people in Moscow will never be noticed. But, if they're aliens, maybe they're difficult to kill. Might that be the case?"

"Well, I don't know about that. But there's another aspect of Sylvie Sensei that's relevant. She's been a strong worldwide proponent of limiting electromagnetic radiation. She's had a great impact on the world's aims in this regard, and even visited Moscow once, and gave much support to our efforts. In her proposed visit she suggests lending support to our plans to impose new limits on the electromagnetic radiation emitters throughout Mother Russia."

Putin asked, "Would that have any effect on the feelings of Russians? Has anyone in our country ever heard of her? Surely if she appeared on Russian TV, speaking in whatever language she is fluent in, that wouldn't sway any Russian opinions."

"Actually, Comrade Putin, she really does have worldwide recognition. Furthermore, I suspect that many Russians have heard of her, and share much of the same respect for her that the rest of the world seems to harbor. Finally, she speaks fluent Russian, or for that matter, any other language she needs to speak at the moment. I can confirm that."

"Well, then, I guess we have nothing to lose by letting her address the Russian people on our TV. I hope she isn't deceiving us and will suddenly start pushing for insurrection. But if she even gives a hint of that we'll simply terminate the show. And probably her as well!"

Her TV address lauded Russia for its efforts to limit the electromagnetic radiation to which Russian people were exposed. She also managed to throw in a few of the things the Camitorians had done to improve Earthling life, especially in recognizing that excessive RF radiation was the cause of the enhanced death rates for many ordinary diseases, and then pressuring the world's governments that had not recognized this problem to reduce their RF levels and, therefore, mitigate that threat.

Putin was stunned when he learned that Sensei's address was watched by more viewers than any program that had ever been shown on Russian TV. By a large factor. That included every sporting event, and certainly included every speech he had ever given. *If she were to stay in Russia, I'd have to have her vanish. Otherwise, she'd be much too great a political threat. I guess that doesn't apply to any of the other aliens, though. I'll just let them continue to exist unless they become too popular. In any event, she did lend strong support to some of my programs. That's got to be a good thing!*

Over a thousand cheering Russians greeted her as she emerged from the TV studio. As she got into her limo and headed for the airport, many more lined the road, not wanting to miss seeing this world-famous celebrity, and cheering their appreciation for what she had done for humanity. Igor Vivanovich rode with her, appearing without his makeup for the first time. Sylvie noted occasional other light green faces in the crowds. Apparently, the Moscow Camitorians were following Igor's lead, deciding it would no longer be dangerous for them to make their origin known. Or if it was, they'd just have to figure out how to deal with it.

"Well, Igor," she said, "I hope you and the others who have emerged from their closets are truly safe without your makeup. I suspect the Russian intelligence has a pretty good idea who all our Camitorians are anyway, so I'm not sure any aspects of your safety will change. Only, hopefully, social acceptance."

Igor was smiling, "I agree with that, except that I think social acceptance will also no longer be a problem. I think you've taken care of that with your address. Many Russians have made a special effort to contact me following your talk to say how much they respect what we've done for Russians and for the rest of the world. You've had a huge impact."

Chapter 44. Decompression

Rob met Sylvie at Charles de Gaulle International Airport. After a big hug and a kiss, "Oh Rob, it is so good to be back with you. I must say I didn't ever feel threatened in Moscow, but there was a tension all the time I was there that has not existed anywhere else, even in the United States."

"I really missed you too, even though it was only for two days. I felt the anxiety also. However, I think you really did make life much more bearable for your fellow Camitorians in Russia."

She took a deep breath, "Rob, I need to decompress from that trip. Let's postpone the China trip for a bit. I'll have to placate Bai Xinyang for a while longer. He won't be happy, but I'm just not up to another trip like the one to Russia, and I think the one to China will be even more contentious. And more complicated; I need to figure out how to make it easy and acceptable for our Beijing Camitorians to skip their makeup. It was difficult enough selecting one thousand Camitorians who had the basic facial characteristics of the Chinese. Of course, we had similar problems selecting the one thousand Camitorians who went to Tokyo, and another one thousand to Seoul. And they're also green, which complicates things for them. All the other places were easier for us to acclimate."

"Agreed on the hiatus. We can continue to think about strategies. But let's take it easy for a week or two. You can visit some schools."

Her expression of concern changed to her smile, "That's a terrific idea!"

As the date for Sylvie's China trip approached, over breakfast during their daily morning coffee, elbows resting on the kitchen table and a worried expression on her face, Sylvie said,

"Rob, we need to have a more detailed discussion about my visit to China. Although I thought that a week or two visiting the French classrooms would redirect my background thoughts from China and reduce my anxiety, that hasn't happened."

"Well, perhaps we need to expand our two-person brain trust to include Linda. Would that be useful?"

"Excellent suggestion. I'll contact her and see if she can join us to discuss this problem. We could do a Zoom meeting, or perhaps she'd like to visit France again."

Upon receiving Sylvie's query, Linda replied, "I'd love to visit Paris again, and you've given me the perfect excuse. It's been at least two months since I was there. That's much too long! I'll send you my dates, and perhaps you can arrange a hotel room for me for a few days. In the meantime, I'll be thinking about the China situation.

Sylvie asked her secretary to arrange for Linda's room. When her plane arrived, Rob and Sylvie met her and, since the French Security seemed to have concluded that Sylvie was no longer in danger, had to summon an Uber to take them to the hotel. The conversation between the three of them on the way was non-stop, as Linda brought them up to date on her efforts with the FCC during Rob's absence, and of the status of the telecom companies' accommodation to the new limits imposed on RFR levels. Sylvie talked about her trip to Russia, and Linda listened intently.

When they got back to Sylvie's apartment, Linda put the discussion back on track, "But, since we're supposed to be brainstorming about Sylvie's pending trip to China, let me offer some thoughts. My understanding is that the situation there is profoundly different from what it was in Russia. The Russians have placed strict limits on RFR levels, whereas the Chinese situation is more complicated. You had an immediate positive connection with the Russians, but that'll probably not be the case with the Chinese authorities. Given that, will it ever be safe for Camitorians to show their light green faces in Beijing?

"I presume that you have interacted with the lead Camitorian in Beijing about this?"

Sylvie replied, "Yes, I've had many interactions with him, mostly about how to mitigate the Camitorians' fear about coming out of their closets. Also, how to ensure they'll not become targets of the Chinese authorities, who must know about most of them from their communications. We've dealt with some other issues too, such as the headaches, brain fog, and other symptoms the Chinese face from the RFR. The Chinese are tight lipped about increases in the illnesses that we found were related to the high radiation levels that occur near the RFR emitters, so it's difficult to talk about how we might decrease those harmful effects."

She developed a concerned look, "But the discussions with Bai Xinyang have dwindled down the past two months or so. I'm not sure why that would occur, but it also seems as if the things we're most concerned about are no longer issues. I've sent him several messages, but all I get back is a message that he is too busy to talk right now, but everything is okay. I don't know what that means. I hope the Chinese authorities haven't found a way to block his messages or, even worse, that he's been incarcerated."

Rob interjected, "I guess that's what your visit will find out as long as it doesn't get you an adjacent jail cell. But that still doesn't solve the problem of how to make it comfortable for the Camitorians to stop impersonating Earthlings."

After considerably more discussion Sylvie concluded, after a quick swipe across her forehead to rearrange the rogue swatch of hair, "As Rob said, I'll just have to answer a lot of questions in my trip to Beijing that cannot be answered any other way. I've another week of visits to schools scheduled, and then I'll just have to, as Earthlings say, bite the bullet. I hope this trip doesn't involve any more bullets; I've had enough of those."

She didn't enjoy her classroom visits as much during that week as she had previously. She had too much on her mind in anticipation of her forthcoming trip.

Chapter 45. Off to Beijing

Sylvie finally sent a message to Bai Xinyang, telling him she wished to visit Beijing, giving her dates, and requesting that he arrange for her to visit at least two Chinese schools. She did get back an enthusiastic confirmation from him. Her flight itself was not stressful, but she was so tied up in knots worrying about what she was about to learn that she was unable to relax. She was met at Beijing Capital International Airport by Bai and was immediately stunned by his appearance.

"Xinyang," she noted with a concerned look, "I see that you're wearing head gear that, I presume, buffers you from the RF radiation levels that exist in China. And I also note that you've given up on the makeup that would hide the fact that you're a Camitorian. Aren't you concerned that both of these will make it obvious that you're an alien?"

He was sporting a large smile, "You've immediately perceived some of the changes that have occurred in Beijing in the past couple of months, and I'm sure you'll see more evidence of these in our taxi ride from the airport to your hotel. These are the most important things we need to discuss, but there are others I've instituted that we'll also need to talk about, and which I hope will gain your approval."

"My goodness, Xinyang, that sounds ominous. Can you give me some hints as to their nature?"

"Oh, I'd appreciate it if you'd just enjoy what you see on the way into the city, aside from the smog. We can discuss the other issues after you've rested a bit, had dinner and breakfast, and we've gotten together tomorrow for our discussions."

What on earth is he hiding from me?

As the taxi sped toward the city, Sylvie had two impressions: the myriad of huge buildings, and the gloom of the enveloping pollution. But once inside the cloud of the city's smoke, somehow it didn't seem quite so oppressive. However, she was quite amazed by two other things she observed as they got into the city. "Xinyang, it appears that a lot of the people I'm seeing are wearing head gear similar to yours. Are these shields that protect their brains from the RF radiation in Beijing?"

"Yes, that would be correct. The head gear has become very popular just in the past two months. They are plastic with embedded metallic fibers, so they are light but effective shields. And you also see that they come in a variety of colors and designs, all of which seem to be popular with the Chinese people."

"That's amazing. The Chinese authorities have set very reasonable ambient RF radiation levels, but they'll obviously be higher near the emitters. Presumably, though, the people have decided they can tolerate the radiation levels they might encounter anywhere, whether near a tower or anywhere else, if they wear the head gear."

Xinyang now had a huge smile on his face, "That's correct, Sylvie. This truly represents a revolution, although the head gear at this point has only become a best seller in the cities."

Sylvie wasn't ready to ignore her concerns, "But I'm seeing something else that surprises me. I've noticed a tiny number of faces that are light green. These must be Camitorians who decided to forego their alien-disguising makeup. Aren't they concerned that identification could be dangerous for them?"

"That is also correct, Sylvie. Very few of our Camitorians use the makeup to disguise their heritage anymore. Their safety is no longer an issue."

"Xinyang, how can that be? You were so concerned about that two months ago. What's happened in the meantime?"

Xinyang didn't even try to suppress his smile, "That'll be the subject of our discussions tomorrow morning. You'll have to wait until then to find out. I don't want to spill the beans yet."

At that point they arrived at Sylvie's hotel. It was ornate, at a level that was emphasized to her when they sat down for dinner, and she saw the wine list. "Xinyang, this is an incredibly elegant hotel. Are you sure we can afford this? I've generally been treated very nicely, but I'm not accustomed to such elegance."

Another big smile, "Sylvie, yes, we can afford such accommodations, especially for your visit. And how that's come about will also become obvious tomorrow morning."

Sylvie slept fitfully, partly because she had overeaten of the delicious dinner and had consumed more wine than she was accustomed to, but also because of the questions that lurked in her mind regarding all the things Xinyang had promised to tell her. She had a wonderful breakfast at her hotel's buffet, following which Xinyang met her in his car, a large Mercedes sedan, to take her to the place where they would have their meeting.

"Xinyang, I've not had much opportunity to learn about cars, but I suspect this is a very expensive one. I hate to keep asking you about expenses, but isn't this overdoing things a bit?"

The smile continued, "Not a problem, Sylvie. This isn't my car, but rather is owned by my company. And that's where we are headed for our meeting this morning."

Xinyang drove into an underground garage in a twenty-story building. As he parked the car, he told her that it was the corporate headquarters of his company. They took an elevator to the top floor, where he led the way to a conference room. It had huge windows overlooking the buildings that dominate Beijing's skyscape. The room's furnishings were elegant, with plush upholstered chairs and a huge oval conference table. Several scrolls of Chinese painting and calligraphy decorated the walls.

Sylvie was allowed to admire the general features of the room for a few minutes. Then they were joined by the president of the company, Mr. Lee Jiechi. After the introductions, and some coffee, Mr. Lee said, "It's an honor for me to meet the leader of the Camitorians. We're delighted to welcome all of you to our city. And, of course, to have Xinyang as one of our employees. In his interview we were impressed with his quick mind and excellent insights, so we hired him at a mid-level position. However, his incredible skills have led to his rise in three-months to Vice-President. Not all of our employees were pleased to see his promotions occur over theirs, but they also are so awe-struck by his wisdom and cleverness that they have accepted the appropriateness of his new status."

Sylvie had found it difficult to get the intonations of Chinese correct, so Xinyang was translating by thinking the translation of Mr. Lee's Chinese into Camitorian. This allowed Sylvie to get his message essentially in real time. Her mouth was slightly agape as Mr. Lee spoke. *Vice-President? Is this what Xinyang wasn't telling me about last evening? But what did he do that got him promoted to such a high level so quickly?*

Anyway, I guess this explains the company car. Maybe even the elegant hotel!

Mr. Lee continued, with a pleased smile on his face, "As I believe you are aware, China has pushed electronic connectivity to an extremely high level. This created some problems, most notably, the plethora of brain related issues. These were created by the high levels of electromagnetic radiation near transmission facilities, of which I'm told you are very much aware. The emitters are very frequent in China, as that is needed to overcome the low radiation levels set by our government. What Xinyang did was point out to us that he wore a metallic helmet to shield his brain. He also suggested that my company might consider producing and marketing lightweight plastic helmets with embedded metallic fibers to the Chinese. The helmets include speakers that connect to the owner's communication device and to an antenna that's external to the helmet. We've named these Pro-Tects. They were an easy thing for us to produce with only modest design work. But we doubted if people would like the thing around their heads until Xinyang suggested that we paint them in many colors.

"What happened next couldn't have been anticipated by even the most optimistic marketing people. The Pro-Tects are certainly a hit, since they reduce the brain related issues by a large factor. Furthermore, their variations of designs have produced an enormously popular fashion trend that features different shapes and colors, as well as flowers, Kanji characters, and inscriptions in English. Our company doesn't produce those, but our Pro-Tects have spawned quite a number of small businesses that do the additional designs, and employ quite a few Camitorians, all of whom seem to be quite creative.

"Needless to say, the citizens of Beijing are grateful to have your Camitorians in our city. They have contributed considerably to the quality of our lives, adding an artistic sense that at the same time solves a significant medical problem. And we are delighted to have you visit so we can show you what your planet's men and women have done for us."

Sylvie was finally able to respond, "Mr. Lee, I appreciate your description of what's transpired, and Xinyang's role in the developments. And I now understand why the Camitorians in Beijing have been able to forego their disguises. But I wonder how this will play out over the rest of China. Perhaps Chinese people in other places will not feel the same sense of gratitude."

Mr. Lee rubbed his chin for a moment, "That's an interesting question, but one that I believe we can address. If the Camitorians took it upon themselves to travel to other cities without their makeup, they might have problems. Xinyang and I have discussed this with our marketing people, and we're planning to market our Pro-Tects in all the large population areas of China. We'll include Xinyang in our advertisements to be sure that everyone recognizes the contributions he and the other Camitorians have played. We sincerely hope this will alleviate any discriminatory problems, at least in the Chinese cities."

During the discussion, Xinyang sat comfortably in his chair with a huge smile.

Xinyang and Mr. Lee also arranged for a presentation by the marketing people to show what they were planning. Sylvie was delighted with what she saw. She exclaimed, "I don't think it could be any better if we designed it ourselves."

Mr. Lee commented, "Well, some of your people were very much involved in creating the presentation. So, you did design it yourselves!"

Everyone laughed.

Mr. Lee joined Xinyang and Sylvie for lunch, which was held in a private room of a formal restaurant. Sylvie had one more issue she wanted to raise,

"Mr. Lee, you mentioned the medical problems resulting from electromagnetic radiation. Perhaps we can follow up on that a bit. Medical evidence has shown that problems can result from electromagnetic radiation on an unshielded brain, but also on an unshielded body. So, I'm wondering if the death rates from heart attacks, diabetes, cancer, and strokes have decreased back to what they were before the ramp up of the electromagnetic radiation over the past few years, or if there's still some way to go."

As Sylvie was posing her question, Xinyang tried to send her a brain-to-brain message to tell her this was a sensitive topic, but to no avail. Mr. Lee stroked his chin for a few seconds, then replied, "Ms. Sensei, this is an interesting question, but one to which we do not have answers. The Chinese government has not indicated that there is a remaining problem after the head coverings, but those have really been applied only to Beijing, and so we don't know yet if there's a remaining problem. The citizens are no longer complaining about the effects of the radiation in Beijing, so perhaps the problem has been solved."

She replied, with Xinyang now shaking his head 'no,' again failing to communicate his concern, "The Pro-Tects certainly solved the problem with the brain associated issues, but I'm concerned that other medical problems are occurring in unshielded parts of people's bodies. This has been shown to occur in medical studies on radiofrequency radiation. So, I wonder if the Chinese might consider reducing their EM radiation levels further, and that along with the Pro-Tects, might solve not only the brain related concerns, but the other medical issues as well."

Lee replied in a less friendly voice than he had used previously, "If there are other medical effects from the radiation, some other solution than reducing the radiation levels will have to be found. I suppose we might consider promoting clothing with metallic fibers. But I don't believe the Chinese government would consider reducing the levels of the radiation. We believe we must develop interconnectivity to as great an extent as possible, and those levels are already among the lowest in the world."

Sylvie wanted to pursue the issue a bit more, but finally got the signal from Xinyang that she had pushed it as far as was going to be socially acceptable. Maybe even a bit beyond that point. So, she dropped further discussion of it.

Following lunch, Xinyang had arranged for her to visit two schools in Beijing. Those went about as they had everywhere else, with the children asking questions about her origins and some of the details about the Camitorians in China. Of course, Xinyang translated. Nothing about Earthling boyfriends, though!

Later that afternoon, in the ride to the airport, she returned to the shielding issue. "I'm sorry I missed your signals at lunch, but I might have pushed for that discussion anyway. I fear that the Chinese have only solved a fraction of the problem. On the other hand, I suppose metallic threads in the clothing really might address the effects of radiation on the rest of the body. Such clothing, including underwear, jackets, and virtually anything you can think of, is already on the market. Any thoughts on that?"

Xinyang quickly replied, "Mr. Lee made an interesting suggestion, and it might mitigate other medical issues, even at the current radiation levels. Pushing for reducing the levels would run afoul of the Chinese government, and then the acceptability of Camitorians might be endangered. So that is much too risky.

"However, let me pursue the business of the shielding in the clothing. It might not work for all clothing; I can imagine swimsuits with metallic threads might not hold up so well. I've already investigated this to some extent and have found the durability issue to be a problem with many of the items.

"But the Chinese are ingenious, and I wouldn't be surprised if we can figure out a way to improve the number of washings the items can sustain. I'd also bet that we can improve the stylishness of all of the items, even including underwear."

Sylvie couldn't entirely suppress her smile.

"I agree, Xinyang. You should pursue that with Mr. Lee. If you come up with any more brilliant ideas he just might resign as President and give the job to you."

He laughed.

"By the way," she added, "I certainly approve of the way you have succeeded. Good going!"

Sylvie's flight back to Paris was as uneventful as the flight to Beijing, but she was relieved by what she had learned there so she was more at ease. *My main concern before my visit, the social acceptability of the Camitorians in Beijing, is no longer an issue. And it appears that Mr. Lee does plan to extend it to many other areas. Of course, that could be damaged by events over which Xinyang has no control, but he's clearly a coper. With impressive success! I can't object to Camitorians succeeding, even to the point of becoming wealthy. And Xinyang might be able to help the Chinese even more with his metallic threaded clothing line*

As she leaned back a bit in her airplane seat, she was grateful that she, Rob, and Linda had raised the possibility with the airlines executives of having shielded pockets on the planes to accommodate especially RFR sensitive people. She hoped they'd quickly install such conveniences. But she'd learned to deal with the problem; her metal fiber infused clothing made it possible for her to get some sleep on the long flight home.

Chapter 46. Role Models

Linda decided she needed a first-hand account of how Sylvie's visits were going. So, she and Rob went to Charles de Gaulle International Airport to meet Sylvie, who spent ten minutes at the baggage claim summarizing what she had learned in Beijing. She especially raved about what Bai Xinyang had achieved just by using his ingenuity to create an essential product, and how that was able to produce a completely unanticipated level of acceptance of the Camitorians in Beijing.

"That's incredible, Sylvie," Rob exclaimed. "I wonder if you could use Bai as an example to show how much approval of Camitorians can be affected when they team up with Earthling companies to help them achieve economic success. Bai and his company did solve a huge problem, after all. Might that same sort of concept work in other countries?"

Sylvie responded, "That's the sort of thing we'd hoped would enable our acceptance when we pushed for limiting RFR. And it did immediately solve the short-term brain related issues and, perhaps, other physiological problems caused by the pervasive RFR in China. However, there is much work to be done. Xinyang's headgear may not have completely solved the problem. There may be additional pieces to the Chinese medical issues puzzle. Shielding of more than just the brain may be required. Furthermore, the head shielding has to be applied throughout the country. Finally, not everyone will be able to afford the fixes, especially when they are packaged in designer colors."

"But" Linda added, "back to the positive side, remember what happened in Japan. Through essentially no fault of their own, the Camitorians started a fashion revolution. That's about as positive a bang for the acceptance buck as one could ever hope for."

Sylvie spotted her bag on the carousel and Rob grabbed it. Then she summarized, "I doubt we can apply anything from the Japanese situation for the other cities, and Xinyang's Chinese solution attacked what was a rather obvious national problem. So, these may not be generally useful. However, we might at least publicize Xinyang's efforts to the other Camitorian leaders to show what creativity can do to improve our acceptance."

As Rob opened the door to the Uber, "I like that idea. Of course, the other cities may already have moved forward with solutions of their own. But you, Sylvie, could at least start a discussion that might be helpful for the other leaders."

When Sylvie contacted the Camitorian leader in Seoul, she learned that the green makeup fashion cult that had made its way through Japan was already becoming high fashion in Seoul as well. "But" noted Kim Ji-yoo, the lead Camitorian in Seoul, "the Korean Camitorians claim to have invented the idea before it hit Japan. No matter, though, it's now raging throughout the entire country. It all started in Korea, much as it had in Japan, with groups of young Camitorians appearing in public without makeup in the places where the young people gather on Saturday evenings. There was little else that was needed to create the fad.

"One Camitorian had been working in a cosmetics company and managed to convince his CEO that the light green makeup fad could become popular. But neither he nor his boss had imagined just how great a hit it would become. The Camitorian is now a vice president in the company. And acceptance of Camitorians, which may never have been an issue in Seoul anyway, certainly isn't one now."

"Wow," Sylvie responded, "that sounds like a huge success. I won't even begin to try to figure out whether it started in Korea or Japan."

A slightly different version of this effect had occurred in Sydney. As reported to Sylvie by Sam Dundee, the head of the Camitorian delegation there, "The sun loving Australians, many of whom have to deal with light skins, rely heavily on their sun block. One of the enterprising Camitorians working in a company that produced the stuff convinced her boss that light green sunscreen could be a popular novelty, so she and a dozen of her fellow Camitorians appeared on a well populated beach one day without their makeup, peddling the novel product. They quickly discovered they had brought far too few tubes with them. The next day they came with many more, and once again sold them all, with many now light green colored Australians inadvertently helping to promote further sales. The product has now gone viral throughout Australia, vaulting the Camitorian who had originally pushed the idea into a high-ranking position in her company, creating new jobs for other Camitorians as the company grew to accommodate its market. The company has become a highly desired stock for investors.

"And, by the way, this made the naturally light green skinned Camitorians the envy of the Australian beach crowd. This has carried our social acceptance to the extreme!"

After adjusting herself to her surprise, Sylvie complimented Sam, "That is a wonderful success story. Please convey my congratulations to the Camitorian who came up with the idea."

"Will do, Sylvie. And congratulations on the successes of all your efforts!"

"Thanks, Sam.

"But, she added, "I also had what might be a useful thought. Perhaps you could coordinate with some of the Camitorians in New York and get them to go to beaches in Florida and California. They could skip the makeup but take some tubes of your Australian sunscreen. I wouldn't be surprised if the Australian company could really enhance their sales by expanding to US markets. It would even be useful that the stuff came from Australia; items of foreign origin always seem to have special appeal to Americans."

"Great suggestion; I'll pass that along. But I've heard they're having trouble keeping up with demand."

When Sensei called Gisele Santos, the lead Camitorian in Rio, she found a situation that was similar to that in Sydney, albeit with a distinct Brazilian twist. "Sylvie," she reported, "we heard about the sunscreen business in Australia, and thought it would be fun to try the stuff on the Rio beaches. Our Brazilian Camitorians don't always use sunscreen, since many of them are darker green skinned, but the light green color of the Australian sunscreen is a huge hit here. Bolivians love strong colors, especially bright extreme ones, and that certainly applied to the sunscreen. So, we went into the sunscreen business ourselves. We quickly found we couldn't come close to having supply keep up with demand. We found that our sales mushroomed when we produced several other colors, all of which are quite popular.

"And, of course, the Camitorians appearing at the beach without their usual makeup have generated considerable envy, especially after the Brazilians discovered that was their natural color. We feel fully loved by the locals! But some of the Camitorians are even indulging in the other bright colors. Rio beaches have become a color kaleidoscope!"

"This is Gunther Zweig."

"Hello, Gunther, this is Sylvie. I was wondering if you had picked up the conversations I had with the leaders of our Seoul, Tokyo, Sydney, and Rio contingents. I have been trying to figure out ways we Camitorians could convince the people with whom we've chosen to live to accept us as fellow citizens. Perhaps you've gotten some ideas from those conversations, if you heard them, or perhaps the German contingent has come up with some ideas of their own."

"As you know, Sylvie, the Germans love the outdoors just like many other peoples on the Earth. Being mostly fair skinned, they have to worry about protecting their skin just as some of the Australians do, even though the intensity of our sunshine is not as great as it is down under. I was very impressed with the Australian's simultaneous solution to the acceptance and skin protection issues, and I've made direct contact with Sam Dundee to see if we could obtain some of the light green sun screen his company is producing.

"Unfortunately, he's been so besieged with orders that he had to put my request on back order. He assures me he'll have some tubes of the sunscreen sent to Berlin as soon as it's available, although that may be a few months from now. But he also encouraged me to develop our own products from German cosmetics companies, so we've begun that foray into the field.

"We're most hopeful the Australian sunscreen will be as big a success in Berlin, and ultimately in all of Germany, as in Australia. And that it will directly lead to acceptance of our light green people. But we've really just begun the effort."

Sylvie responded, "Keep at it, Gunther. It sounds as if you're on the right track, especially given the success of the other places around the globe."

Sylvie and Philippe Dumand had a person-to-person discussion about the situation in France. They agreed that much had already been done, certainly by Sylvie personally, to gain acceptance of the Camitorians by the French. But Philippe also suggested that the acceptance in other countries of Europe would certainly be enhanced by what the Germans were beginning to do with the sunscreen. Philippe decided he would contact Sam Dundee to see if he could also get a shipment of the light green sunscreen. Sylvie seconded the idea.

Sometime later she got an update, "Sylvie," Philippe reported, "Sam's so far behind in filling orders that he encouraged me to see if some French cosmetics manufacturers might want to develop the multicolored sunscreens. However, I'm not sure that will work. French cosmetics people regard themselves as the world's leaders in such things, and might not like to have some upstart, an Australian one or especially a Camitorian one, suggesting how they might evolve.

"So, I ordered a few thousand of the tubes from Sam. I thought perhaps the fashion trend could be established within France but using Australian products. He understood and said he would get the order to me as soon as possible. But he is so heavily back ordered that it will take some time."

"Well," Sylvie observed, "I guess we'll have to wait to see how this plays out. However, do hold on to the idea for the future."

"Got it."

Sylvie recognized that the situation in the United States was complicated. This was the subject for her and Rob in their usual discussion venue, the breakfast table.

"Most of the US Camitorians live in New York City, although some have migrated to other places. But the possible solution to the issue of general approval could ultimately occur on the many wonderful beaches of coastal areas. Thus, total Camitorian acceptance will probably take a while, as the positive feelings generated at the beaches from the Australian sunscreen will require time to migrate to the rest of the country. Surprisingly, New York City will probably be the last place in the US to recognize our Camitorian virtues, even despite our having reduced dangerous RFR levels there."

Rob replied, "Yes, that's sad, but probably true. New Yorkers can be as ingrown as a toenail! Perhaps we should concentrate on San Francisco; they are more open to new ideas."

She developed a slight smile, "Might your west coast biases be showing?"

"Probably."

Sylvie struggled with a means to help the British accept the Camitorians in London. She discussed the situation with William Churchill, the Camitorian leader there. As he said, "Sylvie, I don't believe the Brits would find the color cults of the

Chinese, Koreans, Japanese, Bolivians, and Australians nearly as uplifting as the citizens of those places did. In my estimation, most Brits are just not as taken in by fads as many other Earthlings, although I suspect there are contradictions to that statement, especially among the young folks.

"As I speak, though, I'm recalling that there is a rock band that seems to be gaining acceptance, and a following, that may completely contradict my previous statement. This is a band of four, half Earthlings and half Camitorians, and they call themselves 'The Light Greens.' Their music is largely rock, but occasionally they come up with a piece that deals with climate change. And their fans often turn up with light green makeup. So perhaps acceptance of Camitorians is gaining, even in Great Britain."

"Oh, that sounds both interesting and complicated, William. I'd hoped we could do something that could accelerate our acceptance by all Earthlings, but in some cases, it appears we'll have to let events run their course. We can be patient as long as they don't inflict violence on us."

"I don't believe that will happen, Sylvie. The Brits don't tend to be violent chaps."

Chapter 47. The Future

Rob was in his Sylvie admiration mode. Actually, he spent most of his time there. "Well, Sylvie, in less than two years you've been on Earth you've accomplished some extraordinary things. You've managed to get the entire world, with a few notable exceptions, to limit the levels of RFR that are allowed from RFR emitters of all types and have broken through people's denial of the dangers with their electronic devices, especially smartphones. Meetings with manufacturers of airplanes and trailers have brought about RFR mitigating changes in those, and there's hope the auto manufacturers will improve their products. You've been especially forceful in limiting allowed RFR levels on children.

You and some of your Camitorian colleagues also managed to get most of the world to accept the ten thousand aliens that landed on Earth, at least in the locations where they landed. I'd say those are pretty good accomplishments for under two years!"

Sylvie smiled. "You're being overly generous. I had help from a lot of people getting the RFR limits put in place on most devices and settings, certainly including you and Linda, but a lot of Camitorians as well. Of course, we need to recognize that pretty good limits were already in place in Italy, Israel, and Russia, among others. All I had to do was congratulate them for their foresight and encourage them to tighten their limits even more.

Then she developed a more serious expression, "But we didn't have much time to put these measures in place. The next ten thousand Camitorians will be arriving in another year, and it will remain to be seen how accepting the Earthlings are when it dawns on them that we were just the first of many arrivals. After all, we do plan to transport one billion Camitorians to Earth as quickly as possible. Our engineers have been building new spacecraft, so that we expect soon to decrease the time between successive arrivals to one year. At ten thousand of us per flight, and one flight every year, that will take one hundred thousand years. That in itself raises some issues.

"For example, will Earth still be habitable for Earthling-type creatures then? That brings up two obvious questions. First, can Earthlings keep from destroying themselves and all other life forms for that long and, second, will they have a planet that can support life by that time. Given the contentious existence Earthlings presently have, both between nations and even within them, I'd say they have a lot to learn if civilization is to last one-hundred-thousand years. So, civility is a huge issue for them, and therefore, for us. A major contributor to the current incivility is the disparity between rich and poor; something must be done to correct that. And Earthlings will certainly have to take better care of their climate and ecosystems. At present, Earthling stewardship doesn't give much confidence to Camitorians.

"However, we believe we can help Earthlings adopt measures that will assist in all these endeavors. Regarding global warming, we do know some carbon sequestration strategies that would help, but they need to be introduced along with climate preserving discipline. So, civility becomes the underlying principle for virtually every issue."

This sobering discussion was taking place as they were preparing their dinner table, with their shoes kicked off. Of course, they were enjoying a nice white wine while Rob finished preparations of the mushroom cordon bleu he had prepared. The preceding few days had been so frantic that they hadn't had much time to process events, so they blocked off an evening with a blank schedule just to think.

Finally, the meal was ready, and they had their first few bites. Sylvie commented that she thought the meal was terrific, and that she liked the fact that Rob was such a good cook.

But then the discussion turned serious. Sylvie observed, "I believe the civility issue needs to be addressed first, since little can be accomplished without some reasonable level of agreement, certainly more than exists now. We can be as logical as we wish, but I fear that won't accomplish anything. The deep-seated animosities between liberals and conservatives throughout the world, with a sprinkling of dictators thrown in, will make it difficult to achieve meaningful agreement. The only way I see to attack this problem is if some Camitorians will become involved in electoral politics at leadership levels. Some time will be required for those who are willing to run to achieve sufficient recognition that they could be elected. And for them to achieve enough power to have the impact they would need to really change things. They'll certainly face intense opposition from Earthlings who prefer the status quo, even if it's not in their best interests."

Now Rob leaned forward in his chair, "Sylvie, I guess I need to state the obvious: the only Camitorian on the planet who has risen to the level of recognition that would allow immediate election is named Sylvie Sensei. I think you could run for office in any of several countries with a strong chance of being elected. Not as a leader but, say, as a member of the Senate in the United States or the Senat of the Parlement Français. And this would take no time at all; you are already quite famous in both countries."

Now Rob got a very serious expression, "But would you be interested in running for such an office? You've certainly faced life-threatening danger in the recent past, and I doubt if the potential for that would be reduced if you became a nationally and internationally recognized politician."

She responded quickly, "No, Rob, I don't want to do that. My mission was well defined for me, that is, to achieve a level of RFR that would be survivable and to gain acceptance for Camitorians. Those goals have been achieved to a large extent by the excellent work of the other Camitorians and by some right-minded Earthlings, certainly including you. The next steps will need to involve others. In some cases, those might involve the

Camitorians who are already in place in Earthling cities who have achieved some recognition. They would probably be the leaders in each of the ten cities. They'll need to be careful, but that will not be anything new for them. They have been operating under cautions ever since they arrived on Earth."

Rob had been holding his breath. "Thank god for your response. I wasn't encouraging you to run for office. If you had any inkling to do that, I would strongly urge you not to. I was merely trying to assess your level of interest to see if I was going to have to raise a huge objection. I'm glad to hear we're on the same page."

"I like sharing pages with you, Rob." And she arose, went over to his chair, and sat in it with him. It wasn't really large enough for both of them, so she was really in his lap. That ended the serious discussion for the evening.

Chapter 48. Traveling

As they were just finishing their breakfast, "Rob, I want to go visit Camitor."

Rob didn't even try to hide his shock. "You wanna' do what? Is that even possible? I suppose you could hitch a ride back on one of the next spacecraft to arrive here. When did you say the next ships are scheduled to arrive? Another year? But we're married, and that would mean you'd be gone for sixty or seventy years. I'd probably die without ever seeing you again."

She smiled her lovely smile, "You're missing the point, Rob. I don't want to go alone. You showed me San Francisco, now I want to show you Camitor. And living on a spacecraft for several decades is an experience all by itself. The ships must provide all the necessities for the travelers, including shops, farms, repair places, bakeries, and everything else you can think of. But on the return trip, there will only be the crew. And us! So, we'll have to help provide those necessities. By the way, have you ever done any farming?"

He sputtered a bit, "While all that sounds exciting, I'd probably never see Earth again. I'd be on one spaceship for thirty years, and then on another for thirty more years, and ... . That just seems like something I can't imagine doing. Oh, and I've never even grown a houseplant."

Sylvie smiled again, "I was kidding about the farming. But I think you're underrating yourself, Rob. Your 'best if used by date' may be longer than you think."

Rob paused, then his eyes brightened with realization, "Sylvie, what do you know that I'm only beginning to suspect?"

"You're right, Rob. I put the DNA modification drug into your orange juice a few months ago. I modified the longevity part of your DNA to be the same as mine. You now should live for several hundred years. I also modified the part of your DNA that allows your cells to repair themselves from radiation damage, especially from cosmic rays. That's crucial for extended space travel. So, I think we could have a wonderful round trip.

"I hope you don't mind that I modified your DNA."

She asked nervously, "Will you say yes?"

Rob didn't have to hesitate, "Well, I guess I'll have plenty of time to pack my bags.

"So yes!"

"Wonderful. I'll contact the incoming mission and tell them that the three of us want to go back with them."

"Three of us? Surely you don't want Linda to go with us."

"Oh Rob, you silly fellow, do you remember a few months ago when I told you that I'd taken my chemicals to modify my DNA so that we could conceive? And I'd know in four months if the changes worked? We are now a month beyond that."

He added, "And you said you could confirm in four months if you were ready to conceive. We could start right now!"

"Too late, Rob. I was fertile a month ago, And I'm happy to tell you we succeeded. But we could make love now anyway."

"Oh Sylvie, I don't know what to say, except that I love you. Tremendously. Incredibly.

"But it also occurs to me that by the time we go to Camitor and return, our baby will be older than I am right now. That's pretty daunting."

"Rob, don't forget that you won't age as much while we're moving at high speed than if we stayed here. But it's not a large effect; you'll only gain a year or two. But we might be grandparents by the time we get back!"

"Oh, I'm not sure that could happen. Our baby's DNA will certainly be a confusion of yours, modified, and mine, definitely not Camitorian. Could that possibly work? Would our child ever be able to create a baby?"

"Ah, good question. My paper on what I did to modify my DNA so that I could conceive with an Earthling—you—has been submitted to Nature Genetics. I believe the paper will be accepted for publication. And I wouldn't be surprised if spawned more romances between Camitorian woman and Earthling men. The modifications would be different for a Camitorian man and an Earthling woman. But even without that, there should be plenty of potential mates by the time we all return from Camitor, assuming our adult child returns to Earth with us.

"And, Rob, I wouldn't be surprised if, by the time it's relevant for our offspring, there might well be DNA accommodation centers that would test any mixture of Camitorian and Earthling to see what modifications would be needed for them to successfully conceive."

"Those sound like great reassurances, my Love. I surely wouldn't want to create an offspring that would never be able to enjoy the same pleasures of life that we have."

"Agreed. But I have a blank schedule this morning, so, I suggest that we avoid any further delay and enjoy some of those right now."

But by the following morning, reality had begun to sink in. "Sylvie, what will the world look like in sixty years? We'll be totally out of touch with gazillions of new developments, provided Earthlings haven't destroyed their planet and themselves by then. How will we be able to resume our lives on Earth?"

"Well, I hope that the Camitorians will have put in place some of the necessary institutions to let Earth survive. There'll be hundreds of thousands of us on Earth by then. We'll be getting updates since, by that time, our spaceships will be returning every year, and the crews can inform us as to new developments. Of course, nothing will happen on Earth that wasn't invented and put into use thousands of years ago on Camitor, with the possible exception of Earth-ending disasters. If the fates are with us,

Camitor will give you a preview of what Earth will look like in two hundred thousand years."

"Ah, so the real culture shock will occur when we get to Camitor.

"But, Sylvie, you won't have been there for sixty years. Will you be in for a shock?"

"I can't wait to find out. And to show you all the new developments! And to introduce the Camitorians to my husband!"

Chapter 49. Developments

Rob and Sylvie didn't have long to enjoy their secret. Within another month there began to be speculation in the French purple press about her baby bump, and that news soon found its way to every other such 'newspaper' in the world. Of course, the raging question was, "How could that be? Surely the genes of Camitorians and Earthlings couldn't conceive a baby!"

Indeed, dozens of interplanetary couples around the globe had assumed that they could do whatever they wished sexually without worrying about the complications. The possibility that Sylvie might have gotten pregnant with an Earthling brought a fearful reality home to them. But the magazines speculated in ways that were more insidious. One was that Sylvie had a Camitorian lover with whom she was cheating on Rob. A less nasty rumor was that they had decided to avail themselves of the sperm of a Camitorian male so they could produce a baby.

After a couple of weeks of this, Sylvie and Rob decided they needed to have a press conference to answer the questions that had arisen and lay the nastier rumors to rest. The conference was a spectacle, with hundreds of reporters trying to crowd into the room, and television cameras preparing to broadcast it live around the globe. People were staying up until all hours of the night so as not to miss any aspect of what was to be reported.

Sylvie and Rob walked up to the microphone with broad smiles on their faces. Sylvie began her comments, with Rob standing beside her, holding her hand, "Thank you all for attending this press conference, although I must admit I'm amazed at the interest in learning Rob's and my secret. It has been speculated that I'm expecting a baby. This is correct. Rob and I expect our baby to be born five months from now.

"We know that there's been speculation as to how that could be possible. Those who are wondering if an Earthling and a Camitorian could actually conceive can relax; that can't happen unless there are significant changes in the DNA of one or the other member. I am a geneticist, so I designed a modification to my DNA that would allow conception between Rob and me. My paper on this has been submitted to Nature Genetics, so that the changes for this can be shared with the world. Furthermore, I am sure it will be published; we've done the experiment after all." And she smiled at Rob.

After the laughter died down, she continued, "Earthling capabilities in genetics are sufficiently advanced that with a small amount of new equipment, which will be described in the paper, an Earthling geneticist will be able to make the changes that will enable mixed-race couples to conceive. Although the changes would be different if the Camitorian is the man, those are also described in my paper.

"But perhaps I should stop now and see if there are any questions."

Rob laughed at her comment as dozens of hands shot up.

"Ms. Sensei, are we to believe that any run of the mill Earthling geneticist could make the necessary changes your paper will describe? If I were in a mixed-race relationship in which we were trying to conceive, I think you're the only person on the planet, maybe in the Universe, I would trust to do the modifications."

She smiled, "Well, thank you for that comment but I think you're underrating Earthling geneticists. The strategies for DNA modification are only slightly more complicated than some of those that have been developed on Earth. I'm confident that Earthling scientists will be able to make the modifications."

Another reporter asked, "Just for the benefit of those couples who have viewed your pregnancy with concern about their assumed birth control, would you be so good as to repeat the statement that an Earthling and a Camitorian could not conceive without the modifications described in your paper?"

Rob laughed again.

She smiled, "That's correct. A mixed-race couple would not be able to conceive without the changes I have designed. All you folks to whom this comment is directed can relax."

All the reporters laughed at that.

The next question came from one of the Camitorians, "Sylvie, I can't believe you're having a baby the way Earthlings do. For the past ten thousand years, our people have had babies either as you seem to be doing or conceiving them and letting them grow in gestation pods. As busy a person as you are, I'd surely expect you to opt for one of the pods. Why are you doing things this way?"

Now her expression became serious, "Earthlings have their babies this way, and I've become a citizen of Earth. So, I thought it was only right that I have our baby the way Earthling women do. Besides, I want to have that experience."

That caused a few moments of silence while everyone pondered her response. But then the reporters got back into the question mode, "You and Mr. Thompson are married, but I've heard that Camitorians can live for several hundred years, which is a lot longer than Earthlings live. That doesn't seem like a very good match. Isn't that a concern for you and your husband?"

Sylvie had anticipated where this line of questioning might be going, "We discussed that at length before we married. I was single for more than two-hundred years, so I believe I know how to live that way. But I'm also looking forward to several decades with the most wonderful man I could ever hope to meet."

Rob smiled broadly at that.

"But you modified your DNA so that you could conceive. Why not modify his so he can also live several hundred years?"

Of course, she had done exactly that, but she and Rob had decided not to tell the Earthling world in order to avoid a huge glut at the genetics clinics for those hoping to increase their longevity, as well as an enormous overpopulation problem. So, she replied, "I believe that would be a more difficult modification. But perhaps other geneticists might figure out a way to do that."

But if they're not Camitorians won't not have a chance of getting it right. They would almost certainly kill the Earthling.

With that the press conference ended, although many of the reporters came up to Rob and Sylvie afterward to see if they could get a selfie to send back to their newspapers.

That evening, after they had gone to bed and Rob peered out the bedroom window at the Paris night sky, more implications of his taking a seventy-year trip began to dawn on him. *I'll resign from the FCC; Linda has everything under control. But we'll have to say goodbye to her; she's not likely to still be alive when we return. But my parents, both healthy and vibrant seniors, will surely be gone by the time we return. That'll be a difficult goodbye. And they'll never get to see their grandchild.*

My business will flourish without me; a succession plan has been in place for some time, and the employees will manage just fine. Those goodbyes will be easier.

But what will Earth look like when we return? Will a civilization even exist? I hope some of the Camitorians can get elected to public office and can bring about the changes Earth so desperately need. At least they all have the template for that from their life on Camitor.

And what'll it be like being the only Earthling on Camitor? Sylvie was one of ten thousand Camitorians on Earth, and there were times when I'm pretty sure she was disturbed by her minority status. But being the only Earthling among one billion Camitorians ... ?

"Rob, I can hear that you're troubled by what you'll have to do before we leave for Camitor. And extremely apprehensive about being the only Earthling there!"

"Oh, Sweetheart, I thought you were asleep. Some of the goodbyes will be difficult. But you're right about my not knowing what to expect once we arrive. I don't want to be a one-man freak show."

She rolled over and kissed him. "I'll shield you from any excessive publicity. There won't be any problems we can't deal with, my Darling." Then she cuddled up next to him. He gently patted her tummy and let out a sigh. Soon they were both sound asleep.

Appendix. Some Countries' RFR Limits

As of 2021, most European countries, as well as the United States, Canada, and others, have set a general limit of 4.5 Watts/meter^2 for a broad frequency range. However, there are exceptions. For example, Italy and Russia imposed a much lower limit of 0.1 Watts/meter^2 at the same frequency range. China's level is 0.4 Watts/meter^2. These data, along with many more, are compiled in a report Physicians for Safe Technology | Conversion Chart, World Exposure Limits, Human Exposures EMR/EMF (mdsafetech.org), updated as of October 2021.

Furthermore, as detailed in International-Policy-Precautionary-Actions-on-Wireless-Radiation.pdf (fcc.gov), many of those same countries have imposed much more stringent limits where children are involved. In some cases, Wi-Fi is restricted in schools or even banned altogether for the youngest students.

The latter document also lists locales, in countries that have high RFR levels, where citizens have imposed lower limits than the nation has set. This is especially true of the United States, where many cities have adopted standards that are more stringent than those imposed by the Federal Communications Commission that existed in 2021.

The Council of Europe has issued its (nonbinding) recommendation that lowers the overall RFR limit to be more in line with what many countries have been issuing for their children. Their recommended exposure limit is 100 microwatts/meter^2, or 0.0001 Watts/meter^2, a value comfortably below the level of "Extreme Concern" of 1000 microwatts/meter^2 from BioInitiative 2012, updated to 2020 which, as noted in the Preface to this book, took into account much of the medical evidence obtained up to that time.

Information about Wi-Fi concerns inside aircraft is documented in the report: Radiofrequency (RF)/Wireless Microwave Radiation Exposure from Inflight Mobile Devices and Wi-Fi Connectivity, https://www.safertechsolutions.org/wp-content/uploads/2013/08/New.Aviation.Risk_.Factors.pdf . This report was done in 2015, and it mostly emphasizes that the problem needs to be studied.

Acknowledgements

I have received much information on the effects of RF radiation from the SafeTech4SantaRosa group. However, there are many similar groups around the United States. There may be less in Europe, since the politicians there seem much more aware of the problems with RF radiation. I also profited greatly from the "EMF Medical Conference 2021," which included a wide variety of international experts on the effects of RFR in living systems.

If one wants to delve into the effects of RF radiation, including much medical information, I recommend a book by Arthur Firstenberg, "The Invisible Rainbow, A History of Electricity and Life," which details many aspects of RF poisoning, and references hundreds of relevant research articles published prior to 2017, the publication date of this book.

There are also many organizations around the world that deal with the dangers of RFR. Two excellent websites are http://www.mdsafetech.org, Physicians for Safe Technology and http://www.americansforresponsibletech.org, Americans for Responsible Technology. Perhaps the most detailed source, and the most inclusive of medical research, is BioInitiative 2012, updated to 2020. As indicated in the Preface, it finds "Extreme Concern" from RFR at levels in excess of 0.001 watts per square meter, which is ten thousand times less than the limit imposed by the FCC. An excellent description of not only the RFR limits of many countries, but of some of locally imposed limits as well, is in the Environmental Health Trust document (homepage ehtrust.org) International-Policy-Precautionary-Actions-on-Wireless-Radiation.pdf (fcc.gov) .

A special acknowledgement is due Mary Dahl, an extremely electrosensitive feisty septuagenarian whose battle with telecom has been an inspiration to many.

I am also indebted to Pierre Marsh, who gave the manuscript a careful review, and made several helpful suggestions.

Finally, I am extremely fortunate to live with my editor, that is, my wife, Sidnee, who has done yet another incredible editing job. The book is both much more technically and grammatically correct as a result of her efforts. She also designed the cover.

About the Author

Richard Boyd is an Emeritus Professor, having spent thirty years in the Physics and Astronomy Departments at The Ohio State University. He has worked extensively with collaborators in the United States and Japan, resulting in his authoring or coauthoring more than two-hundred-fifty articles on experimental and theoretical nuclear physics, astrophysics, and astrobiology. "Irradiated, An Alien Perspective" is his seventh book. Two of the books are scientific, one on nuclear astrophysics and the second on the origin of the molecules of life. The others are fictional. Recent ones are "Prairie Renaissance," and "Artificial Intelligence, Mankind at the Brink." These are attempts to challenge some of the basic assumptions of twenty-first century mankind, but to wrap them in interesting stories.

For more information see richardboydastro.com.

Made in the USA
Middletown, DE
29 March 2025